Dedicated to Dad

Changelings

Changelings

By

April Miller

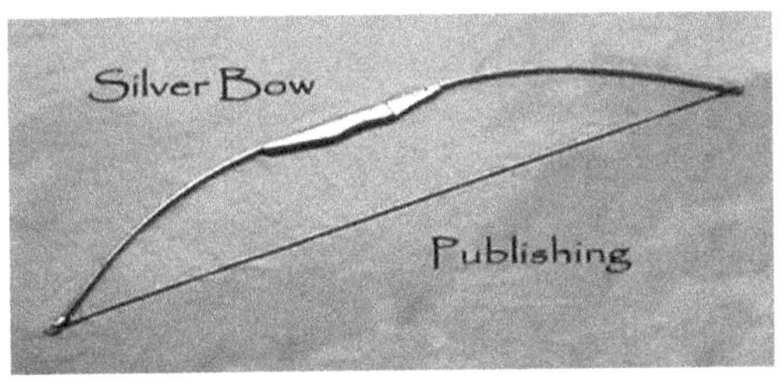

720 – Sixth Street, Box # 5
New Westminster, BC
V3L 3C5   CANADA

Library and Archives Canada Cataloguing in Publication

Title: Changelings / by April Miller
Names: Miller, April, 1965- author.
Identifiers: Canadiana (print) 20190098813 | Canadiana (ebook) 20190098821 | ISBN 9781774030325
   (softcover) | ISBN 9781774030356 (HTML)
Classification: LCC PR6113.I445 C43 2019 | DDC 823/.92—dc23

Acknowledgements

With sincere thanks to Douglas,
Heather & Israel, Kirsty & Mike
and Jodie & Jamie.

Changelings

Chapter 1

PRESENT DAY:

Cerberus circled once more just to make sure it was safe. The motion of his great wings created a breeze that rustled the leaves and made the discarded remains flutter in the street. The few who were still scattered in the streets below did not look up to see what it was that hunted in their night skies. Instead they scurried to the safety of their illuminated homes, preferring not to see his kind; preferring to deny their very existence. Cerberus and his people served without acknowledgement and Cerberus preferred it that way. The day walkers were in his view, contemptible and he wanted nothing from them, least of all their recognition.

Cerberus dominated his domain; he knew every dark corner and hidden act. Any change or fluctuation immediately attracted his direct attention. Tonight, there was no mistake; he could see fresh meat. Faint traces of heat that indicated the animal was recently dead excited his senses and drew him to the carcass. This recent kill was set to draw in one of his kind. It was dangerous to draw too close to human abodes and yet Cerberus found it too exciting to ignore. Caution was called for and curiosity demanded satisfaction.

Hungry for more than the system allowed him, Cerberus alighted on the very edge of the balcony. Tasting the air to check if anyone still lingered, he hopped off the railing and, holding the offering in one great talon, tore into the flesh before him.

"I've been waiting for you," Mike said.

Cerberus jumped and glared at the day walker who had stepped from the dark shadows. The ecstasy as the first strip of warm blood-filled flesh slid easily down his throat had masked the day walker's presence. Now, he was far too committed to stop. Cerberus kept one eye focused on the day walker as he continued to tear the meat apart. When he was finished, he cleaned the blood from his beak, by wetting his feathers with saliva and then rubbing it along the forearm of his great wings. He licked the resulting trail of blood, savouring every last delicious drop, until the evidence of its existence was completely obliterated.

"I would like to talk to you," Mike tried to get his attention, but not too forcefully. The image of this creature tearing him apart as easily as it had the meat made him nervous and uncharacteristically subservient.

"You are," came Cerberus' guttural reply. He had little or no patience for the day walker and one meal bought Mike only the tiniest window into the night stalkers world.

"They took my companion," Mike blurted out. "I came home, and she was gone; no explanation, nothing."

"Get another," Cerberus growled.

"I love her," Mike whispered, running his hands through his dark tousled hair.

Cerberus narrowed his eyes to tiny pin points of intensity and looked for a long time at the man before him, focussing, not on Mike's eyes or face but on the essence of his soul, the inner person. Mike moved uncomfortably from one foot to the other but knowing it was important, did not break his gaze from the once human form. He needed the help of this creature. He needed this modern-day Frankenstein to trust him completely.

How many minutes passed Mike could not tell, but as the clouds drifted across the moon, so something different drifted across Cerberus' brow. Finally, as Mike became aware of the need to empty his bladder, Cerberus simply nodded.

He jumped once more onto the railings and spreading his great wings launched himself, majestically, into the air. Mike rushed to the edge of the balcony as he watched the dark shape fall to the streets below. Then suddenly averting death at what seemed like the very last second, came swooping back up to meet him. Taking an involuntary step backward Mike felt rather than saw Cerberus rush past him and take flight into the night. He stood breathing in and out slowly to calm himself and, as his heart rate slowed, the form of Cerberus became a distant memory against the clear grey of the now revealed moon.

Shaking, Mike slid the patio door shut. Why he had found the brief encounter so tiring he was not sure. He just knew he had to rest, re-charge his batteries. Sinking to the floor he leant his head against the coolness of the glass and, closing his eyes, he allowed it to numb his mind and cool his emotions.

$$****$$

Cerberus flew away from the day walker, he knew he should stay away, but something in Mike's arrogance intrigued Cerberus and convincing him to at least investigate what could make a day walker risk contact with the changed. Whoever he was, and whatever his motive, he had contacted the night stalkers for a reason and Cerberus deeply wanted to be a hero. He wanted to prove his humanity remained in this changed and alien form. Cerberus had a long night ahead; he would send shadows to investigate on his behalf. He flew to the top of Virgin tower and called the shadows that were his to command. Shadows, the transformation mistakes, creatures caught between forms, unable to exist completely in any dimension, their resulting life spans were very brief. Some attached themselves to the Director in the hope that she would be able to restore a kind of life. Others attached themselves to the changed, in the hope that they too would learn to finish their own transformations. Either way, once attached they were loyal to the death. They were a useful tool, shadows, able to move anywhere they pleased, observe, and record any event. Cerberus called them to him. At first it looked like a simple darkening and lengthening of the true shadows of the building, but Cerberus knew better. He waited for them to come together.

"I need your help," Cerberus started. The wind rustled, and he knew it was their reply.

"A man contacted me tonight, sector five. I need you to find out all you can about him. I need to know if he wants my help or is trying to trap me."

Again, it was as if the winds were rustling a thousand leaves, but none grew on this tower and as they had gathered, they began to leave to do his bidding. Cerberus watched them go, until the smallest and last had slid from the roof. The last one was new; too small to have ever been an adult, he was saddened to think that a child had ended its life in this way. He sighed heavily and turned, just in time to see Maia land at the far end of the tower roof. Opening his wings, she came and fitted her body into the space he offered.

"What's the matter?" she asked in a low almost inaudible voice.

"Nothing," he replied as he brushed his wing down the side of her face. It was the intimate times such as these that he missed hands the most. He wanted to run his fingers through the dark curly mane that he was sure had once been hers. Now all he could manage was the briefest imitation of touch and he longed for so much more. Reading the pain in his eyes, she placed her head gently on his chest.

"Cerberus?" she inquired of him.

"Hmmm," he responded, rubbing his beak along the downy feathers of her head.

"We need to hunt," she whispered. "If we don't hit the quota, they will recall us or worse." Her worry hung in the air between them. An unspoken and yet clear warning that they were slaves to the system that had created them. It was their duty to perform the task they had been assigned.

"Perhaps we should test them?" he replied, and before she could respond he released her from his wings and jumped to the edge of the building in one stride. "Catch me if you can," he called as he launched himself from the rooftop.

Laughing, her mood now lightened, she launched herself from the same spot and gave chase. Free falling until she almost hit the street, she swung her wings once in a large arc, giving just enough power to rise and follow Cerberus into the night. This was her time and she was its mistress. The day walkers were all hiding in their cages, the places they called home. They would never know the freedom to fly, swoop and kill. The delight of the chase and the feel of fresh blood running between their talons would be forever denied them. It was in these circumstances she savoured her changed form, enjoying the power it gave her.

✳✳✳✳

How long Mike sat allowing the welcomed numbness to fill his brain he was not sure, but he did know that it was late, far too late for callers. So, the insistent buzz of the apartment's intercom surprised him enough to raise him from his stupor. Forcing himself slowly to his feet, he went to find out who wanted his attention. Leaning against the wall for support he simultaneously pressed the communication button and opened one of his Capstans. He inserted it into the corner of his mouth and inhaled deeply, savouring the sting at the back of his throat as the long-missed smoke filled his grateful lungs. Coughing lightly the bell rang once more, reminding him of the reason for his wakeful state. "Yes!" he said, from the free side of his mouth.

"Detective Sutton, sir, here to investigate the supposed missing persons you reported."

Words swirled round Mike's head, '_Detective_', as he drew once more on the illegal Capstan, 'supposed', as he considered Phoebe and her ways. His brain couldn't or perhaps wouldn't form a reply.

"Sir? Are you there sir?" asked the disembodied voice of the detective below.

"Yes," replied Mike's mouth without his brain condoning the action.

"May I come up?" asked the voice.

"Yes," replied Mike's treacherous mouth and, compounding the problem, his finger pressed the release buzzer that would allow the detective entry to the complex. Inhaling deeply on the Capstan, Mike suddenly galvanised into action, flushing the remains down the toilet. He was dismayed to see the pieces floating on the surface to taunt him. Closing the lid to hide the evidence he sprayed air freshener as liberally as he could to mask the smell and just in time, he was able to open the door to his guest.

"Come in detective," Mike said, surprising himself with how normal he sounded.

"Thank you, sir," Sutton replied as he stepped through the door. Sutton scanned as much of the interior as he could, through long experience he knew these first moments could prove to be useful later. Immediately he detected the air freshener and beneath it the unforgettable aroma of tobacco. How he missed his daily cigarette, still it was illegal and as an officer of the law he could not condone anyone smoking. Rather than use the information immediately he simply stored it for the future. He noticed how messy the flat was, crying out for a woman's touch. Perhaps that was why she had left; an easier offer could have come along. Turning to appraise Mike, he had to admit that if he were a professional companion Mike would be an attractive proposition. Young, obviously attractive and the flat itself oozed wealth, so perhaps she really was missing.

"Sorry it's so late sir, but we have been very busy today. A rogue harvester caused big problems when it entered the city earlier."

"And a missing companion isn't priority," Mike added sarcastically.

"I'm sorry sir, but we do our best," Sutton replied tersely. "Shall we get down to business sir?"

"Yes, yes," Mike said impatiently. "I came home, and she wasn't there."

Sutton waited a minute or two expecting much more to be communicated and when he realised that Mike had finished, he asked, "Sir, is that it?"

"You don't understand," continued Mike, "she's always there."

"I understand you're upset sir, but what makes you think it's a police matter?"

"She's always there!" repeated Mike with more force.

Sighing deeply, Sutton decided a gentle approach might be more appropriate. "OK sir, well I will make some enquiries. Then I'll get back to you." Get back to you some time next year he thought. Then he decided to add, "Perhaps the young lady needed a break, sir. A lot of work for a companion here, wouldn't you say sir?"

"What do you mean? A lot of work? Are you implying something detective?" Mike asked his voice rising with annoyance.

"Well, sir." Sutton drawled.

"Don't *'well sir'* me detective. She is my companion and I expect it to be investigated. Is that clear?" Mike stated with authority.

"Yes sir." Sutton replied, reconciling himself to the subordinate position so he could exit the situation as soon as possible. He had tired of the man already. He had enough arrogant idiots in his life without prolonging his exposure to this one for any longer than necessary.

"Good!" Mike replied as he opened the door and gestured the detective out. Shame he'd wasted the Capstan really, he thought. He should have made this guy wait for him; it would have put him in his place.

"Goodnight sir," Sutton said as he left.

Mike simply closed the door.

****

Sutton sat at his desk; he had ten cases a year where men reported missing companions. Dunking his doughnut in his tea Sutton began to type his night's activities so that hey resembled a report. As he held his soaked doughnut in his mouth, tea dripped down his shirt. "Shit," he said as he reached for a tissue.

"Hey doughnut king, operating with your usual finesse?" Kapowski called as he came into the office to start the day shift.

"Yeah, very funny, any sharper and you'll cut yourself," Sutton responded.

"Guess that sharp wit is the reason you're permanently on the graveyard shift." sniggered Kapowski.

Glaring, Sutton submitted his reports and, still smouldering, he headed for daylight.

"Sutton, you're better than any of them," said the desk sergeant.

"Sure Mac, you and me both," Sutton replied as he left the building.

Stepping onto the pavement he looked up into the rapidly brightening sky, just in time to watch the retreating night stalkers seeking daytime refuge. As he headed for his own fortress and the sanctuary of sleep, he felt somehow connected to those half human creatures in a way that would get him a white room if any of the others were privy to his thoughts. Kapowski, in particular, would have a field day.

****

Stirring his tea, Mike watched as the rising sun spread light and warmth to the coming day. Still, he felt strangely chilled. Finally, when it was light enough, he began to dress for work. Standing in the hall he paused momentarily before heading out. As the door swung shut behind him he felt, rather than saw, his neighbour's eyes on his back. The neighbour's door clicked shut and Mike wondered what else they had seen behind their reinforced barriers. He wondered if they had seen what had happened to Phoebe

****

On the rooftops Cerberus watched as the rising sun spread light and warmth to the coming day, heralding the retreat of his people in favour of the day walkers. Cerberus spread his wings and headed into the rising light and a day's rest.

****

Phoebe knew it must be dawn. It was not the rising sun that brought this knowledge as there were no windows evident, but the increased activity of the staff indicated the morning shift had begun. She simultaneously felt relief and apprehension. Relief at the end of a long night strapped into a hard-wooden chair which prevented any meaningful sleep, and even rest had eluded her completely. Apprehension at what would happen next. She listened carefully to every footfall in the corridor beyond her prison and wondered when they would enter her cell and if the result would be good or evil.

****

Mike paused at the entrance to the IGH, Institute for Genetic Harmony. Just standing near the building made him feel calmer. It was more than simply his place of work; it was his sanctuary and his dream all rolled into one magnificent package. It was the tallest building in Birmingham, standing ninety-two stories; it rivalled anything even the Americans could build. Constructed from panels that converted solar rays to power, it cut a stunning silver streak through the cityscape and lent a futuristic feel to the urban setting. It took his breath away every time he saw it and filled him with a sense of pride to know he was a part of the organisation that saved the civilised world. Not just any part either, he was a principal player. Pushing his way through the revolving doors he entered the Institute. His footsteps echoed on the tiled floor and there, as it had always been, was the Institute's logo set in gold for all-comers to walk on. It was reflected on the far wall for all to marvel. For the IGH had truly saved mankind.

****

Turning the security camera to the best position, Davidson watched from his elevated office. Placing his palms together so his fingers interlinked and extending his two index fingers as he had done in childhood to represent a gun, Davidson touched his lips thoughtfully as he sank backwards into the soft leather of his chair. It was a large swivel office chair made entirely of leather, a rare and precious material in these times.. It raised the level of anyone that sat within its soft confines giving them the aura of authority and putting those in lesser positions in their subordinate place. It pleased Davidson, partly because it was a symbol of his elevated status and partly because others who both envied and coveted what he had achieved were left in no doubt as to his superiority. Today he was concerned with maintaining the position he had worked so hard to achieve. He looked once more at the security cameras and watched as Mike entered the IGH. He continued watching as Mike stopped and stared at the IGH logo. Tapping Mike's open file, he turned thoughtfully back to the work on his desk. Mike was, he thought, getting a little above himself lately. He may have to do something about him, and do it soon, before things got out of control.

Rousing himself from his reverie, Mike strode across the foyer and glanced briefly at the crowded lifts. Uncharacteristically, he decided to opt for the stairs. The exercise, he decided, might help focus his mind. By the time he reached the fifteenth floor he felt as if he had already completed a day's work and he was regretting the impulsive decision to take the stairs. Too out of breath to say hello he simply raised his hand in greeting to Barbara, his secretary.

"Morning Mr Caldwell," she chirped out brightly as he went past.

But Mike was too lost in his own concerns and still far too out of breath to respond.

"Never, mind lover," William whispered in her ear.

Colouring, slightly embarrassed that anyone had witnessed her being rebuffed, Barbara smiled sweetly. "Oh, I wouldn't read too much into it little Will."

"Looked to me like he might want something different this time," William continued, running his hand down the outside of his thigh and indicating his own figure.

Standing and tossing her head so that her hair flipped in what she knew to be a very attractive fashion "I think I have a lot to offer Willy boy," Barbara said as she walked to the filing cabinet while exaggerating the swing of her hips. Once there she turned to face William, and licking the tip of her finger, she touched it to her bottom making a sizzling sound as she did so. Taking the challenge for what it clearly was, William rose to meet it. "Well, you little witch, if it's a competition you want?"

"I don't think it will be a competition, more a walk-over."

"How about putting your money where your mouth is?" William challenged.

"Oooh, the boy bites back," Barbara teased. "50 credits, too much for you?" she continued.

"More like 100," William said, with a flip of his own head, mimicking Barbara's earlier action.

"Hey everyone," Coleen called. "Will and Barb are going head to head for Mr Caldwell." At this announcement, several heads appeared from various corners.

"Is there a book?" called Angela.

"Will be in a sec," replied Coleen.

"Put me down for ten on Barb," Angela called back.

"I'll have five on William," interjected Phil.

"Can I try for a place with Mr Caldwell?" asked Britney, the new office junior. At this they all laughed.

"Let the games begin," Will finished.

****

Sitting at his desk, blissfully unaware of the battle commencing in the outer office, Mike turned to the task of dealing with his mail. Number one he ignored; contending with Phoebe's mother, at this point, was not high on his list of things to do.

He concentrated on the mundane, losing time and resting his brain. As he worked, Barbara slipped in and left coffee at his elbow and a carefully crafted trace of her perfume to remind him that she was still an attractive prospect. It was to remind him that a man in his position needed a companion to smooth the day and its troubles. She was slightly upset that he did not respond immediately to her presence but then she had to be patient. As she left Mike's office, she was so preoccupied with her own thoughts for the future that she failed to notice the inviso-serpent that entered at her feet and slithered beneath Mike's desk. Once there, it coiled around the desk's legs immediately changing structure to blend into the furniture; then, silently, it began to send tendrils around the room. In ten minutes, it had finished and then started to transmit information from all possible sources: the workings of technical equipment, odours and sounds in the immediate vicinity. It transmitted even the quality, type and quantity of Mike's sweat, his heart rate and state of arousal. Soon everything that could be known about Mike was being recorded and analysed in a distant computer. Unaware, Mike lost himself in the routine of his day.

****

Simultaneously, Cerberus curled his supple body around Maia's soft alluring form. The warmth of the sun combined with the heat he felt emanating from Maia lulled him to a land where he was king. In his dreams there were no day walkers controlling his actions. There was just the joys of the hunt and the companionship of his own kind.

****

Mike drank from the coffee Barbara had left for him. As he raised the cup to his lips, he detected the faint trace of her perfume and, smiling, he decided to thank her for her efforts. Rising from the keyboard he was halfway across the room when Davidson entered.

"Your last code is out," he announced with characteristic disregard for social convention.

"My codes are never out," Mike replied, reaching for the printout in Davidson's hands. Taking the sheaves of paper, he returned to his computer and began inputting genetic sequences.

"When did you notice?" Mike asked.

"Not until after it was used," Davidson said quietly. "Yours are usually fine," he added dryly.

"Thanks," Mike replied with no emotion in his voice.

"It wasn't a compliment," Davidson retaliated.

Pulling a face, Mike returned his attention to the screen.

"I'm running a comparison between the version you ran and the one I saved," Mike informed Davidson.

"I can see," Davidson replied tersely.

Mike swivelled to face Davidson. "You wouldn't be unhappy if this proves to be my error, would you?"

"It's not personal Caldwell, you have been distracted of late," Davidson replied with a hint of accusation in his voice.

"Not personal!" Mike repeated loudly, while waiting for the results of the analysis.

"Look Davidson, this could take some time, why don't you wait in your office and I'll come up when the results come through."

Scowling, Davidson nodded, "make sure it's as soon as you get the results!" He turned and stalked out of Mike's office.

"Of course," Mike replied to Davidson's retreating back. Leaving the computer to its work, Mike followed almost immediately.

Walking over to the secretaries' station, Mike smiled broadly.

"Barbara," he said in the warmest tone he could manage.

"Yes, Mr Caldwell," she replied injecting as much allure into her tone as she could. At the same time raising her eyes to meet his and widening them as far as possible to maximise her appeal.

"I want to say thank you for the coffee, it was very thoughtful of you."

"Not at all Mr Caldwell," she continued with a light giggle.

"Don't be so modest, it was thoughtful."

"I'd have popped it in earlier, but Davidson demanded my attention. I noticed he's been around a lot lately, especially since Phoebe was last in," she added helpfully.

Jolting back as if stung, he saw the look on Barbara's face and with effort controlled his reaction.

"Hey," he laughed, "I thought I was getting over her, and there I go getting silly just at the mention of her name."

Smiling, Barbara sat taller in her seat. He had said he was getting over her; it was just what she wanted to hear. "We could talk about things after work," she ventured.

"I would like that," he replied, holding her hand and smiling in return. He wanted to find out exactly what she knew about the comings and goings that had occurred in his absence.

"Oh, Mr Caldwell, you are such a gentleman," she said loudly, just to make sure Will knew she was making an arrangement with Mike.

Later, when leaving his office, Mike held out his hand to Barbara, making it publicly obvious they were leaving together. It had been over a week since Phoebe had gone; any longer without replacing a companion would be rude and thoughtless. Glancing at William on his way out, Mike decided that playing both for a while might be fun. As they passed, Mike winked directly at Will and smiled, indicating that perhaps the game was not yet decided. Slipping his arm around Barbara's waist he called the lift.

****

Phoebe had waited all day for someone to enter her cell. Strapped as she was to her seat, the urge to pass urine had gone beyond what she could bear. Much to her shame she had wet herself. When the door finally opened, she turned away, too embarrassed to look at whoever entered.

"Oh dear," said a cultured voice that could only belong to one person. In response Phoebe turned back to look at the Director. Her face was scarlet with embarrassment, her makeup smeared from the night's tears and her hair frazzled from the struggle when she was first taken.

It had happened at the flat, she had been happily dusting when she had heard the shuffling, snuffling sound behind her. How they gained entry she did not know, she was sure she had locked the door, but it was wide open for anyone to gain entry. A snuffling sound alerted her; out of place in the flat, it had aroused her curiosity. Then she saw the creature that had made the sounds and her mind refused to believe anything like that existed, let alone had found its way into her home. She swooned, almost, but not quite losing consciousness. She was just awake enough to scream as it reached for her. When it wrapped its foul-smelling wings around her, she was finally robbed of consciousness and the world faded mercifully into a black nothingness. She had woken in this room strapped to the chair she now found herself seated in. She had wondered what her fate would be and who would possibly want to abduct her. Now, impossibly, the Director herself was here and although Phoebe was finding it hard to pay attention, it was obvious that the Director was not here to save her. She pulled a stool in front of Phoebe and taking her chin in her hands held her face in front of her own to ensure Phoebe was paying full attention to what she was saying.

"I know this is difficult dear," the Director patted her cheek. "You need to tell me everything you know."

Phoebe's mind ran around inside her head and her eyes projected her puzzlement, "About what?" she croaked. Turning slightly away from her the Director demanded, "Water!" She then dribbled water over Phoebe's dry lips and into her cracked throat. "Is that better?" she asked, and Phoebe nodded. Standing now the Director walked to the edge of the room, "Now dear you need to be sensible." Phoebe was at a loss, "About what?" she asked again. The Director unseen by Phoebe walked up behind her and touched her shoulder with a metal rod. As the current passed through Phoebe's body she jumped and strained at the bonds that held her; once released, she cried out in pain.

"I ask the questions dear," the Director informed her. Phoebe simply nodded as a tear slipped down her cheek.

"Now, tell me why you were looking through my files?"

"I wasn't," Phoebe started to say and stopped as a second current passed through her. She bit her lip and blood slowly dripped down her cheek. When it stopped, she whimpered quietly trying to shrink into the seat; to hide from what was happening.

"The truth is always best," the Director informed her. "You'll find it liberating," she informed Phoebe as she gently stroked her cheek.

"I promise," Phoebe said between sobs. "I was only looking at Mike's work like you asked." The Director stroked her cheek again and shook her head, "Such a shame," she informed the air. "Such a pretty girl," she said as she bent over and kissed her on the lips, enjoying the salty taste of Phoebe's blood as she did so. Phoebe returned the kiss rising from her seat as far as the bonds would allow. "Still if you promise?" the Director continued as she rose out of the kiss and let her fingers drift lightly across Phoebe's lips. Phoebe nodded eagerly, and the Director drew her arm back and slapped her viciously across the face. Phoebe cried out, only partly in pain and partly in the realisation that she was utterly lost. More blood trickled from the corner of her mouth, mixed with her saliva and dripped onto her blouse.

"Find out what she knows," the Director informed a third party in the room. Phoebe had been unaware anyone else was present. "When you know everything, make sure she can't tell anyone else."

Phoebe sank into despair as the door closed on the image of the Director retreating. She briefly considered begging for mercy, but one look into Davidson's cold blue eyes told her it would be to no avail; and, instead, she gave way to her own misery. The tears flowed so quickly they produced a curtain to shield her from his actions. The first blow came as a complete surprise.

Changelings

Chapter 2

THE PAST:

Mike watched his parents' faces as they counted their money to see if they could afford to eat that day. Strain showed in every part of their countenance and he was pensive, not at the prospect of going hungry, that had happened many times, but at the fear he saw in both their eyes. They were the adults, they should know what to do, and for the first time he realised that perhaps they did not. His sister wailed but both of his parents ignored her. The wail grew with increasing crescendo. Finally, Mike reluctantly rose from the kitchen table and went to give her the last piece of bread to suck on. When he returned to the kitchen, his parents were in their own world. Hands entwined, they clung to one another much as drowning men cling to the planks that keep them afloat. They leaned slightly forward with foreheads touching, his mother's eyes turned to the table top rather than considering his father's brown orbs. His father's right hand gently brushed her cheek. A large fat tear rolled down to the end of her chin and fell in slow motion to splatter on the table; adding to the puddle already collected.

Changelings

Mike froze in the doorway, unsure what he should do. He shifted his weight from foot to foot. It was five minutes before Mike's dad noticed he was there. Kissing his wife gently on the forehead, he held his arms open in a gesture of inclusion toward his son. Walking over to nestle into his dad's body, he felt some of the warmth he had known in the past. Despite the physical closeness, somehow his father remained detached, adding to the metamorphosis of the familiar into the strange and unusual, increasing Mike's sense of loss, building his feelings of bereavement.

He watched his father rise from the kitchen table and bringing his baby sister from the other room he kissed her on the cheek and sat her on Mike's knee. He ruffled Mike's hair, told him to watch her and then taking Mike's mother by the hand, he led his wife with tears still streaming down her cheeks to the basement. Mike heard the stairs creek from two heavy steps and saw the door close as his mother was compelled to proceed to her destiny and the fulfilment of their mutual decision. Later, Mike watched his mother return, her eyes dry and somehow hollow as if her soul had left and only her body remained, an empty shell of the woman who had once inhabited her form. She cooked a roast in a mechanical way that would come to be his lasting memory of her. Mike ate and simultaneously wondered when his father would return and where his mother had managed to find meat.

****

The meat soon ran out and his mother took them all down to the headquarters of the new IGH. At that time, it was part of the Law Courts. They stood in a queue and waited. A faint drizzle seeped through his clothing and made him shiver, his baby sister began to cry, and his mother comforted her in her now standard mechanical manner that lacked connection to either of her children. They stood in that cold and silent queue all day long, Mike's mind becoming as numb as his wet and cold body. When the great doors of The Law Courts closed,

26

he simply sat where he had previously stood and dozed in the same spot, waking periodically when he felt the sharp points of rat's teeth penetrating his clothing or to respond to his sister's wails and remove whatever creature was attempting to dine on her tender flesh. He could smell the stench of urine from those who had relieved themselves where they lay, fearful of losing their coveted place in the queue. Finally, he drifted into a restless sleep dreaming of dragons and monsters.

When the sun rose, it shed warmth and a little hope with its brightening rays. Mike looked up into the dejected face of his mother. He tried to tell her it would be fine, but she hushed him and pointed down the street. As he looked, he saw the black limousine stop only feet from where he stood. The sunlight reflected from its polished black surface in such a way that he had to shield his eyes from its glare in order to see the woman who emerged from its dark interior.

"The Director," whispered Mike's mother. It was the first words she had spoken to him since leaving the house.

Mike looked again at the woman who stood in front of him. He could not distinguish any of her features, as the sun was behind her framing her head as if she owned a halo as part of her being. To Mike she looked every bit the saviour of the world that she was said purported to be. The great doors opened once more and raising her hand in salutation to the queue, the Director entered the building to begin her day's work. Mike, returning her wave, fell in love for the first time. The line, held back until now by the police, moved suddenly forward and in an instant Mike, his mother, and baby sister entered almost on the coat tails of the great woman herself.

The queue was tightly controlled by large well-fed police officers who wore stern expressions and carried revolvers in a very prominent and visible manner. The people were efficiently ushered toward reception desks. These were arranged in a long row and had behind each, an equally austere receptionist noting the details of each family.

When it was their turn, Mike's mother sat at the available desk and gave their names and ages, as he continued to comfort his sister. Then came the moment his mother had clearly expected but that he had not dreamed would happen. He and his sister were directed to the left doorway and his mother to the right. She simply stared at their retreating forms with that vacant soul-less gaze that had replaced the mother he had loved with all his heart, and that day, she was removed from his life forever.

Carrying the only relative that remained to him, he entered this new area. It was here he received his first meal in days and then, they took his sister from him. It was his turn to watch as she dwindled in his sight just as his mother had watched him walk away. Moving now as if on an invisible conveyor belt, he was stripped of his clothes, washed, and dressed in white; and with what appeared to be hundreds of other boys, he was numbered, poked, prodded and tested. Then there were the intellectual tests, exam scripts based on logical problem solving. The sampling followed this. Blood, hair and urine were taken in what seemed like huge amounts until he began to wonder if he had any left. At the end of it all he was called to a desk to hear his fate.

PRESENT DAY:

Mike awoke, sweating as if from his worst nightmare; he looked unfocused into the corner of the room, still lost in the landscape of his dream. He could still see the screaming form of his sister as she had been taken away. Why she haunted his dreams he did not know. He only really remembered her screaming and he did not think it was love that he felt for her. Her absence was represented by a welcome silence and a sense of disconnection from reality. He was separated from his roots, disengaged because he had no contact with any living thing that related directly to him. It seemed that he was disconnected from the world. Eternally afloat in a vast sea of nothingness.

Adjusting to his wakeful state, Mike became aware of the form in bed next to him. Her breasts rose and fell slowly; he felt no rising desire at her nakedness. She was not the woman he wanted. Easing himself quietly out of the bed, he walked into the living room and took a Capstan from his secret supply and slipped onto the balcony for a smoke. The first inhalation burned the back of his throat but then the welcoming effect of nicotine filled his mind with a rolling fog that covered the landscape; and hid his thoughts from even himself. He felt the stress leave in its wake.

"Those things will kill you," Cerberus said, emerging from the shadows.

Jumping and almost throwing the cigarette over the balcony. "Shit, where'd you come from?" Mike exclaimed while batting his cigarette towards the window rather than losing it in the street.

"I've already wasted one this week," he told Cerberus in explanation of his acrobatics. He leant on the balcony and inhaled deeply on the saved Capstan.

"I said I would return," Cerberus replied.

"Yes but, I was just expecting some warning," Mike said a little irritably.

Losing patience with the day walker, Cerberus hopped onto the railings readying himself for flight. Suddenly getting nervous that Cerberus would leave, Mike moderated his tone. "Please, don't go," he said, with something approaching humility in his voice.

Nodding, Cerberus jumped from the railing again. "Well day walker, what did you have in mind?" Cerberus asked.

"I don't know exactly, I just want to find her," Mike whined.

"You know as well as I do how long the process takes. It will be another couple of weeks until she enters my world," Cerberus pointed out in a matter-of-fact way. "That is, if she is changed immediately."

Going pale and holding onto the balcony while taking his last drag from the Capstan, Mike replied "I don't really think she has been taken for changing."

"Of course, you do, that's why you want my help." Cerberus mused coolly.

"Why though, and why not tell me? Why would they cover it all up?" Mike continued.

"Those are questions you are better placed to get answers to than I," Cerberus pointed out. "If I do help you find her, changed or not, I want something in return."

"What?" Mike asked.

"When I was changed, I had a younger brother. I want you to look into the records and find out what happened to him."

"But that's illegal," Mike protested.

"So is talking to me and smoking a Capstan," Cerberus pointed out.

Feeling a fool, Mike looked at the smouldering butt in his hand and simply nodded in slow motion. The changeling was, of course, correct.

"Perhaps the new lady in your life can help," Cerberus continued.

Feeling the need to explain, Mike said. "She's an office worker, of no consequence."

Producing a sound as close to a snort as he could Cerberus asked, "And who is of consequence Mr Caldwell?"

Mike didn't know how to respond, so instead he ignored the rebuff in Cerberus' tone. "How long do I have?" he asked.

"Let's say three weeks, by then I should be able to find your Phoebe, whatever her state and you should be able to get my information."

Mike was about to answer when he became aware that Cerberus was no longer listening, having interacted enough with the day walker he had once again taken to the night sky. Mike could not help but feel a little envious of all that power, but only a little, for he knew the dangers of going through that particular change. Many died, or worse, were so malformed they were left mad and deranged.

As Cerberus' form dwindled, a hand lightly touched his shoulder making him jump slightly.

"Nervous?" Barbara inquired.

"No, I just wasn't expecting anyone else out here at this hour.,"

"I sometimes watch them too," she admitted a little guiltily as she nodded in Cerberus' direction.

"What?" he asked sharply, "I wasn't watching the night stalkers; they are none of our concern. I was looking at the stars."

Realising she may have made a mistake she quickly replied, "That's what I meant," and then, to distract him, she let the robe she was wearing fall slightly apart and show her breast and a glimpse of her upright nipple. Moving slowly to the patio door she checked to see if he was following.

Inwardly saddened, Mike had watched her allow the robe she was wearing fall open and reveal her breast. On one level, he had no desire for her, but on another, gratuitous sex was always a little fun. Smiling, he followed her inside.

∗∗∗∗

From the shadows below, the yellow eyes of a lone wolf narrowed. Times, it appeared, were changing and allegiances. Moving like the sands on any beach, they were reforming in new patterns. Perhaps, thought the wolf, a night stalker and day walker could change the world. If that were indeed about to happen then perhaps, he could shape the nature of at least part of that change. Shaking his fir in a ripple effect along his whole body he padded thoughtfully into the night.

∗∗∗∗

Coming up behind Barbara in the bathroom, Mike reached around her to pick up his toothbrush and kissed her shoulder as he did so.

"I see you found the spare toothbrush."

"Yes, I hope that's ok," she said around a mouthful of toothpaste.

"Of course, it is," he replied. As she smiled happily, he continued, "You need to be able to freshen up, before work."

Then looking at her thoughtfully, he exclaimed, "Clothes! You need clothes. You can't go to work in yesterday's clothes."

"No, not really," Barbara replied with a smile. Another victory was about to occur, he was going to buy her, her first gift.

"Debenhams, they will open for me, I'll give them a call and we can drop in before work."

"That's very kind of you," Barbara simpered, finding it difficult to contain her happiness.

****

When they arrived at the office everyone else was there to notice their late arrival, together. Sitting at her desk, she rummaged in her bag for a much-needed pen and being in a rush, she ever so accidentally let her dress poke out for all to see. Making it obvious to anyone who cared to look, and they all cared, that she had not been home. Will found it imperative to do some filing next to where Barb sat. Looking at her feet and so to the place her bag was set, he drew in his breath in a way that made the saliva pass between his teeth and directly communicated his displeasure. Smiling even more broadly, Barbara began her day's tasks, she was sure Mike would soon call her to do some personal errand, an act that would seal her victory over Will.

****

In his own office, Mike was wondering how he could use the rivalry between Will and Barbara for his own ends. By now he was sure Barbara was feeling secure in his affections. Now, all he had to do was hook Will. As a rule, he didn't like to play both sides of the fence but on this occasion, he was willing to make an exception. There was also the possibility that he might enjoy a short walk on the wild side. Looking at the printout of the code comparison from the day before, he noted that the computer had identified the problem. Will and Barbara faded to the back of his mind as he concentrated on the computer's conclusions. It appeared that the amino acids were successfully unzipping the DNA strand but rather than re-ordering the four bases on each strand, an added compound was removing every T base. This resulted in the re-combined DNA becoming damaged; in effect, holes in the DNA had been produced. The outcome he could only guess at and the scientific part of him was very curious as to the nature of the changed organism. He was also curious as to how a compound that attacked only the T base had been produced and wondered if it was possible to attack any of the other bases; and what the resulting effects on the physical body of the test subject would be. The other part of him was simply angry that some unknown adversary had substituted an experimental amino acid into one of his change subjects, making it look like he had messed up his codes. Still it gave him an excuse to search in records for the possible suspect amino acid. Picking up the phone he took pleasure in explaining to Davidson what the problem was and how it was not his mistake. He could not resist asking about the nature of the failed change, just to satisfy his scientific curiosity.

Davidson placed the phone in its cradle and, smiling, went to report to the Director. Entering her room was, as always, an ordeal for Davidson. He was not a man who read people well and in terms of his relationship with the Director this had seriously disadvantaged him on more than one occasion. He still felt the humiliation when as a fourteen-year-old, he and his team of trainee crypto-geneticists had used a well-known obsolete amino acid with disastrous consequences that had cost the IGH undisclosed resources to rectify. The Director had called them all to her office; himself, Maxwell 13, Oldfield 12, and Caldwell also 12. She had spoken to them very calmly, almost friendly. The others had all recognised the coldness reflected in her eyes as a sign of impending danger. Nudging one another, surreptitiously, they quickly agreed through this silent gesture to remain quiet, unless compelled otherwise. They had not included Davidson in their pact. They later claimed they could not attract his attention without alerting the Director. He told her every detail and the more he talked the deeper he dug his own grave. The others, all cowards, simply looked at the floor and when directly challenged by her, simply mumbled sorry. It was clear to her that Davidson was to blame. Two years he had to work under Maxwell before leading another team. Daily he was humiliated by being ordered around by someone his junior. Still, he had to smile, in the end he had paid them back, each one except for Caldwell, and he had a feeling that perhaps his turn was on the horizon.

Bowing slightly in deference, Davidson cleared his throat to attract the Director's attention.

"Davidson, what's the news?" she asked, barely glancing at him before returning to the sheaves of paper in her hands.

"Well, an unknown amino acid was used to destabilise the double helix."

"Unknown?" she snapped, not allowing him to finish.

"Yes ma'am," he replied with a decisive tone; it always worked best to appear confident in front of her.

"Continue," she replied, suddenly giving him all her attention.

Squirming slightly despite his resolve, Davidson continued. "Yes ma'am, as yet unknown. Caldwell is researching the archives to see if it was ever used before. It seems that work is more important to him than his present troubles. I will scrutinise security footage for any sign of deliberate sabotage."

"Excellent, excellent, as usual Davidson."

"Thank you, ma'am," Davidson replied, allowing himself to bask a little in the rare compliment. Waving him away she closed the meeting.

"Let me know any more developments."

Knowing no reply was required, Davidson bowed once again as he left the room. She was already engrossed in her papers well before he closed the door.

****

Mike let his office door close quietly behind him. Looking at the secretaries, he raised a hand in acknowledgement to Barbara who smiled demurely back. He then spotted Will; he was dressed in skin-tight leather, trousers obviously designed to show his slim figure at its best. Mike stopped in his stride and looked for a moment at Will's figure, simply appreciating the obvious effort Will had spent on his appearance. Changing his direction and smiling broadly, he walked straight over to Will. As he approached, he noticed Will stand a little straighter and before he could hide his reaction of obvious pleasure at being approached, Mike caught his eye and smiled in disarming fashion. "Will," he said, "I need someone to come down to archives and work with me for perhaps a day or two, interested?"

"Yes, Mr Caldwell," Will replied in what he hoped was an appropriate manner.

"Mike please!" Mike added. "It might take as long as a week or two, will your supervisor clear it?"

"I am sure it will be fine for you, Mr, ... er Mike, but if you have a moment I can check now?" Will purred in reply.

"Sure," Mike said as he followed Will across the office.

At the end of this display Barbara was bright red and her gaze was furiously directed at her computer screen.

"Wow, you would think Mr Caldwell would have asked Barb," Britney said unthinkingly.

It was just enough to start the tears rolling down Barb's face. Phil, standing from his own station put his arm around her shoulder.

"Hey, it doesn't mean anything sweetie," he said as he handed her a tissue.

"It means I wasn't good enough last night," she sobbed.

"No, no it doesn't, does its Britney?" Phil asked.

"Of course not," Britney backed Phil up.

"I've heard of a lot of the top execs having two companions," Phil continued

"Do you think so?" Barb asked dabbing her eyes.

"I do hon," Phil said as he gave her shoulders an encouraging squeeze. "Why don't you go to the ladies and freshen up?" he asked, "I'm sure everything is going to be fine hon, real sure!" he added with another squeeze of her shoulder.

As she stood, she leant over and gave Phil a peck on the cheek. "Thanks Phil," she dabbed her eyes as she left the room.

"Think nothing of it," Phil replied to her retreating back, and then when she was out of ear shot, "Coleeeen, hon, give me five on Will to win."

Britney just looked puzzled, she wasn't sure what had just happened and when she saw Mr Caldwell get in the lift with Will, both of them laughing, she became even more confused. She went to find Coleen herself.

As Mike's arm circled Will's shoulder, Will felt his spirits rise. Perhaps it would all work out in the end.

****

At the same time, the steel arm of the converter slid along Phoebe's naked shoulder. The touch of the cold metal briefly brought her mind to the surface of conscious thought, but the pain in every nerve of her body forced it quickly and mercifully back into the unconscious realm.

Chapter 3

The archives were in the basement; sub-level 15, almost as low as you could go. There were only two lower levels, but Mike did not have clearance to go all the way to the bottom. As the lift doors opened the archive lights automatically came on resulting in the worker mites scurrying for the safety of the dark shadows. Stepping out first and thus asserting his authority, Mike presented his clearance to the archive hologram.

"I see sir that you have level two clearance and the other gentleman?"

"My assistant, Will," Mike said in his official tone.

"Sir, you do realise that he will not be allowed access to sensitive material."

"Yes," Mike replied. In Mike's view he did not need to interact with a hologram, he could converse equally well with the computer itself and in many ways better, but he also knew that people in general, including Will, preferred to interact with what looked like a person rather than a machine.

"This way gentlemen," the hologram said as it led them to a workstation. "The drones will locate any material you wish to review, and the mites will clear away all used materials."

"What if we wish to keep some material for future reference?" Mike asked.

"The mites will only clear away material when the archive is in darkness sir, which happens once you leave sir. If you wish to retain material for your next session, simply ensure it is placed in the red trays. This will not then be cleared sir."

"Good, thank you archivist, you may retire." Mike informed the hologram.

"Thank you, sir, may I remind you, that it is prohibited to remove any material from the archive or indeed to copy any material while here, although taking notes is allowed." The archivist then walked toward the wall and melted into the structure of the archive.

Relieved at the departure Mike said in a more relaxed fashion, "Ok, first things first, would you get coffee while I make a start?"

"Yes, Mr Caldwell" Will replied, relieved already at not having to spend much time down in the depths of the building. It felt a little like being buried to him.

"Mike ... remember?" Mike corrected him.

"Oh, silly me, sorry ... Mike," Will smiled.

"That's OK, don't give it a second thought. It will take me a while to get started and produce something for you to type. Perhaps after coffee you wouldn't mind organising a cleaner for my place?" Mike asked.

"No, not at all Mr ... er ... Mike," Will answered, beaming. This was his chance to impress the boss and, more importantly, his first visit to the flat.

"That would be a great help, Will. I'll give you my flat keys and you can take the rest of the day to do it and in the meantime, the items I sort here that I want you to type up later will be put in the Red Tray so they will be available to us on our next trip down here."

Changelings

Taking the keys from Mike, Will skipped happily into the elevator. Sighing with contentment he held the keys to his cheek as the lift doors closed.

Alone to pursue his own thoughts, Mike requested the very first news reports from before the conception of the IGH.

As the tape began to play, Mike recognised the shores of Loch Ness and the sound of the news reporter's voice presiding over the unfolding images. This material had formed the basis of Mike's first lessons here at the IGH and he did not expect to uncover any great surprises. He just wanted to remind himself of the familiar so he could identify the strange. He sat back as the reporter's voice permeated the atmosphere.

"Donna Logan here on the banks of Loch Ness, reporting from the ruins of Urquhart Castle, where tragic proof of the existence of the cryptid known as the Loch Ness Monster has been washing ashore almost daily. These huge creatures resembling in part the plesiosaur are scattered everywhere. They confirm the popular theory that they are refugees from the dinosaur era. They are in various stages of shape metamorphosis, with some creatures having easily identifiable characteristics of the horse. Locals have claimed the creatures could transform themselves into horses and it appears that this latest evidence adds validity to the Kelpie legend. However, the scientific community remains somewhat sceptical and carcasses are being removed for further study. The public are advised to stay away from the area as any public health risk is still to be ruled out. This is Donna Logan reporting for the BBC."

Archivist note: In total 157 cryptids were removed from the shores of Loch Ness, each having unique combinations of amino acids able to unzip the DNA chains and recombine them to allow shape shifting in an individual animal. In total five amino acids were identified with 120 possible combinations, 120 possible effects. No other cryptids were ever found.

Mike yawned. He had never wondered where the IGH had gotten the original amino acids and now his own lack of curiosity puzzled him. He was determined to understand the history of the organisation he worked for was now a priority. The next BBC inclusion jumped forward several months:

"Donna Logan reporting from Kendal in the Lake District; in scenes reminiscent of Alfred Hitchcock's fictional Birds, the usual picturesque scene is blighted by the bodies of thousands, possibly millions of birds across all species. Locals are at a loss to explain the phenomena, as is the scientific community. Clean up operations are set to take several days, and many crops will have perished beneath this macabre carpet. The public are advised to stay away from the area as any public health risk is still to be ruled out. This is Donna Logan reporting for the BBC."

Archivist note: In subsequent days, all bird life on the planet became extinct for no apparent reason. Like the Loch Ness cryptids, all species of birds were now extinct. Genetic material was archived for future reference and experimentation.

****

THE PAST

Cerberus turned in his sleep; he and his brother were watching from the window of their shared bedroom. Watching, as birds fell from the sky like a macabre rain. Cerberus slipped his arm around his brother's shoulder in a show of affection and protection. Jamie was two years younger and Cerberus was aware of resenting his presence at times. Before Jamie the room had been his alone and the toys had never had to be shared. Still at times like this, when the younger boy was afraid, he felt a surge of the desire to protect him. He supposed it had always been the same for brothers; they could fight with each other to their hearts content, but if an external threat occurred then they banded together for mutual support. He looked down at Jamie and shuddered as he saw his hand transform before his eyes. Shaking in his sleep, his mind rejected the transformation and his hand was once more restored to what it should be. His parents where downstairs arguing loudly with their father's brother. Dad believed that recent events were a clear sign of the end of the world. Justified outcome for the sins committed by humanity. Uncle Tom called him a fool. He was sure it was all part of a huge conspiracy by the government, a way to reduce exploding populations. Mum was simply begging both to stop arguing.

The boys listened to the disintegration of their family and watched the end of their world as more birds dropped. Cerberus was about to suggest they play marbles when he saw the black van turn into their driveway. The tyres bounced as they made their way slowly over the small bodies which littered the area. The van continued forward crunching over gravel and the bones of the dead. The van came to a halt directly in front of the living room window and as the door opened the voices below stopped arguing. The adults became aware of the intrusion that was about to occur. The whole house drew in its breath in anticipation of the intrusion. Reflecting the tension, both boys held their breath also. The knock, when it came, made them all jump as it resounded throughout the house with an air of authority. It demanded entry to their home. Sneaking to the top of the stairs, the boys peeked at the scene unfolding below. Cerberus held his hand over his brother's mouth and warned him not to make a sound. Whatever was happening was obviously serious. One look at the dark suited strangers was enough to convey that simple message.

One of the suits stepped forward and demanded Uncle Tom go with them. Uncle Tom however had other ideas. He took one look at these intruders and exclaimed, "Hell!" and ran for the back door. It was then that the boys' world truly fell apart.

The back door collapsed under the force of three armoured guards the sight of which stopped Uncle Tom in his tracks. Coming to his brother's aid Cerberus' dad placed himself between danger and his brother. The gesture was futile as he fell under the hail of bullets which announced the arrival of the backup team. Their mother screamed, and Cerberus clamped his hand even tighter over Jamie's mouth dragging him backward into the bedroom and then into the cupboard which he hated being left open at night. More gunfire was replaced by an ominous silence which was quickly broken by the sound of footsteps in every corner of the house; and finally, by the squeal of tyres on gravel as the intruders withdrew. Running to the bedroom window, the point at which they had started the day, the boys were just in time to see the van leave their driveway. They stood frozen for some time, both afraid to see what waited below and both hoping their mother would call upstairs that everything was alright now, and they could come down for breakfast.

Finally, when the call failed to come, they descended the stairs together; hand in hand they went downstairs. The spray of holes the bullets had left was clearly visible along the hallway. The bodies of both their parents became visible to the boys. Jamie, at the same time silent, pulled closer to his elder brother and began to suck his thumb, something he had not done for more than a year. Placing himself between their bodies and his brother Cerberus guided him into the front room. He put his brother on the settee to watch television. He put cartoons on so that Jamie could pretend all was still well with their world. Bringing a sheet from upstairs he rolled his mother's body onto it and then dragged her to the bottom of the garden. He then repeated the operation for his father and then his uncle. Exhausted he wanted to curl up and simply cry but he knew that he had to look after Jamie and so he began to clean up the blood. He scrubbed the stains without looking at them directly, as if looking at them would make them worse. When he was finished, he went to the kitchen and stood the back door against the hole it had originally vacated. He then made sandwiches for them both and finally brought their duvets downstairs, so they could huddle together in front of the television.

****

PRESENT DAY:

Still in the archive, Mike flipped through several similar reports, all by Donna Logan. He wondered if she ever tired of reporting the demise of her world. Looking at his watch he also wondered where Will had got to with his coffee. Taking out his mobile phone he was about to use it when Will came skipping out of the lift holding a large gingerbread latte and sporting a smile. Just the sight of him made Mike smile and his mood momentarily lightened. Accepting the coffee, Mike felt no need to converse with Will, and as Will skipped back to the lift to follow the rest of his orders, Mike returned to work.

"Donna Logan reporting from Staffordshire; the fields around Lichfield are the sight of the most bizarre scenes to date. Crops that were ready to harvest have virtually disappeared overnight. Locals have reported being besieged by waves of giant insects. Scientists have yet to verify their existence or identify their origin. The public are advised to stay away from the area as any public health risk is still to be ruled out. This is Donna Logan reporting for the BBC."

Archivist note: The rise in insect life was noted worldwide. It was presumably a result of the loss of the main predators. The absence of bird populations also led to greater numbers, although the increased size of the insects needs further scientific investigation. Genetic material of the new species was archived for future research.

Mike tracked the death of the old world through the news reports of Donna Logan. He thought about how she must have felt reporting each disaster and if she had suspected where it would all end. He wondered if she had guessed where it would lead? He began to watch for signs of strain on her face.

"Donna Logan reporting from Staffordshire; the initial rise in insect life has been astounding. However, as quickly as they arrived, they are dying in the millions. Children are ploughing through the exoskeletons as they once did through autumn leaves. Scientists discourage this practice and are advising the public to stay away from the area as any public health risk is still to be ruled out. This is Donna Logan reporting for the BBC.

Archivist note: the death of excess insect populations was initially heralded as a positive new development. It soon became clear that this was not the case.

Mike switched to the next report.

"This is David Stringer reporting for the BBC..."

Mike wondered what had happened to Donna Logan. Turning to a second computer he searched for her. He found a short piece in the Times obituary section.

"Much loved presenter Donna Logan was found in her apartment this morning having died in her sleep. No other person is being sought in connection with her death and family have asked that instead of flowers

well-wishers make a donation to Barnardo's the famous children's charity, and a cause close to Donna's heart."

Suicide, Mike presumed. Back then suicide still carried stigma and was not often reported directly. Presumably she had tired of reporting the death of her world.

Mike stopped the tape and rubbing his eyes he tried to make sense of what he was viewing, to put the information into order. Viewed together it was obvious that disaster was just around the corner. The only puzzle was why the authorities of the time had missed the signs. He knew, only too well, that portended disaster had arrived in the middle of his childhood and continued well into his adult life. The eco-balance had been lost, but how it had all started remained a mystery. He decided it was time to go home for the day. Perhaps something would occur to him overnight as to where he should search next. As the doors of the elevator closed he saw the lights of the archive blink out and heard the faint scurry of the mites as they came to clear away his day's debris.

****

Outside the IGH, he caught the first indo-bus that came along and, sinking into the soft seat, he closed his eyes and relaxed his mind. The bus monitor would let him know when they arrived at his apartment block. This was one of the advantages of a reduced population. Large numbers no longer had to cram like sardines onto small claustrophobic conveyances where personal space was a myth. Now, you just hailed one of the numerous individual units and gave your grid reference. Complete privacy on a public system, true perfection. The lull of motion relaxed him further and he began to dream of the Loch Ness creatures swimming in the depths of the lagoon. He thought he heard their mournful cries as they called for the last time to one another. The cries of a dying species. Then, as he watched, they began to change, not into the horses of legend but a more human shape and then impossibly the creature before him emerging from the water was no longer a lost legend but that of Phoebe, his lost love. He stretched his arms out toward her but once again she began to change, this time to a figure that was half Davidson and half bird man. Jerking backward, he woke himself and, disorientated, took several seconds to reconcile all his senses and understand he had simply dozed for minutes rather than directly experienced the things he had seen. Shuddering slightly, he looked out of the window and still, half asleep, he fancied he saw a cryptid swimming through the shadows of the streets. Shaking his head to clear away the last shreds of the dream, he stepped out of the bus as it stopped in front of his building.

****

Clearing away the last remnants of sleep, Sutton heaved his body upright and sat for a moment at the edge of his bed. Taking a swig of whisky to give himself a kick start, he belched and simultaneously scratched his stomach. Rising slowly, he went to what passed for a bathroom in the pit he called home and put his head under the tap. Every day it seemed harder to rouse himself from sleep and once again he wondered if he ought to call it quits and take early retirement. Then he remembered Kapowski's sneering face and that was all the motivation he needed to get himself into working mode once again. Galvanised to action he prepared himself for the graveyard shift.

****

Cerberus shivered in his nest and withdrew from the world of dreams. Saddened by the events he experienced while sleeping, he turned once more to Maia for comfort and for a time all was well with the world as he nestled amongst her soft downiness. She gave him the support he needed and knew by his mood that it was his brother that was foremost in his thoughts.

****

Mike opened the door to his apartment and stopped on the threshold. He needed to take a second, look and check it was indeed his place. The lighting was subdued with a hint of red, a rose scented aroma reached his nostrils and a scantily clad male held a glass of wine out toward him. Smiling, he came through the door and accepted the wine.

"This is all very nice Will" he commented.

"Oooh, thank you Mike," Will simpered. "Dinner is almost ready if you would like to freshen up first," he continued.

"Yes, I think I would, is the bath ready?" Mike asked.

"Oh yes, Mike," Will replied, still smiling he was sure all his efforts were being appreciated.

"Well I'll slip into something more comfortable then," Mike said as he exited the main room.

Will began to hum as he busied himself with finishing up the dinner preparations.. It was obvious that Mike was testing both him and Barb. He felt he had the advantage though, as he was something a little different for Mike and he was determined to make that fact very special.

Stirring the sauce, he called through to Mike, "Shall I come and wash your back?"

"Sure," Mike called back "and bring some more wine, will you?" he added.

Turning everything on the stove down to low heat, Will happily hooked the wine in his right hand with his own glass and skipped into the bathroom. Mike was sat in the centre of champagne bubbles. Will leaned closely toward him and refilled Mike's wine. Then, setting the bottle and his own glass on the toilet seat, he picked up the sponge and began to wash Mike's back.

Later, Mike leaned against the balcony rails with his third and final Capstan between his lips. Will came out behind him with another glass of wine and silently held it out to Mike. In return, Mike held out the Capstan. Inwardly thrilled, Will took one pull and handed it straight back. Folding over in two he began to cough, and tears streamed down his face.

"Sorry Mike, I've never had one before," Will spluttered.

"No, I'm sorry," Mike replied, "I should have thought, it must be a week's credits for you."

"More like a month," Will replied with a wry twist at the corner of his mouth.

"Hmm, they don't pay you guys much do they?" Mike asked.

"Oh, I can't complain," Will was quick to make that clear "We make enough to eat, which isn't true for everyone."

Mike turned to face Will directly. "I thought the hunger problem had been solved?"

"Oh yes, yes it has mostly, it's just people find it a little hard to make ends meet, that's all," Will added quickly.

"Not you though?" Mike asked.

"Sometimes," Will replied.

Mike turned and looked out into the evening, lost a little in his own thoughts, thinking for the first time about what it was like for those less well-off in the Director's brave new world. As the sun went down upon the city scene, he watched the shadow world descend to claim its territory for the night. He was truly in his own world and for a time he forgot about Will behind him.

Mike wondered, what the 'changed' dreamed of. Did they have the same desires as the fully human? For a long time, he had simply viewed them as commodities. Raw material to produce useful and functioning units and now as he watched the city, he wondered what happened to their souls. Unaware of Mike's thoughts, Will simply observed, not wanting to break the intimacy that he had felt with Mike; not wanting to bring Mike back to the present. Mike also wondered about Will and Barb's feelings. Did they really want to be with someone like him or was it simply the best they could hope for? It had been a long time since he had wondered about the feelings of others and once more, he saw his screaming sister being taken from him. Should he have fought to keep her he wondered. Had he lost something else, an essential part of himself by letting her go? Rousing himself from unproductive thoughts he smiled at Will and holding out his hand he led him inside. Time, he decided for another walk on the wild side, perhaps it would cure his sadness and give a second boost to Will's self-esteem.

****

Phoebe ran her hands through her hair; it felt as it usually did, and she decided to open her eyes. The pain was gone, and the world did not seem as bad as it once had. When she looked around the medics were all there looking back at her and writing on their clipboards. One of them looked sorrowfully at her and turned away. She wondered what kind of monster she had become and decided to follow this woman to find out. The others blocked her way and she was led to a mirror and it was there she began to scream. Every molecule she had left to her screamed in response to what she saw but no sound disrupted the world around her. She had joined the shadows, and in her distress, she dove into this new world and left the old one behind. Mercifully, none of the scientists who had created her had the power to follow.

Changelings

Chapter 4

As the sun left the horizon and the shadows settled to the pavement for the night, Sutton entered police headquarters for his shift. His timing was just a bit out, as usual, and he passed Kapowski on his way home.

"Hey, Sutton, we left you some doughnuts to pass the time." he called.

Sutton just glared as he went past and Kapowski giggled, pleased at having elicited a reaction. Cursing himself, Sutton slipped into his chair. Immediately he felt at home in the familiar setting. A part of him loved the night shift, he had the office virtually to himself and could fix his own pace of work. He could even forget about work altogether if he wanted. No one really cared what the night shift guy did; he was just marking time. Picking up the first file from the 'in' tray, he settled down for the night. As was his custom, he read all the incoming reports before deciding where to make a start. The one he decided to follow up first was a report about a confused Butterbee, changelings that were modelled on the deceased butterflies and bees. They were designed to pollinate crops, but because they were derived from the youngest of raw materials, they could often become confused and try to attach themselves to others. This complaint was from a citizen that was being followed by a Butterbee. The confused creature had been sitting on their balcony crying for hours and disturbing the family. The first port of call had been the wardens, but they had been unable to track the creature and now it was suspected that another citizen was feeding and sheltering the Butterbee within city limits. This was why Sutton was involved, harbouring confused changelings was illegal and could result in the citizen being fined or even reassigned themselves. Putting on his coat, Sutton left to see if he could pick up the Butterbee's trail.

Curfew meant Sutton should only come across changelings when out on the streets. Experience told him that others,' intent on hidden business, would also be prowling. It was those he needed to be careful about. The changelings tended to avoid human contact, but a cop could be in all kinds of danger on the dark streets if he stumbled across the deviants. Sutton thought announcing his presence helped. He found that his footsteps echoed disproportionately with the time of day, giving his night-time jaunts an eerie air, much like the atmosphere encapsulated in the old-time horror movies. Sutton found a strange comfort in the sound of his own steps and liked the way they proclaimed the emptiness of the night streets. The fact that he could make an impression in this foreign landscape confirmed that he was indeed present and alive. He was prominent in a world most of his kind liked to lock out and ignore until the sun rose and reclaimed the day for them. Rounding the corner of the Art Gallery, he was surprised to see Simon, a gentleman of the night. For a long time, the numbers of people living rough had rapidly decreased, many falling victim to the rising tides of rat armies that patrolled all the major cities. Of those who managed to stay alive, a large percentage had entered the IGH for the promise of a good meal. Others who had not wanted to go voluntarily had been escorted by the legal system as a way they could contribute to society.

Simon was an oddity, and since Sutton himself fitted into this category he was always pleased to see him drifting along the clean streets. Tonight, since he was on police business, Sutton did not want to stop and chat, so he simply raised his hand in recognition as he passed. From across the street, Simon raised his hand in return, immediately going back to his search of the bin that was occupying his full attention. Sutton continued down the street, he knew it would be quicker to catch a bus, but he preferred the feel of the night, its sights, sounds and smells. He enjoyed the solitude of the darkness and the relaxed silence enabled him space to think. He often thought thinking was an under-rated skill that was drowned out in the day to day business of most people's lives. As he walked, he watched the rats begin to emerge from the sewers, cautiously sniffing the air and hesitant but they soon gained confidence, when they believed no danger existed. Suddenly, from above a dark shadow glided soundlessly past and then swooped and scooped a rat in each talon. Stopping, Sutton frowned, slightly worried at how close the owl had come. Some of them took liberties with the freedom they had in the night streets. They knew they were expected to stay away from human contact and yet they seemed to come deliberately close as if asserting their own authority and power in the night time economy. While he was lost in his thoughts, the owl swooped a second time and forced Sutton to take a step backward and he called out loudly.

"Watch it!" he shouted.

The owl did not deign to reply but it did drop one of the rats it was carrying. It hit the pavement with a sickening thud and struggled a little in front of Sutton. Then several of its own kind emerged from the sewer opening and dragged their comrade away. Probably, Sutton thought, to cannibalise the flesh and prolong their own lives rather than offer the stricken any help or solace. There was little waste in this world and the sacrifice of the individual for the good of the group was common. The problem as far as Sutton could tell was whoever decided what was for the greater good may well just be deciding what was good for themselves and not the majority. Shuddering slightly, he dismissed his own thoughts as unhelpful and continued on his way.

He realised he was in Caldwell's upper-class district. It didn't surprise Sutton that, yet another complaint had come from this area. It seemed to him that the more people had, the more they expected and the more they complained so those expectations could be met. He looked up toward Caldwell's balcony and thought he saw the brief flicker of red produced on the end of a cigarette as someone inhaled deeply. He remembered smelling burnt tobacco when he had entered Caldwell's apartment and wondered if it was Caldwell who was smoking again. As quickly as the thought entered his head, he dismissed it, for Caldwell to be smoking again so soon he would have to be far richer than he appeared. It could not be Caldwell, Sutton decided. It must be another fine upstanding citizen and even, he knew part of his vehemence was due to his own jealousy. He would love to inhale tobacco once more and savour the burning sensation at the back of his throat as the smoke filled his lungs. Perhaps he could catch Caldwell in the act and confiscate his stash. At least he could dream!

Walking a little further, he came to a building identical to Caldwell's and, here, he could clearly see the offending Butterbee sobbing on a balcony about eight floors up. Finding a comfortable spot to watch and wait, Sutton began his vigil. Unlike the wardens his intention was not to catch the creature but to catch the human sheltering it during the day. As he watched he began to note every detail, this one was very small and was probably the changeling of a three-year-old or less. It must have been an orphan and that would explain why it was following a woman, it probably wanted its mother. However, it was no longer human, not worthy of his sympathy. As he watched he noted its beautifully coloured wings. They reminded him of the tissue paper stained glass windows he had made as a child. Delicate, with many colours, they were attached to the now green body that turned daylight into energy, for these creatures needed little in the way of conventional food. One of the biggest changes was in the nose. This had become an elongated proboscis that could take the nectar from the flowers they pollinated. In a way, they were beautifully constructed, and it was amazing that science had produced them and not the natural world. Leaning against the building Sutton found that after a while his mind began to wander.

Looking back toward Caldwell's building, he wondered if the companion had turned up. Perhaps, if he had time, he would drop in on the geneticist. Turning back toward the Butterbee, he was just in time to see it disappearing around the corner.

"Hell," he cursed and set off at a trot to try and catch it. By the time he got to the corner it had already turned around the next building. Puffing, he cursed again, perhaps he should drink a little less and exercise a little more. By the time he got to the next corner his breathing was so loud that any element of surprise was surely lost to him. It was then that he noticed something was not quite right. The Butterbee was built to go for a long time, either running on its ultra-light frame or flying, yet it was slowing, almost as if it was waiting for him. Bending over and holding his knees to catch his breath, he watched it more closely and as he straightened to resume the chase it started to move again. He tested this at the next intersection and once again, as he slowed so did the creature in front of him and as he resumed motion, it did too. Now totally focused on the creature, he neglected his own rule of keeping half an eye on the landscape around him. He failed to realise that the neighbourhood was changing, significantly, and not for the better. Almost ready to call it a day, he saw the Butterbee duck into a derelict building. Perhaps he had been wrong, perhaps it wasn't being helped and was simply hiding out by itself. Arriving at the entrance he pushed aside the rotting timber that once kept the curious out of this plot. Slipping through the fence Sutton was surprised to find himself in a courtyard leading to a main entrance which was framed with stone pillars. The large oak doors were even more conspicuous by the fact that they were still hanging in place. A building this old would usually have been scavenged on several occasions and solid oak doors would have provided firewood for a whole community. Sutton wondered what had prevented their theft. Walking up the steps, He heard the soft scrunch his feet made as the dry leaves littering the floor were reduced to powder beneath them. Reaching the huge doors, he realised they were even bigger than he had first thought, standing at least three times his own height. Expecting to have to push hard in order to open the ancient wood far enough to allow his admittance he braced himself for effort and was startled when it opened easily on a well-oiled mechanism. So unexpected was this that Sutton lost some of his balance and swinging round self-consciously he stumbled before regaining his feet. He was glad that no one witnessed his inelegant dance. Kapowski and his crew would snigger about it for a week if they found out. Entering the great hall, he turned to study the way he had come and noted the system of weights that balanced the weight of the great doors and enabled them to open so smoothly. He also saw his own footsteps in the dust; his and no one else's. He wondered why there were no other visible prints prior to his. It was very evident that even if the Butterbee had flown in here, no citizen was helping it. At least no one was walking into the building this way; that was certain. It would be impossible not to leave a trail in what must have been a decade's worth of accumulated dust. He really didn't need to go any further into the dark interior of this derelict shell. Yet he wanted to explore further, he was fascinated by the majesty of the place and amazed that he had not noticed it before. However, the sensible side of Sutton knew that any further exploration would be best done in daylight. He decided to come back with the right equipment on Saturday, his day off. Turning reluctantly, he started toward the door and as he left, he heard a distant wail that could or could not have come from deep within this monument to the past. The sound made

Sutton shudder. It was as if the past were in distress and reaching out to him for comfort that he could not give. It confirmed his decision to investigate in the light of day. Swinging the doors closed, just to make sure nothing could follow him out of the building he made his way back to the pavement.

As Sutton stood on the pavement, Cerberus watched the watcher, one wing sheltering the Butterbee from sight. It worried him that this one walked the streets at night policing both changeling and human alike. Other officers were uncomfortable around his kind and left them alone, which suited Cerberus. This one was different. He seemed to be actually doing his job, almost as if he believed what he was doing was right, and Cerberus had no respect for such a depth of delusion. No respect for a man that chased children and upheld the rules that held Cerberus' kind as slaves. Bending to caress the Butterbee, he lifted the tiny creature onto his back and flew across the rooftops, out over the fields and into the night. He flew to return the tiny creature on his back to a place where it would be safe.

Tonight, he would be short of his rat quota, but if the others covered for him then it would not be noticed. Tonight, he had other business, and at the same time he may as well shelter the pathetic creature he now carried. It had lost in the process of change, but it was not to blame for what it had become, 'they' had all lost in the process in one way or another and they all shared the responsibility to protect the weakest. Cerberus felt anger surge through his body like molten fire through his veins and it made him fly faster to try to retrieve the soul he felt was stolen from him. His anger roiled against those who had stolen it and designed this world to favour only the elites.

****

Mike sat up in the bed. He watched the form sleeping next to him and smiled to himself. Tomorrow he would continue looking for Phoebe but for tonight he would enjoy the interlude. He stroked Will's cheek as he slept and sighed with contentment. Will smiled in the dark. Mike decided he could get used to the two different kinds of companion. Checking the clock, he decided to watch the sun rise over the city and slipping on his wrap, he stepped onto his balcony. Looking at the horizon, he was mesmerised by the splash of colours. The mix of yellows, oranges and reds was beautiful and unique. He had always enjoyed watching the day paint itself anew; one of the few constants in a troubled life. It brought hope to Mike and he never grew bored of this daily miracle.

He felt the heat of the sun as it rose above the horizon, and just as he was ready to go inside, Will stepped out beside him and offered him coffee. Smiling he accepted it wordlessly and decided in that moment to have the both of them as his new companion. It would look as if he was completely over Phoebe. He drank and then held it out to Will for him to take the cup. Pleased, Will drank then gave it back.

"Is coffee all I get?" Mike asked.

"No, I can make a full breakfast," Will laughed, enjoying the lightness of the moment.

"Great, I'll get a shower then," Mike said.

****

The wolf padded silently through the dark streets. Hunting alone he watched the night's dramas unfold before him. Unlike the owls he did not stick to just the rats. He considered everything that wandered in his realm fair game. No one complained when the disenfranchised failed to turn up in the morning. He simply solved a problem; a problem others would have to deal with if he did not. He had watched the two men on the balcony and wondered if either dared tempt him by an early morning walk. He was not pleased when they returned inside as his time on the street was almost over. He was convinced he would hunt them one day soon. They were placing themselves on the edge of matters they did not understand and that would eventually bring them into his realm. With that comforting thought he padded away to his daytime lair.

****

Sutton finished his shift and, with relief, managed to avoid any interaction with Kapowski. Last night's inability to track even a harmless Butterbee would have added further fuel to Kapowski's already extensive supply with which to ridicule him. Although Sutton worked hard at not to show it, being universally considered superfluous did get to him from time to time. He knew himself to be an excellent detective, he just had to convince the rest of the world it was still true. He wondered if it was just his age. In a world that idolised youth he felt side-lined and forgotten. Walking down the awakening street, lost deep in his own thoughts, he failed to notice the changing shadows on the buildings as he passed them. It was as if they were tracking him, and not with benign intentions. The shifting patterns of darkness were almost indecipherable from the true shadows cast at this time of day, but they were very visible in the pools of light left by the rising sun. Ordinary shadows did not exist here, and those following Sutton could be clearly seen if anyone had been watching. But humans had a great talent for ignoring the things they did not wish to acknowledge.

Sutton shuddered slightly and pulled his coat more closely around himself; a sudden breeze chased a leaf down the street ahead of him and he became uncomfortably aware of just how alone he was; alone and vulnerable.

****

Mike and Will arrived at the office together. As triumphant as Barb had been the day before, Will bounced out of the lift with a huge smile and,

"Hi ya all," as he skipped to his desk.

Mike smiled, enjoying once again Will's outgoing nature, enjoying his exuberance until he saw Barb hurrying to the ladies. Mike went to follow her when Coleen stopped him.

"I'll sort her sir," she said.

"You don't understand," Mike replied, "I was going to hire both."

"Oh, that's wonderful sir," Coleen simpered.

"Should I talk to her?" Mike asked.

"I'll sort it sir," Coleen said "I'll be happy to explain things. She can come to the office for a chat when she feels better."

"Are you sure that's best?" Mike inquired.

"Yes, sir. She will feel better talking to you when she's freshened up. Believe me sir," Colleen explained. "I'll be happy to make things clear," she added. Coleen was more than happy they both won, then neither had beaten the other and she didn't have to pay anyone out. She had just made a tidy sum and that made her magnanimous.

"Well, if you are sure," Mike finished "I'll wait in the office then."

Mike left Colleen to sort Barb and bring them both to see him. In the meantime, he busied himself with his overnight e-mails. Happy, he hummed as he worked, and the serpent started transmitting for the day.

✳✳✳✳

Barb and Will were excused to work out the joint living and working arrangements, Mike returned to the archives. He moved away from the stored news footage and began to trawl through the first records of the IGH. It appeared that at the time the world was dying, the IGH, as such, did not exist. He tried to trace the Director herself but kept coming across security issues. Her private life was out of bounds. Logical, he supposed, as particularly in the early day's she must have attracted all kinds of interest, not all with good intentions. Moving on, he decided to look for the first experiments involving the collected amino acids. As he reviewed the material, he began to wonder when it had occurred to the scientific community to start trying to change existing organisms. Once again, the records were unclear.

The first experiments he found were already experiencing success in changing or partially changing the rats they used as raw material. They had formed the first test subjects; their numbers had exploded inversely proportional to the decline of other species by feeding on the dead. Also, the animal rights activists did not find them cute enough to protect. Experiment with hamsters and everyone complained, but rats were fair game. It took five years for the first human subjects to be used. It had become evident that rats could not plug many of the ecological gaps that had appeared at an alarming rate. The only other organisms in ready supply were humans.

The government passed the first conversion laws allowing any person at risk of starvation to offer themselves for change and hence survive; albeit in a different form. Their family would also receive food vouchers. For many it meant instead of being a burden they could be a provider in a single act of final sacrifice. As far as Mike could tell, there was no scientific reason why the rat conversions had been abandoned. The conclusions that had been drawn should have needed another five to ten years research to back up the change to human testing. Admittedly time was a constraint. A solution was needed and needed quickly but the move could equally have backfired instead of proving to be the right strategy. Somewhat puzzled, Mike decided to stop for the day and think about what he had discovered. The answers had to be in the records somewhere. It was just a matter of conducting the correct searches. Deep in thought, he made his way back to his office and as his door closed, Davidson stepped out of the lift into the archives. Caldwell was over stepping his boundaries but for some reason the Director protected him. However, Davidson knew if he put the right evidence in front of her she would act.

Changelings

✶✶✶✶

Sutton tossed and turned, tying his bedding into knots around himself. He found it increasingly hard to sleep even with blackout blinds. He decided to get up and watch a little TV. Sitting in his dilapidated armchair, he poured himself a generous whisky. Fortunately for him when the public health laws criminalised smoking, alcohol had escaped untouched as its benefits were seen to outweigh its deficits. It could also be made by completely synthetic means.

Flipping through the channels, he wondered why daytime TV which was such rubbish remained a constant when so much else had changed in the world. Sighing, he decided to watch the Jeremy Westlake show, this one was called, 'Forbidden Love; my companion is an Owl'. After a while Sutton drifted into sleep and began to dream that he had undergone the change himself. He felt younger and more alive than he ever had before. He could run at breakneck speed and delighted in the feel of the wind as it caressed his body. He could see clearly even though it was dark. It seemed natural that he was a night predator and it suited his own view of his personality. He ran through darkened streets on all fours, and he presumed he was a wolf. Although, as far as he knew, no formula existed to change a man into a wolf. It had been briefly considered but abandoned as unnecessary and even dangerous to resurrect such independent carnivores. He caught the scent of his prey on the light breeze and howling his delight, set off in pursuit. Rounding a corner, he saw what he was hunting, huddled by a far wall. As he approached, the figure slowly turned its face toward him. Waking with fear tumbling through his veins, he realised he had been hunting himself.

Sweating and shaking, he cursed himself for the fear he could still feel. That would teach him to allow himself too much whisky in the future. Rising stiffly from the chair, he failed to notice the shadow creature swim out of the open window and into the shadows of the city. Rinsing his head

62

under the tap he checked the time. There were still several hours before his next shift started and he decided since he was awake, he should make the most of the day and go back to the derelict building from the previous night. He hesitated slightly on the steps of his flat. He was unaccustomed to being a part of the daytime world and was slightly startled by the sheer numbers that now thronged the streets. It seemed to him the population had increased rather than been decimated. Usually he saw these streets either in an empty state or with the first of the day walkers taking possession. Now the streets were crowded and, strangely, the one thing he noticed most was that in vast numbers like this, people smelt and smelt rather badly at that. No wonder both he and Simon preferred the night! Taking a deep breath, he entered the throng. Moving swiftly to the curb, he gratefully entered an indo-bus and letting himself breathe again, he gave his destination.

The bus moved slowly through the crowds until it took a sudden turn onto the street he had walked just the night before, but instead of crowds, this street was empty. Getting out of the bus, he decided to walk the rest of the way. Glancing back the way he had come, he could see the busy street he had just turned off, it was almost as if the people represented a flowing river and a glass sheet prevented them from turning down this way. He wondered if they could even see that the turning existed. As the thought crossed his mind, Sutton was mentally telling himself off for being so fanciful. It was not like him and he wondered if the whisky he had been drinking had contained any impurities or if possible, he was still actually asleep in his armchair.

As he walked, he examined the fence on his left. It was through this fence he had chased the Butterbee, however in daylight it was becoming very difficult to identify exactly where he had entered. Turning the corner at the end of the street, he became aware of a feeling of being watched. From the corner of his eye he saw the shadows moving on the building opposite to his right. Distracted, he almost missed the loose boards, almost but not quite. Stopping, he examined the fracture and pushing slightly, was able to make the opening large enough to allow him to pass without too much effort. Looking up and down the street to make sure he was not observed. Sutton entered the courtyard once more. It was like stepping back in time and just to make sure he had not done precisely that, he put his head back through the fence and reassured himself the world, as he knew it, was still there. Then, turning his back to the opening, he strode quickly across the courtyard to the great doors. He was so determined that he failed to notice the moving shadows in hot pursuit.

In daylight, he could clearly see the remains of an engraved sign above those doors. They read, 'Law Courts' and he was somewhat surprised that this was still here and that he, a city veteran, was so completely unaware of its continued existence. Trials that had once weighed the evidence against a law breaker and judged them innocent or guilty had long since become redundant. It was far too costly in terms of housing the accused while a decision was made and also too costly in terms of the extra manpower to guard them while the process unfolded. Now they were simply changed as a matter of course, moving them from a drain on society into a useful productive niche. In Sutton's opinion, it was the right thing to do. Pushing once more, this time lightly on the great doors, he entered. Even in daylight the interior was dull, and he felt the need for the torch he had brought. Walking quickly across the entrance he had seen the night before, he paused for a moment at the foot of the stone staircase checking he was indeed alone and then beginning his ascent at a more leisurely pace, watching and listening as he went. Every part of him on alert. At the top of the stairs, he entered a large chamber, with small chambers leading off through various impressive archways. The floor was littered with debris and dust, the only footprints evident were his and again he wondered how long it had been since another had walked these halls. The walls were empty, all that was evident of the paintings that had once hung there were the discoloured rectangles of various sizes that littered the expanse. The smell was one of mustiness, of dried age-old rubbish, of long forgotten memories that no one cared for and had been tossed in a corner by historians. Unimportant and forgotten, it was a sad place that should have decayed some time ago. Why, it was fenced and preserved was the question that bothered Sutton. As he walked the halls, he became increasingly, relaxed in his surroundings. Reaching what appeared to be the end of the floor, he saw a small door and he pushed until the ancient lock burst open and allowed him access to stairs leading upward to an, as yet, un-hinted second floor. These stairs were very different from the main stairway he had used to gain entry to this floor, they were smaller and curved round upon themselves as he climbed, leaving him with a disoriented feeling and a little unsure as to the direction he now faced.

This floor too was different. Instead of one large visible expanse, there was simply a corridor, the end of which he could not see, with doors leading off each side. The floor was also clean as if looked after by an unknown custodian. Progressing forward cautiously he tried the first door, it opened easily, and he could see a room full of display cases. Stepping forward, he wiped the dust from one of these. On display were; medals, awards for bravery for the police force and other officers that supported the old regime. Some he presumed were once valuable, others just of interest. He moved on to the next room, similarly, filled with the artifacts of a bygone age. Room after room, each offered its own look into the past. He supposed he opened between twenty to thirty rooms before he began to tire. Close to giving up, he saw the end in front of him and as he approached the final doors some of his earlier disquiet returned. Pausing, he watched himself reach for the door knob as if he was watching a film in slow motion. The handle turned, and the door clicked open, allowing unexpected light to tumble into the hall, immediately rendering his torch obsolete.

"Come in detective," an unidentified voice said.

Stepping cautiously into the room, Sutton identified the voice as coming from a chair which was facing a fire. He could not see the owner of the voice, but was happy to step forward. Even if this individual proved a foe, it would still be one to one combat and despite his negative billing, Sutton could still handle himself.

"Evening sir," Sutton started.

"Good evening detective," the voice replied with a hint of amusement evident.

Glancing round, Sutton took in the desk and the book filled shelves that lined the room, unusual in this day when few read for pleasure. "You like books?" He inquired.

"Yes," the voice simply replied, waiting for Sutton to decide what he wanted to know.

"Have you lived here long sir?" Sutton inquired.

"Yes," came the simple reply once again.

Sutton tried to conclude something from the voice. Its tone was light with an educated edge, almost soft and vibrant. It was self-assured and knew it was on home turf.

"Who are you?"

"At last detective, a question worth answering, please take a seat," the voice said while a disembodied hand gestured at the chair, which faced his own. Sutton walked over to the offered seat and saw what he could only describe as a well-groomed old-fashioned gentleman. He was smiling at Sutton's evident confusion.

"Please, don't be confused detective. I am not clairvoyant, look," and as he spoke, he pointed a remote control at the wall. The wall rose to reveal a series of screens each depicting various areas from the building's exterior and interior below. "I have just been watching, that's all detective."

A little embarrassed, Sutton fidgeted on his seat, "I thought the place was derelict, sir."

"Oh, it's fine detective, if I had wished I could have locked my front door from here," the old man replied, with that edge of amusement evident once more in both his tone and in the gentle crinkle around his lively sparkling eyes.

"Why, then did you let me explore without identifying yourself, sir?" Sutton pushed.

"I thought you may enjoy discovering my home," he replied, and then rising to his feet, continued, "forgive my rudeness detective, can I offer you some refreshment?" he inquired, indicating the glass of wine in his own hand.

"Yes," Sutton replied and then noting the quizzical look on his host's face, he realised further explanation would be necessary. "I mean, I enjoyed exploring and I would very much like a glass of wine, thank you," he finished, thinking his resolve to stay off the booze had not lasted long.

"You are welcome," the cultured voice assured him "and while we drink, would you like to tell me what brings you here?" he enquired.

"Yes sir," Sutton replied, sinking back into the red velvet of the armchair and wondering if it were real. He strongly suspected it was, as this abode was very different from any he had been in before, the smell was of real wood and leather. Unthinking Sutton stroked the velvet and he could feel its opulence. He realised his host was wearing what used to be known as a smoking jacket and once again he briefly yearned for the taste of tobacco. Accepting the proffered wine, he knew he should begin to talk, but somehow the silence was so peaceful and perfect, he did not want to spoil the moment and be the one that forced them both back into the present. His new companion appeared to agree as he wordlessly raised his glass and smiling took a companionable drink. Completely relaxed, Sutton raised his own glass and even while a part of his mind warned him not to, took a long drink. The liquid slid easily down his throat and left a warm trail in its wake. It was full bodied and for a moment Sutton enjoyed the fruity aftertaste and warming sensation the wine gave him. As he savoured the wine, he became aware of his grip on reality slowly slipping away and as his eyes closed. He felt rather than saw the old man catching the glass just seconds before it shattered on the floor. He had broken the first rule of policing and accepted refreshment from a suspect. Although, what he suspected the old man of, he was not sure.

Chapter 5

As the night wrapped the city in darkness, Cerberus returned to his territory. Flying silently into the city he was focused on returning to Maia and failed to notice the lone wolf as it padded across the park. Intent on following its own path it remained unseen by many more creatures than Cerberus. It was its own master; and had its own intentions. Unaware of conflicting interests and forces Cerberus flew directly to the nesting zone.

"Where were you?" Maia asked.

"I had to go out of the city limits."

"Why?" She asked turning toward him so he could see her anxiety.

"What worries you?" he replied, tilting his head to express the confusion he felt. The female of all species were often a mystery to most males and Cerberus was no exception. He did not know what he had done that could have unsettled her.

"Oh nothing," she replied, with bitterness evident in her voice. She turned from him to hide the tears that were welling up in her eyes. "If they recall you, what will I do?" she blurted, unable to stop the tone of her voice rising as she spoke. Stepping toward her, he stretched out his wing to meet with her shoulder.

"You worry too much Maia," he whispered to calm her.

"I worry too much," she snorted, pulling away. "You worry too little. They will kill you if they think you are a threat, make no mistake," the first of the tears rolled down her feathered cheek.

"Oh Maia," was his simple reply as he pulled her even closer to him. This time she let herself lean into his embrace and with the tears falling faster said, "Don't you understand Cerberus, I can only just bear this life with you here?" Once again, he comforted her, running his beak across the top of her head and making comforting noises as if comforting a small child.

"Let's hunt together, my love," he finally said, hoping to distract her further. Nodding, still with tears in her eyes, she leant her head one last time against his chest and then together they launched themselves into the air. First, he rose and then her, each flying the same path, she seconds behind him. She was like a smaller echo of him with reduced power and presence. As he flew, he increased his speed and she in turn increased hers so that she kept pace with him. Faster and faster they flew, spiralling toward the sky and then hurtling in unison down to the earth. In an elegant aerial dance, they separated and spiralled away from one another gaining height in unison. They flew closer and closer intertwining in their paths so that they appeared to join as a single animal. They turned and tumbled one over the other, both now breathing heavily and yet excited at their exertions; it was as if they had reached a strange orgasm. Then, falling away from one another, all power now gone from their movements, they appeared relaxed and almost calm. They dropped, almost but not quiet to touch the street below. Instead of resting on the ground however they each scooped a rat from the street and coming close together again, swapped prey in a macabre game. Laughing, Cerberus swooped once more to the street and then others of their kind began to join the dance game with couplings and retreats becoming ever more complex. Soon the night was filled with strange shrieks and the moving tumbling bodies of the owl kind. Exhilarated Cerberus stood on top of a block of flats to catch his breath. His eyes shone with pleasure. It was times like this that he felt he'd been made to experience.

He was sure they had already reached their quota for the night and yet he felt like he could hunt like this for hours to come. Then seeing Maia below, he leapt and darted straight down to brush past her. Laughing, Maia called "too slow," as she dodged out of his reach. Cerberus, flexing his shoulder muscles and raising his great wings in a graceful arc, set out to pursue her.

Landing lightly on pavement to pause and renew his energy levels, he heard the distant sound of a flute and it chilled the blood in his veins. The sirens were swimming through the shadows. All playfulness left him and suddenly he became serious. Searching the sky for Maia he tried to catch her attention. He did not have to try for long and she immediately became aware of the change in his body language and demeanour. She landed lightly beside him, "What is it?" she asked him, all her previous worry and anxiety visible again in her eyes.

"Time to go," he told her as gently as he could, not wanting to increase the pain and unease she so obviously felt.

"This time I come too!" she insisted.

Opening his mouth to object, he stopped for he could see by the stubborn stance and glint in her eye that clearly told him protestation would be of little use. She was determined to remain by his side, and he found he was comforted by her loyalty.

Landing softly in the alleyway, Cerberus waited. It was not long before a running shape turned into their field of vision and Maia drew in her breath in evident surprise. Before her, stood a large wolf. She had thought them long dead and yet, there it stood, its mouth slightly open as it panted to cool itself from its recent exertions. The fur was a mix of black and white with a white collar and black muzzle. Her eyes were drawn to the sharp teeth that were very prominent because of the bright red blood that dripped from the creature's fangs. A shudder ran down Maia's back and she understood why the wolf had not been reproduced through the changelings. It was a lone hunter with no ties to others and as a result it was dangerous; it would take risks others would not consider because of the consequences for those they loved. It was a maverick breed and all her instincts told her she could not trust it. She wondered where this one had come from. Then, to Maia's surprise it spoke, showing with no room for doubt that it was indeed a changeling.

"Is this your companion?" he asked. The voice was surprisingly cultured, and Maia was reminded of an ageing, kindly professor, an image totally at odds with the predator she saw in front of her.

"Maia, she wants to help," Cerberus replied. "Maia this is Thanatos," and the wolf bowed in Maia's direction touching his nose to his front paws, an elegant but strangely displaced gesture. Its oddity threw Maia off balance.

"She is beautiful, but does she know what she is getting into?" Thanatos asked.

"Yes, she knows," Maia replied, stepping out from behind Cerberus, "and she has a voice too!" She was a little too forceful as she tried to compensate for the confusion, he caused her.

Throwing his head back, the wolf creature laughed and howled at the same time, making Cerberus check for signs that this exuberance had been noticed. Thankfully, no windows were thrown open to admit curious gazes into their domain. Cerberus was almost tempted to tell the wolf to tone things down. However, he knew Thanatos would not take the suggestion well, he always made Cerberus uncharacteristically nervous and he wanted to avoid antagonising him. Cerberus also recognised that Thanatos could be very unpredictable. Even so he was much more pleasant to interact with than the full humans and much more desirable as an ally. Cerberus would put up with a multitude of uncomfortable moments to retain him as a friend.

"Did you take the boy back?" Thanatos asked.

"Yes," he replied, "but it was a narrow escape, a detective almost caught us both."

"Almost isn't caught," the wolf growled. "What was he doing in the city anyway?"

"Just confused," Cerberus informed him. "Many of the vulnerable are becoming increasingly confused and they can sense something on the wind I think."

"I know, I feel the city changing beneath our feet as if re-ordering itself, it knows change is almost here. I even smell new changelings, have you detected them too?" Thanatos inquired, inclining his head to the right as if he were listening to the same distant song Cerberus had heard earlier. "Do you not hear the cities new sounds?" he whispered almost too low for Maia to grasp every word he spoke. Whispering was not essential but somehow seemed appropriate to all of them, as if talking of the new sounds and smells would magically speed up their ownership of the city. Whispering was childish, and it exposed their fearfulness. Yet all of them were drawn in to the dramatic effect.

"I hear," Cerberus replied, "but I don't know what it means or who is responsible for its broadcast."

"Me neither," Thanatos whispered once more. "Give your tame day walker a nudge, he may come up with something we can use."

Cerberus nodded. Further words seemed gratuitous.

Understanding the meeting was over Thanatos bowed once more to Maia and said, "Until we meet again fair lady" and with that he turned and disappeared into the grey light that the dawn brought with it. Maia watched him go and for a minute could have sworn she saw not a wolf in the sun's first rays but the shape of a man. As far as she knew returning to human form was not possible. If she had hands, she would have rubbed her eyes to clear her vision, instead she shook her head and turned to find her nest for the day. At least in daylight she knew where Cerberus lay, intertwined with her own form, lending and taking heat and comfort from her and she from him.

****

The new day found Mike back in the archives. He was frustrated at his inability to find any records relating to the earliest of the clinical trials. Finally, admitting defeat he called the librarian. Annoyingly the hologram appeared immediately with professional speed and asked courteously, "May I help you sir?"

"Yes," Mike replied, "the records seem a little incomplete".

"Incomplete sir? May I enquire what information you think is missing?"

"Firstly, are all the experimental records for the IGH available to me?" Mike asked.

"Yes sir, you have accessed all that is available to you"

"But is there more I cannot access?" Mike asked again.

"I am afraid I cannot give you that information sir," the librarian stated with an infuriating tone.

Taking a deep breath Mike continued, "Did the IGH, conduct all the changeling experiments?"

Again, the librarian replied, "I cannot give you that information without a higher security clearance, sir." That was a no then Mike thought.

Tapping his fingers on the desk and frowning Mike finally asked, "Is the information held anywhere else?"

Smiling so that Mike felt like frying all of its connections, the librarian replied, "At the Law Courts sir".

"The what?" Mike asked.

"The Law Courts sir," the librarian persisted.

"I thought they were demolished?" Mike asked.

"They were preserved sir, for posterity," the librarian informed him helpfully. Mike thought perhaps he would not fuse all its circuits quite yet. Just the ones that made it smile.

Already gathering himself to leave, Mike was unaware the hologram remained standing behind him as it should have put itself away. Mike made his way to the lift. Pressing the call button, Mike froze with his arm still extended and looked around in surprise. The lights had gone out! The lights only went out when no one was in the archive. Obviously, a technical fault, and while these thoughts were going through his mind, he heard the mites scurrying out to clean up. Pressing the button again he idly wondered how long it would take the mites to clear his debris away and whether they would finish before the lift came. It was taking the lift longer than usual and as he waited in the dark, he leant against the wall, turning over in his mind the new information he had gathered.

He suddenly felt one of the mite's brush past his ankle and in the dark, it made him jump. Then he felt the sting of steel as his right ankle was gripped in the mandibles of the mite. Squealing loudly, he kicked out and smashed the mite with his other foot. Shocked, he felt his ankle in the dark and was a little concerned to feel something warm and wet. He decided to light his lighter and look. This proved to be a mistake as crouched on the floor he became aware of a line of mites directly in front of him. Rising slowly, he turned to look around and he saw he was surrounded by the small robots.

His mouth fell open and a part of his brain thought this is impossible, while fear crept into another corner. Just before the heat became too much for his fingers, he saw the librarian in the corner. It looked like the hologram was watching the drama unfold with interest. Then, as his lighter went out, he heard the scurry of metal legs advancing on the tiled floor. The part of his mind concerned with survival screamed "RUN" and he did. Launching himself into the air and landing on the study table, he held the edge to steady himself but had to pull back quickly as steel mandibles reached for him once more. He could hear them advancing and knew there were far too many of them to fight off. As one jumped toward him, he batted it away with a heavy leather-bound journal he had read earlier.

He wanted to call out to the librarian to turn the light back on, but he had no time as the assault moved on. The next mite managed to tear a long incision down his forearm and just as he was sure he was going to die, he remembered the red trays. Jumping to the next table he placed a red tray on the top and stood inside it, once again lighting his lighter to see if it had any effect.

Miraculously, they were retreating. All he had to do was stay where he was until someone came to find him. He could feel his heartbeat slowing as relief flooded over him. He felt rather than saw the librarian still watching from its corner and he knew that rescue would not come from that corner. He really would see its circuits fried he decided; the thing had lost any mind it might have had. At the same time, he knew he was not being logical. If the librarian was acting outside of its brief, someone must have programmed it to do so. It had no free will. What really bothered Mike was who would re-program it to do him harm. He decided he would have them changed. He would see Davidson had them in custody as quickly, or even better he could have that useless cop, Sutton earn his wages for once. He comforted himself with thoughts of retribution and the peculiarly designed changelings he could create from their treacherous DNA.

After a while, his ankle began to throb, and both legs began to ache. Just as he was wondering how long he would have to wait, the lift doors opened with a ping and the lights once more came on. Out of the lift skipped Will, who immediately stopped and dropped the papers he had been carrying.

"Er Mike?" was all he could manage when confronted with the image of his boss battered and bleeding on the study table, standing in a red tray.

"Help me down." Mike snapped unable to stop himself from sounding peevish. He stepped out of the tray gingerly, wincing every time he put any weight on his injured ankle. He only just managed to stop himself from audibly moaning.

"Of course, sir," Will said, rushing forward to help him down from the table. Then taking his arm and supporting Mike's weight Will helped him limp slowly to the lift and supported him as it carried them straight up to Mike's office floor. Almost falling out of the lift, Will and Mike drew the attention of all the office staff.

****

"Best not ask," Coleen commented. She had always disapproved of the couples who enjoyed the rough side of play. "Obviously not our business," she finished with a sniff as she turned back to her screen.

"Don't be silly," Barb said, grabbing the first aid kit, and running after them. "There has obviously been an accident," she added over her shoulder.

"Obviously," Coleen echoed in a sarcastic tone. Barb just shook her head; she did not have time to argue she needed to help Mike and find out what had happened.

Will supported Mike until he found his seat and as he did the surveillance snake continued to transmit data, letting its master know about Mike discomfort and anxiety.

****

Davidson cursed and threw the report he had been reading across the room. What had Caldwell managed to get into now? He seemed to be nothing but a problem at the moment. Making his way out of his office, he kicked the cleaner bot that was picking up the discarded report and felt a little better at releasing his anger. He comforted himself with the thought that if Caldwell got into enough trouble he may be removed altogether. At least he thought his own problems would be lessened with Caldwell out of the way.

Although he knew such a scenario would irritate the Director it still lifted his spirits and made him smile as he made his way down to Caldwell's office. It was his job to know if the Director asked.

Barb carefully undid Mike's shoe. "Sorry," she said as she saw him wince. Then gently, she removed his sock and as she started to bathe his foot, Davidson came charging through the door.

"What happened?" he asked.

"The lights went out," Mike said through clenched teeth, "the library mites tried to clean me away," as his voice rose slightly at the end of his sentence, denoting his discomfort.

"That's impossible," Davidson said with a hint of incredulity in his voice.

"It should be," Mike said and now that he was safe, he felt anger rising "You need to get the techs to scrap the lot," he added a little petulantly.

"I'll get them to look," Davidson said in a conciliatory tone. "But you know Caldwell perhaps they were just doing their job".

"What do you mean by that?" Mike asked, jumping a little as Barb touched a sore spot.

"Nothing, I was just commenting that's all, no harm really," Davidson said.

"Well keep it to yourself," Mike retorted and then a little irritably, "isn't it clean yet Barb?"

"Oh, I am sorry Mike" Barb replied, "I am trying to be gentle." She continued in the kind of tone you would use to an irrational child. However, it had the desired effect and Mike leaned back in his chair and allowed her to clean his ankle.

"By the way Caldwell," Davidson started once again, "since I am here, can I ask if you found the problem with the codes?"

"No, not yet," Mike replied, "I could do with full access though, some of the original experiments are classified Grade one."

"You know only the Director has that level of clearance, but I will see if I can get you any relevant experimental data," Davidson conceded, with an emphasis on the word relevant. "Oh, and maybe you should be more careful," he added.

"Maybe you should check out the librarian," Mike retorted. "I am sure it was watching the whole thing."

"Now, you are being ridiculous," Davidson told him coldly.

"Ridiculous? Does my ankle look ridiculous to you?" Mike asked as his voice rose once again. He also wriggled in his seat as Barbara bandaged his wounds.

"No," Davidson replied calmly, "but you are making ridiculous accusations."

Mike wriggled some more and opened his mouth to retort, but Will stepped between the two of them.

"How about a strong tea?" he asked both Caldwell and Davidson simultaneously. "It's great for a shock to the system," he added helpfully.

Both men looked at him as if he had lost his mind, Will didn't mind as his comment had stopped the arguing. Davidson capitalised on the lull and commented, "Perhaps you ought to go home," as he left Mike's office.

Once Davidson was out of the office, Mike had no reason to protect his manhood and he slumped backward into the chair. The colour drained from his face and the energy seeped from his body as the full effect of what had just happened sunk into his conscious mind. He sank backward and gratefully allowed Will and Barb to take charge. They supported him as he made his way to an indi bus and the sanctuary of his bed.

As Mike drifted into sleep, Cerberus' thoughts turned to the last time he had seen his brother. Alone, without parents he had to turn to illegal means to feed the two of them. He stole near to home and that was his big mistake. He was easily tracked down and when they came back, they came for him. They looked the same as the ones who had killed his parents, only this time they did not knock before entering.

They simply burst into the living room as he and Jamie drank the pint of milk he had managed to steal just that morning. They laughed at the fear and shock they saw on the boys faces. Jamie curled into a tight ball, sucking his thumb and he hid his face between his knees. Cerberus tried to stop them, but he was too small. They simply laughed even more as they pushed him from one to another until tiring of the game, they threw him into the back of the van. His last view of Jamie was watching him rock backward and forward in the corner of the room. The room that had once witnessed the happiness of his family and now saw it literally lost forever. It was the last time he saw Jamie and he had always wanted to find out what had happened to his younger brother.

$$****$$

THE PAST

During interrogation they had goaded him, telling him Jamie would be changed and probably become a shadow. They called him an imbecile and an idiot. They said it was the mentally defective that could not complete the change. It was this that haunted Cerberus' nightmares. He was the oldest and should have protected his brother. It was not a shadow that made him scream, it was all the other possibilities of what could have happened to the brother he loved.

They found his anger amusing and yet it was exactly his anger that helped him live through his own change. The owl was one of the most difficult and painful changes to endure, almost half of those initiated failed. It was his anger and hatred for those who had hurt his family that kept him alive. The anger and the thought of revenge. As the process ripped apart his DNA molecule by molecule, he screamed with pain. His scream was directed at the detectives and doctors. He saw in his mind's eye his new form ripping them apart. He saw their blood fill the changing rooms until it flowed from the institute and touched all those responsible. He saw those it touched wither and die, large boils taking over every available surface of their skin. For a time, he became insane, revelling in horrific images of death and wondrous destruction.

Slowly his mind awakened to his surroundings and he became aware of the lack of pain. He was stiff and sore as if he had over-exercised. He tried to rise slowly and wobbled unsteadily; his new talons made standing on a flat surface much more difficult than in the past where soft feet had been able to help him balance. He brought his hand up to brush away the hair from his eyes and cried out in shock as a wing rose into his line of vision.

They released him to the streets in that confused state of mind, later he realised it was because they were afraid of the power the owls could command. Fear and the fact that they had lost techs before once the new owls gained more confidence and hit out at those who had caused them pain. The talons he now had were deadly and he found them fascinating.

Cerberus had enjoyed becoming familiar with those talons and their use. He still had the desire to rip the doctors into tiny pieces, but he was wise enough to know that such a course of action would only lead to his own demise. He was biding his time and he could feel his time getting closer. Soon he would know what had become of Jamie and he would know what his destiny was to be. This knowledge made him both excited and apprehensive. It promised both freedom and danger. Both seduced him.

Changelings

Chapter 6

PRESENT DAY:

Sutton turned over and fell out of his narrow bed. Surprised, as he realised where he was, he sat on the floor to gather his scattered wits. As far as he could recall he had been somewhere drinking wine. Scratching his head, he tried to make sense of the fragments of his memory. He was convinced he had fallen asleep in an armchair and not his own battered apology for an armchair, but a well stuffed and sophisticated specimen far better than anything he owned. Come to think of it he had been speaking to someone who was sophisticated too. Now, taking in the drabness of his own abode and letting reality seep into his mind he supposed he must have been dreaming. He had not been back to the Law Courts after all, had never met the old man who must have been his subconscious idea of an old-fashioned caretaker. He hadn't realised he had such an active imagination.

Pulling himself onto the edge of the bed he reached for yesterday's clothes and as he forced his right leg into the trousers, he saw a bright shiny object fall from the pocket. In slow motion it rolled beneath his bed. Still with only one leg in his trousers, he returned to the floor and began searching the rubbish that had found its way into the dark space. Pulling out discarded items from his past, a dust filled sock and empty toilet roll, he wondered at his own slob-like qualities. He didn't even know what the function of some of these things were. A piece of strangely shaped metal and a slim piece of plastic with numbers embossed on the surface, he had no chance of understanding why he had kept them. Grimacing, he recognised the moulding peel of an orange. It sounded common enough, but he could swear he had not eaten an orange within the last two years. He shuddered at the thought of exactly how long it had been rotting undetected in the dark. Finally, he found his prize and walking over to the window, he did something else for the first time in a few years, he opened the curtains. The last of the day's light illuminated the coin in his hand. He studied its surface for a minute, remembering how he used to purchase items with tokens such as these. It made him feel weary; weary at how long ago it all now felt. It had been a shiny life, almost as shiny as the coin itself and no-one had appreciated how much they really had. It was a life that had simply been reality, until it had suddenly stopped and left the human race feeling confused and somehow abandoned.

Coins were an enigma of that past, a token people exchanged in return for all kinds of goods and services. Coins had become obsolete during the great famine. No amount of money could purchase the food an individual needed. They either had skills that made them worth feeding well, or received basic rations, a level of subsistence that barely allowed survival. Money had quickly become a redundant symbol of a useless and decadent society. A society where excess and overindulgence could be purchased; very different from the lean society that replaced it. It was also proof that Sutton had paid a second visit to the Law Courts.

Looking at the 20th Century coin in his hand, he remembered picking it up from the dust strewn floor, placing it securely in his pocket. He thoughtfully completed the action as he finished putting on his trousers. The question now, was who had brought him home and why had they gone to the bother? He remembered the sweet tasting wine and wondered what they had mixed it with to make him sleep and forget his wanderings. He frowned as he determined to face his unknown antagonist. This time it would be official, citizens could not get the idea they could go around drugging the constabulary.

∗∗∗∗

Still limping, Mike shone his torch on the fence in front of him. It was here the archive said the Law Courts stood but all Mike could see was this fence. He continued to walk around the perimeter but was very aware of the throbbing in his ankle. He wished now he had decided to bring Will with him, at least this far. He had decided against including him because he had not thought he would be of use. However, he now realised that Will could have completed the reconnoitre and reported back as to how to get in. He began to wonder how much of this expedition had been a good idea. The place he was looking for was somehow lost or left behind in another time behind this eternal barricade. He began punching each fence panel in frustration. It was more as an act of revenge on the barrier that kept him from his goal, rather than a conscious desire to test its strength and resistance. As a result, he almost fell through the fence head first when the loose panel swung forward. The only thing stopping him falling through completely was that he was a little large for the opening. His fall came to an abrupt rest when his body slammed sideways into the remaining secure section. His shoulder jarred painfully, and he winced both at the physical pain and the feeling he had just a made a complete fool of himself. He quickly looked left and right to check that his humiliation had not been witnessed, while at the same time massaging the feeling back into his throbbing shoulder. The last thing he felt he needed now was an audience amused at his comic dance and foolish motions.

Giving himself a shake, he gingerly tested the fence once more and then with effort, squeezed through the gap sucking in his stomach as much as he could to allow himself access. It was a tight fit and he made a mental note to go to the gym with Barb and cut down on his alcohol consumption. On his way through the barrier, something was disturbed and scurried away from the noise he was making. Repulsed, he hoped it was a rat and not some genetically created creature he could not define.

Looking from the identical angle that Sutton had first observed the building, Mike too was struck by its commanding nature. Why he wondered, would this place be quarantined ... to protect it or the city in which it stood? Walking up to the great doors, he was reminded of his dream and with a certainty he did not know existed, he realised that this was where his mother had brought him and his sister the last time, he had seen either.

For a fraction of a second dream and reality collided, he saw a line of dishevelled starving people shuffling silently forward across the dusty hallway. They were dream creatures who left no sign of their progress and as quickly as they appeared, they melted away into the walls of the great hall. As the ghosts from his past faded, Mike's attention was drawn to the one set of footprints that went in a straight line across the hall and up into the dark recesses hidden above. There were no other footprints, no accompanying set to indicate the owner had left and so Mike had to conclude he would encounter company on the top floors. Company more solid than the ghosts of his past that haunted his mind.

Unwilling to announce his own presence, Mike made his way around the outer edge of the hall. He had no desire to explore the levels above or meet the owner of the footprints. He remembered that when he entered this place, everything relating to the IGH had been on the lower floors and it was these that he wished to explore now. He made his way to the rear of the ground floor, to where he knew the access to lower levels lay. He felt strangely chilled walking in the footsteps of his own past. Once he found the dark passageway that led downward, he felt somehow more secure, more protected, and less vulnerable. The Law Courts had welcomed him home. He made his way down five flights of stairs to the lowest available level. It seemed to be a universal rule that the darker secrets were kept out of sight in subterranean vaults that only the initiated could access. It was secrets such as these he wanted to bring into the light.

Stepping into the first room, he was surprised to be greeted by electric light. Turning his torch off, he still grasped it as if it were a talisman that could protect him from any possible evil. The room in which he found himself was in opposition to the chaos above. It was, or had been, a lab. All the experimental equipment was in neat rows in glass cases. Although well preserved, it was evident that they had remained untouched for as much as a decade. The lighting system was obviously the same as the library, it came on automatically when someone walked into the room. Thinking of the library he unconsciously checked the floor for any sign of mite activity. He had no desire to repeat that particular experience in a hurry.

As he walked across the room, he ran his hand along the work surfaces and then raised it to examine the dust he had collected. 90% of dust was human skin and he wondered how many genetically different specimens were represented in the sample on his fingers. Reaching the door at the end of the room, he was admitted to a second corridor with six further doors leading to yet unexplored chambers. He tried the first to find it locked and with sinking spirits he found they were all locked against the curious. Why he had thought it might be different he had not known but he stood for a minute feeling foolish in the tight confines of this secret corridor. Mike was a compliant, rule-following member of society; it took a while to occur to him that he could try to force entry to the locked rooms. Balancing his weight on his still sore ankle, he kicked as hard as he could with his good foot. Although the door did not fly open immediately it did give a satisfactory shudder and throw several years dust into the air at the same time. Smiling with the glow of partial success, he had to give two more kicks before the door finally separated from its frame and allowed him access. The resulting clouds of dust caused him to cough and sneeze profusely which in turn made his eyes water and added to his difficulties to clearly see what he had uncovered. He was not proving to be a natural at the subterfuge, hell he thought he was outright clumsy. It was a good job that whoever else was in the building was too far away to notice all the noise and commotion he was making. Once inside the new room, he found more scientific equipment alongside what appeared to be shackles attached to the walls. He supposed that this was where some of the first changelings had been held. The atmosphere in the room made him shiver slightly as if, as the old saying went, someone had walked across his grave.

Disappointed at finding nothing he closed the door and thought he could perhaps contain some of the ghosts that seemed determined to unsettle him. He forced entry into two more rooms and found more of the same. The fourth room was completely bare, and he entered simply because he was feeling frustrated. He thought this search should have been much simpler. Once inside the room, something at the edge of his conscious mind alerted him to the fact that this room was subtly different. Stepping outside he re-entered the room and experienced the same vague misgiving. Opening the door to the adjacent room he put his head into one followed by the other, hoping to judge what was different and then he realised, it was smaller. There was no apparent reason it should be, but it was inarguably smaller, the rooms on either side had several feet more depth.

✳✳✳✳

Sutton stood at the entrance to the Law Courts. He could clearly see the footprints from his previous visit leading up the stairs. It unnerved him a little that it was very evident that neither he nor anyone else had left by this exit. Whoever had returned him home had done so by a different, yet unidentified route and that meant a whole army of subversives could be using this place. Swinging his torch slowly around the hallway, Sutton meticulously illuminated its full expanse, looking into its every detail to see if it told him anything about the caretaker living above. As the beam returned to its starting position, he saw the set of footprints around the edge and traced them to the rear of the building. He had no way of determining how long they had been there or if indeed their owner had already left by a different route, but his gut told him they were recent, and his gut had saved him from sticky situations in the past. Heading toward the stairs he decided to follow the second footprints later. For now, his pressing business was with the grey-haired caretaker.

****

Unaware of Sutton's arrival Mike began to explore the far wall of the room tapping along its whole length. He believed that it was the right thing to tap and listen, but he had to admit he had no clue as to what he was listening for. He stood back and scowled at the rear wall. He thought if he looked at it long enough it would put its hands up so to speak and just open to offer its secrets to him, in a gesture of surrender. The wall simply remained as it was and looked straight back at him. He thought he was wasting his time. He turned to go but something stopped him from walking away altogether. He decided to examine the two remaining walls before going home empty handed. His hunch paid off and before long, a panel slid open revealing an access pad. All he had to do now was punch in the password. He tried his own and the light on the panel blinked red. Access denied was a universal concept represented in this one colour. He then tried Davidson's password, something he had stolen many years earlier. Once again, the light blinked red. He decided to think laterally and tried several clever combinations from the Director's daughter to the anniversary of the founding of the IGH. Each time he was rewarded with the red light, access denied. Then, almost on a whim which he would later claim to be brilliantly deduced logic, he tried the word, Cryptid.

The access panel blinked green and the whole wall in front of Mike slide smoothly away.

****

Sutton stood outside of the caretaker's quarters and reluctant to simply barge in, found he was knocking politely instead.

"Come in detective," the calm, cultured voice filtered through the oak door.

Sutton turned the handle and stepped directly into the previous night. Once again, he was confronted with the caretaker in the costume of old. Smoking jacket already around his shoulders, he simply asked, with an amused air "Wine detective?" as if they were old friends meeting for a regular appointment.

"After the last time?" Sutton growled.

"I suppose not," the caretaker said, turning, and placing the wine bottle back on the silver tray.

"A few questions if you don't mind sir?" Sutton enquired in an official tone he reserved for intimidating possible suspects. However, it did not have the desired effect. Throwing his head back the caretaker laughed,

"I seem to have upset you detective." He said with a smile.

"Not at all sir," Sutton continued while glaring in the caretaker's direction, communicating his displeasure that he was not being responded to with enough deference. "Just enquiries sir." He clarified, keeping his tone sharp and crisp.

"Enquiries, detective, then please let me see if I can help." The caretaker gestured toward the same seat Sutton had occupied the night before. Determined to remain in control, Sutton walked around the caretaker and sat in what was supposed to be his host's seat instead. With a slight shrug, to indicate it was not a problem, the caretaker sat across from him.

Looking at his notebook as if checking something he had previously written there, Sutton looked up and said, "Now I must caution you sir, anything you say could be taken down and used as evidence." Sutton was pleased to watch the power base shift in his favour. It was a subtle change and the caretaker sat slightly taller in his seat, put down his drink on the table next to him and lost the smile from his face.

"Now detective, there's no need to get all official about this, is there?" he asked. The disconcertment was evident in the timbre of his tone, perceptible only to those who were sensitive to detecting weakness in others. For Sutton, it was like hearing a siren. Confident now, Sutton leaned back in the chair, spreading his arms to include ownership of the physical as well as mental space he occupied. He was in charge and he was going to make the most of it.

"Well sir, there is the little matter of drugging an officer of the court, not to mention removing him without permission from a line of enquiry. Obstructing the course of justice is a serious offence." Sutton wanted to inflict the maximum discomfort, then when he relented a little the caretaker would be in his debt. He would owe him something and in Sutton's experience that always paid dividends in the long run.

"I thought I was helping you detective, not interfering," the caretaker tried to explain.

Sutton interrupted him. "How sir, is drugging an official helping?"

"Oh, but I didn't, you see, it's just the wine."

"What do you mean?" Sutton asked.

"It's homemade" he explained. "A lot of people find it too strong. All I did was make sure you got home safely, so you see ... just a misunderstanding."

"Homemade?" Sutton exclaimed. "What do you mean homemade, you can make wine yourself?" he continued with disbelief clearly evident in his tone. "Do you take me for a fool man?" Sutton felt his anger rising, the man thought he was a fool obviously. Even if the wine was extra strength a couple of mouthfuls would not have knocked Sutton out so quickly. He had spent years building a resistance to alcohol. Recently he had to drink almost a full bottle before achieving a comatose state.

"No, no, please, don't get upset, I'll show you" and with that the caretaker rose from his chair. Sutton had no choice to follow and wonder after his careful manipulation, quite how this man had managed to regain his lost control. It should be Sutton directing things not this elusive character whose name he still had to discover.

✶✶✶✶

In the basement, Mike was looking at row after row of filing cabinets. More information than he had ever seen collected in one place before. He opened the first drawer in this series and picked up the first file. It belonged to a company called Progen and the motto defined it as a landscaping venture. At first, he was baffled as to why a gardening company would seal its records away from prying eyes and in a written form that was unreachable by hackers. He quickly understood that the landscaping was not to do with changing gardens but re-ordering organisms. He knew immediately that however long he had, he would not be able to sort this information before he was disturbed. He needed something to carry the files back to his flat. Retracing his earlier movements, he was sure that he would be able to find what he needed and before long he had returned with a hover box. He loaded in the contents of the first and half the second cabinet before it was full. Looking at the remaining cabinets he shrugged his shoulders. If he needed to, he could always come back. Stepping away from the cabinets, he closed the false wall and the room looked as it always had. Except the floor was, he realised, littered with his footprints and he decided to erase them before he left. He swiped his foot across the floor and soon large sweeping tracks were the only evidence that anyone had been here at all. It was the best he could do. He realised that to distract anyone he needed to do the same in at least a couple of the other rooms he had disturbed. He was already tired and decided that this subterfuge stuff really wasn't him at all.

Manoeuvring the hover box along the corridor and then the narrow staircase was difficult, but manageable with care. Mike did not want to lose this cargo. Once back in the hall he saw a second set of footprints headed upstairs and thinking it would not matter now with the increasing traffic, he walked across the centre of the great hall, announcing his presence to anyone who cared to look. At least, if he needed to come back it would be less obvious amongst the rising comings and goings.

****

Sutton was on the roof of the Law Courts and feeling decidedly uncomfortable. To his right there sat several bird people, watching him with the caretaker who was in front proudly showing him some plants?

"Do you know what these are detective?" he asked.

"Plants" Sutton replied in a surly fashion. Things were not going his way and he did not like the latest developments. He also was not inclined to look at organic matter which was completely irrelevant to his enquiries.

"Very good, but what kind of plants?" the caretaker asked again with the patience you would display for a truculent child.

"Why are they watching?" Sutton countered.

Turning, the caretaker became aware of the bird people.

"Oh, forgive me detective, you get so used to them you forget they are there, this is just a vantage point, they sometimes use," the caretaker explained.

Many people found the changelings unnerving and this discomfort manifested itself in dislike and an urge to maintain distance between them. For Sutton it was slightly different, it was the watching that unnerved him, not the genetic differences.

"Shouldn't they be hunting by now?" Sutton asked.

"Oh, they know what they should be doing, believe me they will be gone soon." Feeling a little frustrated, the caretaker continued, "detective have you ever seen such beautiful grapes before?"

"I don't think I've seen real grapes before" Sutton said in a disinterested voice, keeping a wary eye on the bird folk. "What are they for?"

"Those, detective, are what makes wine."

"That's nice," Sutton said without conviction and then continued, "this is all very well but what does it have to do with your drugging me?"

"Everything, you just don't see it, you see real wine fermented from real grapes is ten times stronger than the chemically produced stuff you are used to. You just fell asleep."

"Maybe," Sutton conceded, "but even so it does not explain why you moved me".

"I thought I had explained detective," the caretaker said in a matter of fact tone "I thought you would be better off at home."

"How," Sutton continued, "did you know where to take me?"

"That's easy, Cerberus told me." The caretaker told him.

"At the risk of sounding obvious, who, is Cerberus?"

"The leader of the bird people, they know you because they see you at night all the time" the caretaker told him with a smile. "You're a kind of favourite teddy to them; they would miss you if you weren't around" he concluded.

Great! Thought Sutton. Now the changelings were patronising him, this one really would make Kapowski's day. Hell, he thought, it would make his century.

"You do know," he said, "that citizens should not be fraternising with the changelings; it could get you into trouble," Sutton warned.

"I'm not though," the caretaker stated.

"Well, you must talk to them to get this information. As I said earlier at the risk of being obvious, isn't that mixing?"

"Yes, but you see detective, I am not a citizen," he told Sutton.

Sutton just looked at him with his mouth slightly ajar. This character was really on the edge and perhaps not entirely stable. He checked his gun was still safely in his holster and within easy reach just in case he needed it.

"Can I ask you then, what exactly you think you are sir?" Sutton asked in what he hoped was a soothing tone.

"I'm one of the first changelings, Thanatos. Pleased to meet you," the caretaker said as he held out his hand.

****

At the same time, the banshee swam through the shadows only its destination in its mind. Phoebe was not fully living and so her presence behind it did not register. She followed as if her very existence depended on it, and in a way, it did. The mission gave her a reason not to fade too quickly into the shadows and disappear altogether. She swam through the shadows of the everyday world and mourned her loss as she went. Soon she began to recognise her surroundings. She was moving through the shadows of the buildings she had once occupied and without doubt heading for the centre of all things, the IGH.

She slipped through the cracks of the door and flitted past the security officers chatting at the desk. She was pleased that her progress was undetected and amused that the great IGH had no defence against such as her. They had in their arrogance failed to see them as a threat and she had to admit there was little she could do other than watch.

She followed the banshee to the very top of the building and to the quarters of the Director herself. It came as no surprise that the vile creature in front of her belonged to the woman she had once respected. It was as if all the Director's inner evil was expressed in this single creature that formed her personal guard. Phoebe wondered how many there were.

The banshee slipped into the Director's quarters as if she also lived here and Phoebe slipped in behind her. They were in the living area, a fire burned, and the lights were dim. It was obvious that no one was presently in the room. A shirt was discarded on the floor and a little further away one shoe and then another. The discarded clothes formed a trail which led the follower through into the bedroom. First banshee and then Phoebe followed the trail left for them. It was irresistible as if they were both being reeled in on an invisible fishing line. Once the banshee passed through the doorway the interior of the room became visible to Phoebe. It was what could only be described as sumptuous; deep red lined the walls and thick carpet lay on the floor. It looked so welcoming that Phoebe wanted to remove her own shoes and feel its depth and softness between her toes. That was until she remembered she had neither shoes nor in the real sense toes to do either anymore. Instead she crept into a corner and watched the scene unfold before her.

The Director was on the bed, but she was not alone. Two blonde haired young companions were obviously earning their keep. It took Phoebe a while to realise only one was a male and it was not him the Director favoured. All three failed to notice the banshee as she crept to the bottom of the bed. It was the Director who noticed her first and she did not have the reaction Phoebe had expected. Instead of fear she smiled and beckoned the banshee forward. The vile creature crawled forward across the top of the silk covers. It was the boy who noticed her and as surprise registered in his eyes the Director pulled back on his hair exposing his throat to the oncoming banshee. It was an invitation that did not need to be offered twice and the banshee had his throat between her teeth well before the girl began to scream. Blood gushed down the boy's neck and across the remaining occupants and silk sheets alike.

Rising from the bed the Director wrapped herself in the sheet, she paused to pat the banshee on the head and then entered the bathroom. She left the girl cowering in the corner. The banshee ate her fill from the boy and satiated wandered aimlessly away. The girl remained silent in her corner, shock evident in her eyes. Before long a cleaning crew entered and removed the boy's body. The girl was led away to where Phoebe could only guess. She was still trying to make sense out of this nonsensical situation. She could not understand how a scene of love could turn to a scene of such carnage so quickly. She did not think it was her diminished self that was the problem. She was convinced that the saviour of the modern world, was, in reality, an insane monster. She remembered the kiss the Director had given her just before they had changed her. It made no sense either but put with the scene she had just witnessed it was clear that something was very wrong with the Director and those around her rather than helping were trying to cover up every despicable thing she did.

Phoebe, determined to make the loss of her life count for something, left the IGH to find someone or something that she could do to change the things she had seen. She had to contact the changelings and show them what she had seen, although it was possible that many already knew what she had just newly discovered.

Changelings

Chapter 7

As Cerberus landed on the roof, Thanatos and the lawman were going back inside.

"What were they doing?" he asked Maia

"Talking about wine and Thanatos told him he was a changeling, why did he do that? He could have passed as full human."

"He isn't daft, he knows the lawman can find out who he is, and besides, what citizen would live here?" Cerberus said.

"I suppose," Maia said "but, I don't like him."

Cerberus pulled her close and his heart as always lifted when he felt the warmth of her body. "He probably feels the same, about you" he teased her.

Pushing him in the chest and throwing her head back in a display of contempt she marched to the edge of the building and launched herself into the air for the nights hunt. Amused Cerberus followed without comment, women had their feelings and Maia was no different than the rest of her gender.

****

Changelings

They flew in a companionable silence through the empty streets. Cerberus knew she was not really upset at his teasing, but he also knew that sometimes she preferred not to use words to communicate her feelings. She felt that words represented the human world and there was only a residual part of them that was still human. Most of their makeup was instinctual and wild. She and Cerberus both missed some of the human traits they had lost but at the same time savoured the skills and abilities they had gained. The pure joy of being aware of how you fitted into the whole could not be communicated to those who lacked the knowledge. A pale reflection was the experience of walking in the first snow of winter and then on returning home being aware of the smell of frost and flushed with the feel of the cold. Day walkers only experienced it a few times in their lives, if at all. For Cerberus, he could feel and smell the world with every fibre of his being; every second of his life.

He became aware of a commotion below and circled around to see if he could work out what was happening. Alighting on top of a nearby residential block he observed the scene below. Several dark shapes were collected around something on which they were all intent. Around their feet were several smaller creatures milling around. Cerberus watched, at first out of curiosity over the unusual, and because the scene had a sense of familiarity about it. Then, as memory revived and collided with understanding, he swooped lower to get a better look. The dark figures resembled the day walkers in size and stature but were indeed subtly different. Their eyes were narrowed and red to see in dark places, their noses broadened to almost a muzzle which allowed them to smell far more than humans ever could and their ears were elongated as bats to hear even the slightest of treads or swish of wings. Around their feet milled the hounds that helped them in their quest. They were a tracking pack. Cerberus felt the feathers along his back stand on end and he involuntarily pulled back into the shadows lest they detected his scent on the changing winds.

Changelings

It was these creatures that were sent to find the changelings that were no longer of use or had deserted their designated place and function. They tracked the dangerous or those deemed dangerous to the state. He had only seen them once before and that had been at a demonstration just after he had been changed. Every batch of changelings were shown what would happen if they became useless in the eyes of the IGH. An expendable member of the group was placed in a maze, the rest watched from a balcony. In the centre of the maze was an escape hatch. If the hapless creature could reach it then they would escape to live another day. From the opposite side of the maze just one tracker and its hound entered and began to track the creature condemned to death. Even though he had no time piece, Cerberus knew that the creature below was trapped. The hound was upon its quarry keeping it corralled until its master arrived. The tracker had about it an air of unhurried inevitability. It sauntered to catch up with its hound, confident that its quarry would be unable to escape its clutches. If it could have smiled Cerberus knew it would have done so malevolently. Once at its destination, its quarry froze as if from sheer terror and the tracker walked over and wrapped the creature in what Cerberus had thought was its cloak but later transpired to be great leathery wings. They all watched with dawning horror. When it was finished the tracker stepped away and its victim fell to the floor obviously from its pallor, now dead. The only sign of injury was one single trickle of blood slowly dripping down its neck and even this was strange since such a neck wound should have bled profusely. The answer was because the master had finished bleeding it, the hound moved in to feast on flesh and as it tore a limb from the dead creature it was evident that no blood flowed in its veins. The tracker had drained the ebb of life swiftly and with little waste. It was an efficient creature, perfectly designed to deliver death.

As Cerberus watched the throng below, he was reminded of other images he had been buried in his subconscious a long time before. It was a collective memory of swamps and vile creatures. He could see perhaps ten trackers with twice as many hounds and they were intent on a piece of clothing one of them held. Curiosity kept Cerberus watching as no changeling he knew wore clothing and yet it was inconceivable that these, things, had been released to track a human. Then they once again began to move out, as if their momentary confusion had been overcome. Cerberus saw that what he had thought to be gliding in the mist was in fact cruising because of the silent movement of the leathery wings. He also saw that they were less human than he had supposed, their hind legs held clearly defined talons and a tail was visible emerging from the base of the wings. Indeed, Cerberus would now classify them more gargoyle or demon, than human. Instinctual revulsion sent a shiver down his spine. He also made the connection to his previous experience; the scene he was watching looked exactly like a hunt he had watched when still a boy.

Even though he knew it to be very dangerous, Cerberus set out to follow the pack and discover what it was they were chasing. Keeping himself downwind and in the shadows so that the trackers could not find him, he followed through the deserted night and he wondered how sound the citizens of this city would sleep if they saw the trackers skulking in the streets. He wondered if mothers would lie to their children and reassure them that monsters did not exist so they could sleep soundly in their beds.

After about ten minutes Cerberus became aware of single trackers, each with a pair of hounds, leaving the pack and going in different directions down darkened alleyways. They were spreading out, clearly indicating that their strategy was developing and that they had more than the physical ability to detect. They also had a level of intelligence that could plan. Sickened in his spirit that such things not only existed but had been actively created, he could conceive of no worse a creature. He had yet to meet the banshee that sang so well and drew his soul to join it in imagined friendship. Cerberus found himself compelled to follow the macabre scene unfolding ahead.

Soon only one tracker with its two hounds remained for him to follow. Then, as if reacting to a signal only it could hear, it changed direction not once but several times until Cerberus remembered that bats used sonar to navigate and he supposed that it was sonar that was directing it. Cerberus flew higher to see if he could get a view of the others and their actions. As he flew, he located all ten trackers, they had formed a wide circle that was now converging on the south side of the great park.

It took Cerberus two passes to locate the creatures the trackers were chasing. Landing lightly a little away from them so as not to cause alarm he addressed them directly.

"There is little time left, the trackers are closing in, do you know what they want?"

"Yes," the man replied, "they want the boy," and he pointed as he spoke. The boy looked directly at Cerberus and all Cerberus could see was fear.

"Why?" he simply asked, "you are not changed"

"I don't know," the man replied almost crying. "They said at his school that he must go to the IGH. I was afraid to take him and then they came to the house, now we will both die" he finished with a hint of a sob.

"I'll take the boy," Cerberus offered, "but we will have to hurry."

Nodding, the father picked up his son and placed him on Cerberus' back. "Thank you," he whispered. The tears fell from his eyes as he watched Cerberus fly away with his son just as he had flown with the changeling child only a few nights before. Then, as the father turned from them, he was knocked to the ground by a pair of hounds and the first tracker was upon him before he could draw breath. Almost simultaneously others arrived to take their share and he was empty of blood in seconds. As their hounds feasted on the remains, they tasted the air for the boy they were seeking and found the sweat of the owl. This interference would need reporting, perhaps they would taste the blood of the owl also.

Cerberus flew almost vertically to put as much distance between them and the trackers as he possibly could. He also wanted to spare the boy of having to see exactly what would happen to his father. In silence, Cerberus concentrated on his flight. He hoped that the trackers would need to seek instruction and be unable to follow until the next night. His plan was to fly to Manchester, the place he had taken the Butterbee, well outside the city limits and he hoped that those who lived there would take as much pity on the unchanged as they had on the changed child.

Looking back, he realised one tracker was following at a safe distance. The rest must have returned for further instructions and this one had orders simply to follow them. Thankfully, it was not trying to close any ground. If he simply flew to his intended destination it may not be able to follow that distance from the city. Cerberus was still unsure. If it did follow, there was no telling what damage could be done. He decided to consult Thanatos.

＊＊＊＊

Sutton sat at his desk catching up on paperwork and thinking about the caretaker. He could not think of him in terms of the changeling name he had identified. He seemed more human than most of the real variety Sutton knew. He decided to pay a visit to the police archive and see if he were telling the truth or on a flight of fancy. Perhaps the old guy had just spent too much time on his own with only the owls for company. Perhaps he was just confused and wanted to belong so badly he had convinced himself he was really one of them. Sutton knew what a serious disease loneliness could be and to what lengths people would go to alleviate it.

As he walked past the desk, Mac called to him, "I thought you had been put on desk duty?"

"I'm just popping down to the archive," Sutton replied.

"Ok, I'll log you away from desk but still in the building then; that way Kapowski won't be able to moan in the morning that you're not following orders."

"You're a lifesaver," Sutton called as he exited through the double doors. In truth, going to the archive did involve going out on the street

As he stood on the steps of the station and fastened his coat, he was astonished to see two dark hounds run past swiftly followed by a creature that spoke to his primeval memory and made Sutton withdraw involuntarily. Immediately he forced himself to step forward surprised at such an instinctual reaction and curious to identify the creature that aroused it. He was just in time to see the tracker turn the next corner. He wondered what business they had in the streets this night and why he had not been informed they were hunting. They usually informed whoever was on duty when the trackers were hunting. Then, making connections, he realised that was why he had been told to stay on desk duty, so his wanderings would not interfere with their goals. Confirmation that his superiors thought of him as a fool; a fool that might interfere with the most basic of operations.

$$****$$

Mike sat at home reading the stolen files. The more he read, the more he wondered if they were not part of an elaborate joke. Any minute Davidson would leap out from behind his settee and shout, fooled you. If they were real, the story they told was incredible and unbelievable and true. He felt himself slip further away from finding Phoebe. It was as if he was negotiating a maze that kept changing its shape and moving the boundaries. There was a solution that was just out of focus and if he concentrated enough he would be able to see it clearly. Mike just wasn't sure if it was the right solution; the one he needed to lead him to Phoebe. He could not be sure if he was being led away from her. Sighing deeply, he lay the file on the seat next to him and stepped onto the balcony for some fresh air. Leaning against the railing he determined to find another cigarette no matter how much it cost. He needed some serious de-stressing.

Looking down at the street below he was surprised to see two large dogs run by as if they were in chase of some hidden prey. He had not realised that any dogs had survived or been recreated. He made a mental note to check in the archive tomorrow. Then he saw a bat like creature follow and he felt the hairs all down his spine stand on edge. He gave an involuntary shudder and stepped back, away from whatever it was. Then, just as Sutton had done, he leaned forward curious as to the nature of a creature that could produce such instinctive revulsion. He had time to note the leathery wings and forked tail before it disappeared from sight. He decided to check both sightings out in the morning. Chilled, he returned inside and decided to stop for the day.

****

Sutton entered the archive and began searching the records of the first IGH changelings. As he expected, Thanatos was not amongst them. The man was really starting to get on Sutton's nerves. He was obviously playing some game that he found amusing and Sutton wondered if anyone had put him up to it. He would not put it past Kapowski to be in some corner having a good giggle at having Sutton run around in circles over nothing. Still, while he was here, he decided to investigate fully and began to research the name Thanatos as well.

Thanatos, it appeared was the Greek god of death, and he had a brother called Hypnos who was the god of sleep. Sutton thought the caretaker was deeply disturbed if he had chosen the name. Uninterested in Greek mythology, Sutton continued to search the archives. He found that the first changelings were named after the Greek gods and this would seem to bear out the caretakers claims to be one of the first. Sutton cross-referenced his search with changelings and was rewarded with a picture of the caretaker. It appeared that he had started the search from the wrong angle. Thanatos was one of the first changelings, just not one of the IGH's first. He was registered to a company known as Progen. Sutton had never heard of them before and began a simultaneous search relating to their activities.

****

Cerberus landed once more on the roof of the Law Courts and the boy slid from his back. Cerberus turned to appraise him for the first time. It was lighter on the roof than in the park, he could clearly see the boy's distress. Tears had left grubby track marks down each cheek and he pensively bit his lower lip. Even so he looked Cerberus clearly in the eye and did not waver or cower as many adults would in a similar situation. Cerberus was about to speak with him when he saw the boy's attention diverted to behind him and from the shock reflected on his face it was not a friend that had just landed. Swivelling swiftly to face the demon behind, Cerberus was just swift enough to avoid contact with the tracker's poisonous fangs.

"Inside," Cerberus called to the boy as he deflected another blow from the talons of the tracker. He was able to see the boy leave the roof as the fight began in earnest. Both creatures used flight to gain an advantage over the other. Time after time talons clashed and bodies entwined. It seemed for a time that they were well matched, but things began to turn against Cerberus. He began to tire and at each clash he became weaker and it became harder to break free from his opponent. Then the tracker struck a blow the full length of Cerberus' thigh and a stream of red coloured his feathers. Letting out a long screech of frustration, he renewed his efforts and forced the tracker back to the edge of the roof. Suddenly, Thanatos in wolf form leapt on its back and together he and Cerberus were able to overcome the creature.

Cerberus collapsed to rest on the roof and catch his breath. Thanatos followed and as he collapsed, he transformed back to his human form so that by the time he collapsed on the rooftop he was fully human once more. The boy stood by the roof garden simply watching the fight unfold and as he saw Thanatos change, he twitched as if slapped.

"Come and help boy," Thanatos called and reluctantly, at first, the boy came to join them. He had to trust them; they were his only protectors.

"What can we do?" Cerberus asked.

"We need to burn it," Thanatos replied, jumping to his feet. "Come on boy," he continued, "I need you to help me carry things" and with that, Thanatos hurried toward the roof door with the boy trailing behind. Cerberus lay back and closed his eyes. Weariness overtook him, and he drifted into a semi consciousness that was comforting in its own way.

****

Sutton returned to his office from the archive to find Kapowski sifting through his files. "Hey, what are you doing?" Sutton called.

"What I like, doughnut boy," Kapowski replied sarcastically.

He held one file in his hand and as he spoke, he allowed it to fall to the floor where it shattered into a thousand pieces.

"What did you do that for?" Sutton challenged him.

"Because I don't like being called in to cover for the likes of you," he replied, as he let a second file shatter.

"Those will take hours to retype," Sutton informed him.

"Well perhaps then you will follow orders and, stay, at, your, desk" Kapowski spat each word as if they were insults. "Instead of acting as if you are some great detective ready to solve an eternal mystery."

"I only went to the archive," Sutton explained.

"Only disobeyed orders as usual," Kapowski countered.

"So why is my being at my desk suddenly a big deal?" Sutton asked.

"Don't flatter yourself, we are just sick of you never doing anything and seeing yourself as so much better than the rest of us" Kapowski emphasised his words by pointing at Sutton as he spoke, jabbing the air as if to reinforce what he said.

"I don't," Sutton tried to explain.

"Oh, but you do," Kapowski continued, warming to his theme "Every boring little poxy job you treat like a major crime and try to solve it. Why can't you just accept that the glory days are over?" Kapowski stepped forward, "Frankly it's embarrassing to the whole squad."

"I know that!" Sutton replied with an edge of sarcasm, "I'm only trying not to die of complete boredom."

"Do us all a favour and die quietly, at least that way you will be less of a laughingstock," Kapowski added.

"Is that what you all think?" Sutton asked tight lipped as he sank into his desk chair.

Softening a little, Kapowski laid a hand on Sutton's shoulder "Look old man, just type your reports and leave the real stuff to the day shift"

Sutton nodded, "you're the boss," in a much more subdued tone "I didn't think they were all laughing at me," he added uncertainly.

"It's not that bad, yet," Kapowski conceded, magnanimous now it was obvious he had won, "but it will be if you don't slow down."

Nodding again, Sutton started up his computer. "Better start typing those damaged files," he said to the air.

"Good man," Kapowski said as he headed toward the door. A smugness crept over his whole demeanour. He was obviously pleased that his message had been so well received. Kapowski had thought the whole thing would have been much harder, the old man was obviously further gone than he had suspected. Kapowski thought it was sad and they should have retired him a long time ago.

Sutton watched him go. If he thought, for one moment, a late-night warning would stop him Kapowski really did think he was an idiot! The visit made him even more determined to find out what the mystery was about. Someone like Kapowski did not come out in the middle of the night to give a friendly warning. He wanted to know what Sutton had and that made Sutton very curious to know what was being hidden. The first thing he needed to do was figure out how Kapowski had known he was out of the office and for now, he needed to look like he was taking the friendly advice to heart. That meant typing for the rest of the night. The things he did for the love of this job he thought as he began work on the first of the two damaged files. It was around the time of his visit to the Caldwell residence, the point at which things began to get strange.

****

Cerberus watched in an almost dreamlike state as Thanatos and the boy doused the trackers remains and set them alight. As the creature burned, Thanatos cleaned the wound on his leg.

"Feeling out of it old friend?" Thanatos asked. All Cerberus could do

was nod. "It's the venom in their bite; that's why their victims never struggle."

For Cerberus, it made a bit of sense, but he was struggling with the concept of rational thought and he simply did not care about anything else at the moment.

Patting his leg, Thanatos said, "lots still to do, you'll be fine." Then, talking to the boy, "help me get him inside, and then we will finish clearing up."

Chapter 8

Mike considered phoning in sick. He had never done it before but the files in his room needed reading and he needed time to do it. Neither companion had shared his bed the previous night and so he was sure he could fool both, but he knew it would have to be good to trick Will, Barb and Davidson. He thought the best move was to make himself sick. He looked around to see what he could find and eventually settled on the idea of swallowing spoiled milk. Stealing himself over the sink, he poured a capful, then mentally counting to three he poured it in his mouth. He held it there for a second and then before he could talk himself out of it, he gulped and allowed the liquid to hit his waiting stomach. The reaction was almost immediate, his stomach violently objected to the presence of the liquid and in projectile fashion, it came right back out of his gut. Grimacing, he wiped the foul-smelling fluid from the mirror with toilet tissue. He briefly wondered how it could smell like vomit even though it had spent less than thirty seconds in his system.

He rinsed the gruel-like fluid from the sink, washed his hands and tried a drink of water. This, too, returned to the world very quickly, but this time he was expecting it and he leaned into the sink and avoided splattering the mirror with any more effluent. Examining his reflection in the mirror he was pleased to be confronted with a very ashen image. He was ready to face his audience.

Barb was making breakfast which made him feel worse and Will was getting ready for the office. One look at him and they both came running over, full of concern about his well-being.

"Oh Mike," Barb fussed, guiding him to an armchair.

"It's all right," he insisted, holding up one hand to fend them off. "I just need to stay in bed today."

"It's both our days at the office," Barb announced in somewhat plaintive fashion. "Don't worry," Mike continued, "I don't want any company, just sleep."

"Oh, but one of us should stay and look after you," Will interjected.

"No, I won't hear of it." Mike insisted, "I will only be asleep, and the codes need typing and checking again." Then, just to appeal to their vanity he added, "Someone else might mess them up; it would give me great peace of mind if I know both of you are on the job."

Flattered, they both began to assure him that they would give it their full attention and all he had to do was get better. Barb popped into his bathroom to give it a quick clean before she left even though Mike said he would clean it himself. It was good, she thought, that he knew she would do anything for him. Once they were out the door all he had to do was phone Davidson. The beauty was that, even if he decided to check Mike's story, both Barb and Will would be able to testify to how ill he had been that morning.

Making himself coffee, Mike returned whistling to his room and the, yet to be read, files. He drank two more glasses of water before he stopped vomiting and thought it safe to drink his coffee. He was beginning to piece together a surprising chain of events. He discovered that the cryptids had yielded not five but six amino acids. The Director had found these when she worked for the company called Progen. They had been experimented with extensively, well before the world crisis had been reached. None of these initial experiments had involved human subjects. The extensive animal trials had resulted in some very interesting DNA shifts. At some point, they had stopped using the sixth amino acid and the reason remained unclear. References were made to high mortality rates, but actual numbers were not quoted. Another strange convention was that the subjects were referred to via species numbers rather than species names. This meant he could not be sure what the starting raw material or finished product were. One thing was evident he needed to return to the art gallery to collect more material. Placing the file on the bed next to him he was surprised to see that the morning was about over. Getting out of bed, he went in search of more coffee. Just as he was filling his cup, he heard the front door close quietly. Curious he entered the sitting room expecting to see either Will or Barb returned to see how he was doing. Instead, Davidson stood by his fireplace. Taken aback, the first thing Mike could think of saying was, "How did you get in?"

Smiling a little creepily, Davidson replied, "Its company property, remember? I have full access to everything that belongs to the company."

"I didn't realise that meant you had access to my flat," Mike said warily.

"Don't be naïve" Davidson snorted "I have access to where the Director wants me to have access and today it's here."

Completely put in his place, and on the defensive, Mike felt like a chastised child and he decided to change the subject.

"Did you come to see how I was?" he asked.

"Of course," Davidson replied in an oily tone which showed he was clearly enjoying the situation. "It doesn't look like you have spent much time in this room?" he half-stated, half-asked.

"No, in fact I've just got up," Mike answered helpfully. "I feel a lot better than I did this morning".

"Good," Davidson stated. Obviously disinterested in how Mike felt, he began to move around the room looking at ornaments and even opening drawers. A little puzzled, Mike asked, "Is there something I can help you with?"

"Now you ask." Davidson literally purred, and Mike's sixth sense screamed be careful. "I was wondering if you had found anything in those old records?"

On safer ground, Mike replied, "nothing concrete but I have a couple of interesting leads, I could fill you in when I come back to work tomorrow."

"That would be lovely," Davidson replied. "I wouldn't want to think you were holding anything back."

"Why would I do that?" Mike asked, genuinely puzzled.

Davidson shrugged. "People do and, when they end up in all kinds of hot water, they blame everyone but themselves." The menace was unmistakable and then to really give Mike the chills he finished, "remember Maxwell and Oldfield?" He paused then added, "Poor chaps."

For the first time Mike wondered what part Davidson had played in their downfall. He was left in no doubt that Davidson had been involved and if he wanted to be sure of his own personal safety then he would have to play the game Davidson's way. The threat was clear.

Having completed his mission and warned Mike, Davidson began to leave. "See you tomorrow," he said, "back at work as you should be." was the parting instruction.

"Yes sir," was all Mike could think of, but the reply pleased Davidson as it reaffirmed his position as the chief and he left with a smile on his face.

Once he had gone, Mike returned to the kitchen to re-warm his now cold coffee. Davidson had obviously come to warn him, but why ... that was the worrying part. What had he done to make Davidson believe he was up to no good? He began to analyse his recent behaviour. As far as he was aware, any change in his behaviour had been negligible. The second worry was, why mention Oldfield and Maxwell? Both had been good crypto-biologists until each had decided to break the law.

Mike did not even know what changeling position they now held. He decided that perhaps he ought to know, something else to add to his to-do list. Find out what had happened to one or both without alerting Davidson further. Just as he was deciding what was for lunch his entry system intercom sounded. This place was beginning to resemble a food distribution centre, but at least this time whoever it was had the courtesy to ring before entering.

"Yes," he said into the speaker.

"Doctor Caldwell? Its Detective Sutton sir, I wondered if you had a moment to answer some questions?" he asked.

"Of course, detective, come up." why not thought Mike, the more the merrier. He should have a day off more often. Mike buzzed Sutton in. As Sutton entered, Davidson took the door from him and passed into the street. Vaguely recognising him, Sutton made a mental note to identify him later. He wrote down the exact time so that he could easily locate satellite footage and print a picture when he returned to the office.

Mike invited the detective in. Unable to resist the temptation, Sutton commented, "Much tidier than last time sir, did the young lady come back?" Not in the best of moods and still smarting from Davidson's visit, Mike was quick to reply, "That rude tone could get you in trouble detective," with a hint of menace in his voice.

"No disrespect meant sir," Sutton replied offended.

"Good, good," Mike continued, pleased to have someone over which to exert his own authority. "What can I do for you?" gracious now; it was clear he was the one with the power.

'Idiot!' thought Sutton as he said, "Just a couple of questions sir?" He asked carefully keeping his tone neutral and his thoughts to himself.

"Get on with it then." Mike replied somewhat impatiently.

Pretending to consult his notes, Sutton deliberately strung out the moment just to wind the man up. He really did find him excruciatingly annoying. "Yes, let me see," he said. "The young lady, Phoebe," he continued.

"Yes, yes get to the point," Mike interjected while rolling his eyes.

"Yes, sir, well if you will interrupt my train of thought, it's bound to take longer," Sutton said.

Longer! Mike thought it had already taken an eternity, the man was a complete buffoon, no wonder they had delegated him to the night shift.

"Yes, let me see," Sutton continued with a straight face while inwardly laughing at his own comic ability. "I was wondering sir, if the young lady or even yourself, had any links with a company called Progen?"

Almost choking on his coffee, Mike could not hide his surprise. Was this man spying on him? Did he know that Mike had the files? More importantly, were they legal? Suddenly Mike panicked, and he saw his future unfold, it was a future where he chased rats for a living under Cerberus' command. It was a possible future he did not want to become a reality. His reaction however was already producing curiosity from Sutton as he watched Mike with an expression that was difficult to discern. Mike decided that truth or rather partial truth was probably the best policy; that and counterattack.

"Where did you hear that name detective?" he asked.

"Just on routine enquiries sir," Sutton replied, inclining his head slightly, waiting patiently for Mike's reply and revealing nothing of his hand. Mike collected his wits.

"In fact, I have," he replied coolly.

"May I ask in what context?" Sutton asked.

"I believe it was the parent company to the IGH" Mike replied.

"Do you know anything else, sir?" Sutton pushed, putting emphasis on the else in the sentence as if he were expecting extra information.

"No," Mike replied, shaking his head, then turned away from the detective to hide any tell-tale sign that might appear on his face. "May I ask a question?" he continued.

"Absolutely sir," Sutton replied, struggling to maintain his civility.

"Do you have any leads on Phoebe's case?"

"Enquiries are ongoing sir," was the only reply Sutton was willing to give.

"Does that mean no?" Mike pressed.

Sutton sighed. This was the part of the job he disliked. Other people's emotions were always difficult to deal with, you never knew what lay behind them and as a result it was easy to offend. Normally, this would not cause Sutton a problem. If people became offended, they could either get over it or not. However, Caldwell could complain directly to his superiors and the way Kapowski was acting, any complaints and he would be straight down the changing booths. No, he had to keep Caldwell happy and that was why he was sighing; he found such things, very hard work.

"Not necessarily sir, just that things have not come together yet that's all." Sutton stated.

"Oh, I see," Mike said in a tone that meant he did not understand at all. Sutton however wanted to move on. "You work with the changelings, don't you sir?"

"If a sculptor works with clay, then I guess I work with the changelings," Mike answered tersely.

"Sorry sir, I was just wondering if you could explain the process?" Sutton asked.

"Not quickly, detective," Mike replied off handily.

"Perhaps though?" Sutton pressed.

"Oh, Ok I suppose so," Mike replied while also looking at his watch to reinforce the impression he was short of time. "There are five cryptid amino acids, it is these that unzip the DNA and recombine it in new forms. Do you know what these amino acids are detective?"

"Yes sir, I think I can manage that much," Sutton replied, a little peeved that the man thought he was that simple.

Mike continued, "It is these amino acids that we combine in different ratios to produce the effects we want. It's simple really. The artistic bit comes into play when deciding how much of each amino acid to combine and how long to expose the organism," he concluded rather smugly.

"Thank you, sir," Sutton concluded while folding his notebook. He would download its contents when he returned to the office. He understood what Caldwell was on about but had wanted to hear it directly from the man himself. He had wondered if Caldwell would really explain the process or simply try to hoodwink him with science.

****

Once out in the hall, Sutton decided to look at the floors above. The first three were identical to Caldwell's level, but the next one had only two flat doors instead of the four on Caldwell's level, indicating the occupants were more senior. Taking a closer look, he also noted that a metallic key operated the locking mechanisms, very old fashioned. He wondered who the occupants were; they must be very senior to have such limited access. As he looked around the hall, he noticed two further doors, one labelled 'services' and the other 'fire escape'. He tried the services first and, although it was locked, punched in the police override code, and was rewarded with the door opening. Inside were the cleaning materials he had expected and the usual array of cleaner bots to operate them. A little disappointed, he turned to go but as the door closed behind him, he thought he caught movement out of the corner of his eye. Jumping back into the closet he was rewarded with the definite changing of the shadows which froze just a fraction of a second too late. Was this Kapowski's source he wondered, tracker shadows reporting on his movements. Something, instinct, or his gut, which according to Kapowski was so big he had to listen to it, told him it was someone else, something else that had him in their sights. Watching the shadow closely he withdrew an instrument from his pocket that resembled a small torch. He aimed directly at the shadow in front of him and hit a trigger. The effect was dramatic. The shadow screamed, a high pitch somehow melodic sound and then it leapt away from the wall, momentarily taking on a three-dimensional form. It was not that of any creature Sutton had seen before and he fell away from it in surprise. The head was small and resembled that of a boxer dog he had once owned, and it was also reminiscent of a gargoyle. The head was perched on top of a long neck. The rest of its form was hidden in the darkness of the ordinary shadows.

For a moment, he was transported to the depths of a lost swamp and he could even smell the green plants steaming in the heat of the day. The creature then turned and swam away from him through the thick sea of shadows which rippled as it made its escape. Jumping, Sutton was determined to follow the creature and running down the hall he was just in time to see it flee through the fire escape. Following at a run, he expected the door to give at the pressure of his weight, but instead he was thrown back onto the floor. Cursing, he kicked the door. He could, and perhaps would, prosecute the building supervisor for having a locked fire escape.

Overriding the lock mechanism, he leapt up the stairs two at a time and burst onto the roof right into the middle of a barbecue. At least six people turned and stared at him directly and one walked over to talk to him. He had an uncanny resemblance to the caretaker, even down to the cravat around his neck and Sutton had to do a double take before he fully comprehended that he was a different person.

"This is a private function," he said with authority.

"I am an official," Sutton said flashing his ID. The last thing he wanted was for these people to know his name. He should be home asleep, not as Kapowski would say ... snooping.

"I am sorry, detective?"

"Kapowski," Sutton said before his brain could fully justify the move.

"Ah, yes, I have heard of you Detective. How can I help?"

"Just now, I was chasing a shadow. Did you see it?"

"No, but I can ask the others," he offered helpfully. "Hey everyone, did anyone see a runaway shadow?"

A chorus of negatives were the result of the enquiry.

"If it was here, no one saw it, Detective."

"Thank you anyway sir," Sutton said respectively. "May I look around anyway?" he asked.

"Of course, perhaps around that way; we would not have seen it if it went that way"

"Thank you," Sutton said as he headed in the indicated direction.

The area he was directed to was where the utilities were and as he skirted the air conditioning unit, he saw one living shadow hiding in the corner; but the tag was showing his shadow was already some distance away. It wasn't the one he was chasing so he ignored it. He went to the edge and peered over. He was rewarded with the sight of a long arrow tipped tail fleeing down the side of the building. 'Shit,' he thought. Well at least he had tagged it; he would know if it came back. Sutton made his way out of the building.

****

Maia was finding it difficult to sleep as she lay quietly next to Cerberus. She did not want to disturb his dreams. He was sleeping very soundly next to her. She watched the regular rise and fall of his chest and found comfort in his calmness. He had been having disturbed dreams recently; it was calming to watch him sleep so soundly for a change. Recently everything was unsettled, changing and it made her uncomfortable and jittery.

She closed her eyes once more, if she did not get some serious sleep she would suffer when it came time to hunt. She tried to think of herself asleep, visualising her own sleeping form. On some days, this had worked and sent her into the land of dreams but today it was having no effect. She turned over and tried again, she sometimes reached the dream state if she told herself a story. She often chose a scene from her own childhood and today her mind slipped into a familiar groove. She saw two children in the distance they were building a sandcastle on a beach. It was one of her favourite memories but today something didn't quite fit. The children were wrong she realised but she did not know in what way. She watched a while and laughed at their games; it was just as she had remembered childhood holidays with her parents. The feeling that something was wrong grew stronger and her pleasure drained away. It was not until the boy stood and ran to the water's edge that the wrongness was clarified in her mind. These children were owl children, not as she had thought of herself and her brother. But the wrongness did not end there as she realised, they were not just random changelings. They were connected to her. When the knowledge they were her own children surfaced in her conscious mind she woke once again. Tears fell freely from her eyes; the denial of her own unconscious desires hurt more than any physical pain ever could. She had dreamt of her own children; a reality that would never be, for changelings were always infertile. She lay next to Cerberus' sleeping form and cried for all that could have been.

Chapter 9

Cerberus slowly became aware of his surroundings. He was inside. It had been some years since he had been inside a building and he suddenly realised how uncomfortable he felt. It was no longer his domain.

Thanatos walked into his peripheral vision. "Awake at last?"

Cerberus just grunted.

"The boy helped me clean up the roof." Thanatos nodded in the direction of the couch, where Cerberus saw the boy; he was reading.

"He talked to you yet?" Cerberus asked as he raised himself into a sitting position.

"No, I thought I would wait for you to come around before I asked questions," Thanatos said.

Cerberus stretched his wings but was unable to extend them fully as the furniture and trinkets were in his way. "I forgot how restrictive the indoors are," he said, almost apologetically.

"Don't worry about it" Thanatos said. "I have a feeling I won't be living here much longer. Who's the boy?"

"I'm not sure," Cerberus replied. "I found him with his father, the trackers were chasing them, and I took the boy. That's where we picked up the one you disposed of for me. Others will be chasing it; I think I better move the boy soon."

"The trackers won't be able to pick up your scent from the roof," Thanatos reassured him.

"You can put them off?" Cerberus asked, with a hint of disbelief in his voice.

"The smell we eradicated with industrial bleach and I have speakers up there. When I play music, it will disrupt their sonar, they are basically bat hybrids you know." He told Cerberus.

"I didn't know," Cerberus replied, "How do you?"

"I've been around a long time, that's all."

"Let's talk to the boy then."

The boy knew no more than his father; he was running away because his dad thought it was the best thing to do. They had a blood test at school, and everything had started to go wrong straight after that. Thanatos took a blood sample from the boy and looked at it under the microscope. What he saw surprised him so much that he cursed. Reaching for a test tube full of an unidentified chemical, Thanatos mixed it with a little of the boy's blood. He then placed it a machine that span the blood very quickly. Thanatos looked at this under the microscope and exclaimed, "No way," in a tone of wonder that surprised Cerberus.

"What is it?" Cerberus asked unable to wait any longer.

"He has the same amino acids in his blood stream as I do," Thanatos told him.

"How, he's not a changeling." Cerberus asked obviously confused.

"That must be why the IGH want him, to find out how that could happen," Thanatos hypothesised.

"But he can't have been accidentally changed," Cerberus insisted still confused.

"No, not accidentally. It is logical, and really, it was only a matter of time," Thanatos rambled as he drew his own blood for comparison and then Cerberus' with an air of distraction that clearly indicated his thoughts were elsewhere. He displayed all three results on the computer screen.

"Do you see?" he asked and then went on to explain that although all three had similarities they were also clear differences. Cerberuses had missing DNA bases and clearly two types of associated amino acids. Thanatos explained that was because he had both distinct human and cryptid DNA strands. The cryptids being the additions made during the changing process and the missing bases being removed allowing the physical changes to manifest themselves. Thanatos had no missing bases and less human amino acids, enabling him to unzip and reconnect his DNA strands almost at will. He also had a greater number of cryptid DNA strands that floated free when not in use. This allowed him to move between human and wolf shape. The boy's DNA was even more intertwined with cryptid biology. Both cryptid and human DNA floated free and the cryptid DNA was more varied. It must have happened at conception that kind of complexity would have killed him if it had been changed so extensively after the original organism had been created. Thanatos pointed out the new hybrid free floating DNA components that were evident in the boy's blood stream.

"The IGH did it, is that what you think?" Cerberus asked.

Shaking his head Thanatos replied, "I don't think so. If it was deliberate, they would have known about him. No, I think he is a naturally occurring mutant. Like I said, logical really, we have been introducing the cryptid gene sequences into the environment for years. Rather arrogant of the IGH to think they can control all the effects.

Before the disaster they had a problem in Australia with a certain insect infestation." Thanatos told Cerberus.

"What's that got to do with this?" Cerberus asked.

"Just this; they introduced the American toad species to control the insects, but they had not thought the situation through. With a plentiful food supply and no predators, the toads bred so prolifically that they were soon a bigger pest than the original insects had ever been. They were arrogant in thinking they could control nature." Thanatos finished his story and looked thoughtfully at the boy.

"That's the IGH for you," Cerberus replied. "Arrogant to the last."

"We need to get the boy out of the city. He will be very valuable to them." Thanatos told Cerberus.

"I can fly with him tonight," Cerberus offered.

"No, I think someone else should take him. We need you to get your guy in the IGH to start giving us information. If we can prove the IGH has made illegal changes and show the ability to change is leeching into the natural population, we have a real chance of improving things for us." Thanatos said.

"I'll pay him a visit," Cerberus said as he turned to go.

"Wait," Thanatos called. "You need to leave by the tunnels downstairs, so the trackers don't pick up your trail."

****

Sutton turned over recent happenings in his mind and decided Kapowski could go *'make himself happy'*. Sutton was going to find out what was at the bottom of all this. He decided to pay the IGH a visit and start by looking at the records associated with Caldwell and his companion. His instincts told him the events were all connected; he just had to work out the nature of that connection. Then he would be able to see the whole picture and decide which pieces of the puzzle were important and which were irrelevant.

Sutton stood in the entrance to the IGH. He had to admit, whatever you thought of them, they knew how to make a good first impression and the gold crest was spectacular. Walking across the foyer was a rather attractive young woman; blonde, shapely and sporting a PR badge. He knew they would have looked up his preference the second he had requested information. It was all part of the service, ensuring he was served by someone he found attractive. It increased his chances of remaining under the IGH control. Smiling, he followed her across the hall to an interview booth, all the way dutifully admiring the swing of her perfectly proportioned rear. Who said there were no benefits in his job?

Once at the terminal he requested staff lists. Who worked for the IGH had never been considered sensitive material and so he had free access. Firstly, he looked Caldwell up and confirmed he had been a child recruit as had his sister. Strange … he had not mentioned a sister before. Still, not entirely unusual, especially if she were self-sufficient. Sutton made a note to visit her later. He then looked Phoebe Johnston up and was again a little surprised to see her listed not as secretary or companion which he had expected. It was common for executive types to take secretaries as companions, but under the watchful eyes of security. And, it appeared they were watching Caldwell unaware of it. Now that was interesting. He requested her whole file and was somewhat annoyed when directed to the head of security. It would take days to go through official protocols. While thinking about his next move, he began flipping through staff list after staff list and his half alert brain began to see a pattern emerging among certain staff.

Every couple of years some staff were marked *'employment terminated'*. In the good old days that would have meant very little, but now people did not get fired or quit. They were demoted or transferred but definitely not terminated. He decided to do a file sort of terminated staff. What followed could have been coincidence or a simple error, however Sutton believed in neither of these. When he asked for the sort, he forgot to define dates and as such obtained a list that dated back to the early days of the IGH. He was about to redefine the data parameters when he noticed the first name on the list, David Grey. It was not the name itself that caused him to stop, but the additional knowledge he had. This had been the man that was now called Thanatos. He saved the list to his notebook. He would check these names against the changeling list held at headquarters.

He returned to current staff lists and again began to simply trawl through to see if anything else jumped out at him. Surprisingly, it did. Listed on payroll was the name Kapowski. A conflict of interest that supposedly was not allowed, he had always known some officers must have been on the IGH payroll but had thought it would have been better hidden than this. It just showed how arrogant the corporation had become if it believed it did not need to be careful. He put a request in for this file also.

Leaving the IGH, he entered an alley at the side and ignited a de-tracking bomb. This would ensure that trackers would be unable to follow him later and that any tags would be rendered useless. He wanted no unwelcome eyes knowing what he was doing. Unfortunately for Sutton, his hardware was useless against watching shadows; and watching they were. The de-tracking device not only rendered any tags on Sutton useless but the tag he had placed on the watching shadow was also deactivated.

****

Across the city Mike decided to return to the Law Courts, taking back most of the files he had previously removed. Now he knew what he was looking for. The cross-reference list that would help him identify the species being changed in the first experiments. Somehow his agenda had moved on from Phoebe to simply trying to understand what it was that the IGH was built on. He had based who he was on seeing them as the good guys. He wanted to be on the winning side and was only now beginning to realise that those who were winning were not necessarily the good guys.

He retraced his steps without difficulty and replaced the files in order. He was a meticulous man. He then began searching the files for the species list and finally he found what he wanted. Using it to guide his choices, he began to load all the files relating to human experimentation. It was surprisingly heavy work and he paused to wipe the sweat from his brow as it obscured his vision. As he paused, he heard a faint sound that put him on alert. Creeping along the hallway, he peered into the first laboratory. He held his breath, lest it betray his presence. A strange trio entered from the main doorway. First there was an aging man who appeared to be leading the way. He was quickly followed by a blonde child and then ungainly and unsuited to walking was the unmistakable shape of Cerberus. Pulling himself further into the darkness of the hall he wondered what this unlikely alliance meant. For a minute, he panicked because it appeared there was nowhere else for them to go than down this short hallway. Mike wondered where he could hide. He then realised the old one in the lead was intent on the furthest wall from his hiding place. A second hidden mechanism sprang from the wall but this one revealed, not files, but a hidden stairway leading even further below the city. Mike watched as they disappeared, and the wall rolled back into place. This new exit route may prove useful in the future. He was tempted to follow Cerberus and his friends a little further but decided to return and finish the task he had set himself first. Unless absolutely necessary, he decided it would be unwise to return here again. Whatever was happening had an edge of danger and putting himself in personal danger had never been high on his list of things to do.

✳✳✳✳

As the strange trio made their way into the staircase, they were all overwhelmed by the stink of rotting flesh and long dead fears. The rails were slimy from years of neglect and the stairway was slippery underfoot. It was Cerberus who struggled the most with negotiating the route. His wings, unsuited to gripping, could only act as a balance moving across the top of the rail and the talons on his feet were unable to grip the stone on which he walked. They went down for what seemed a very long time, and Cerberus began to wonder if it would ever end. Finally, they reached the bottom.

Changelings

This proved to be a tunnel, in fact a storm drain which led to the river. Once there, they would be met by a changeling who would take the boy outside of the city, possibly to Manchester, possibly not. It was best Cerberus did not know where the boy would finally end up. He would be free to return to his flock and if questioned even under the influence of a truth drug he would be unable to give them what he did not know. Leaving them both at the end of the tunnel Thanatos returned alone the way they had all come.

* * * *

Thanatos entered the lab and sniffed deeply to see if the human was still there. He could smell the sweat and the fear that emanated from Caldwell and gave away his presence. Going down the small hall, he investigated the archive room and nodded in satisfaction. He had obviously found what he was looking for. All the threads seemed to be coming together at last. He had waited a long time, ever since he had been changed, for the truth to become exposed once again. He knew it could mean his own existence may be in jeopardy, but personal danger never worried him. Whatever happened would be for the best and perhaps balance would once again be restored to a scarred world. He took his time in the rooms leading from the lab. It was here that he had created some of the creatures that now walked in the world. Would he do any of it differently he wondered? He would like to think he would be less self-seeking, but he was not at all sure of that.

What had brought him to this point were his own failings. He knew with a certainty. He would have ideally liked to have had someone else to blame, but the guilt was all his own. His, and possibly one other. He ran his hand over the desk where he had once sat and remembered better days with those he had thought to be his friends. Memories floated around as if they were ghosts, ghosts only he could see. He could not change what had been, but only what was to come;

130

and soon he hoped to restore what should have been his all along.

****

While Thanatos struggled with his personal demons, Mike struggled with the files through the hallways of the gallery and beyond. From halfway up the central stairway Sutton watched Caldwell struggle. The story, it seemed, had several intertwined strands and for some reason the Law Courts were central to it all. He wondered if buildings did indeed absorb what happened in their walls and if they did, could they be persuaded to tell their secrets. Bouncing up the stairs, Sutton went to confront Thanatos.

The door to the caretaker's quarters stood open, and Sutton entered presuming Thanatos would be home. What he found disturbed him and he withdrew his weapon as he began to investigate further. The neat nest of tables was overturned, and its contents spilled across the fireside rug. A bowl of water mixed with what looked like blood sat at the foot of one chair. Sutton walked across and touched the bowl. It was warm and indicating that whoever had been injured had left not long ago. There were also other signs of foul play, scratches on the polished floor that were out of place in this usually pristine abode. A drink overturned and simply abandoned and there were the remnants of a hastily consumed meal, some of it raw. The general chaos was out of keeping with Sutton's impression of the immaculate Thanatos.

Sutton cautiously approached the closed doorway, slowly opening it into what he saw were further rooms. Slowly turning the knob of the first door, he suddenly pushed hard and quickly entered what turned out to be the sleeping quarters. If anyone had been there, he wanted to retain the element of surprise by entering quickly.

The room itself was surprising. Expecting an old world feel similar to the living area, he was a little taken aback to find utilitarian functionality. The bed stood in one corner. It was a single metal frame, neatly made with a white duvet and white pillow. Against one wall stood a single silver wardrobe and no other furniture was present in the white room. Sutton walked over to the wardrobe and opened it. Inside were two pairs of trousers and the smoking jacket on a hanging rail. Four drawers completed the contents. Opening each in turn, he encountered an array of socks and underwear, nothing unusual. The bathroom which led from the sleeping area was equally sparse and uninteresting. Returning to the main living room he remembered the hidden monitors. Walking over to the fireplace he began to search for the control unit which Thanatos had used. Almost immediately, he felt the hairs on the back of his neck rise and a cold shiver run down his back. Turning swiftly with weapon ready to fire, he momentarily felt a little foolish as he could see nothing to be afraid of. Nothing until the shadows in the hall began to move. Curious, he holstered his weapon and went to look at what was causing the shift.

As he looked at the inky blackness, his eyes narrowed to try to process what he was seeing. He thought he saw movement and was convinced that this was the same shadow he had seen before. He had no concrete evidence to support his view but still he knew he was right. Someone had a shadow following him. Stepping out of the light he walked to where he thought the movement originated, completely unaware of the danger solidifying behind him. Running his hand over the surface of the wall he was intrigued to watch the living shadows withdraw from direct contact with him, and then he felt the same sensation at the back of his neck that had drawn his attention to this spot. Turning and keeping his back against the wall for security, he thought nothing could sneak up behind him. He was shocked to see how far away the living area and light now appeared to be. A massive shadow obscured the light; obviously the creature that had been observing him. He pulled back pressing harder against the wall and as he did so, he became aware of his movements becoming restricted. Looking down at himself he saw shadowy fingers encircle his arms and as his brain screamed *'impossible'*, yet another appendage covered his mouth removing his ability to create sound in the real world. Looking toward the great shadow in front of him he saw the world turn black and felt conscious thought flee his mind. If anyone had been watching they would have seen Sutton dissolve into the very fabric of the wall. Once the drama was complete, the hall returned to its dull grey ambiance and the living shadows departed for other haunts.

Phoebe was compelled to follow Sutton into the shadow world. It was still new to her too and she had seen the fear in his eyes as his familiar world disappeared before him. She thought she could perhaps help another accept his fate and help herself come to terms with her own destiny.

$$****$$

Mike lugged his burden through the doorway of his flat. He realised if any of the neighbours were watching then he may be in trouble, but he was too exhausted to care. He banged heavily as he made his way through the communal areas. He was so focused on completing his task he failed to notice the glint of metal as a small creature scuttled quickly past him. He also failed to hear a second such creature pass overhead. The pair of mites entered his flat as Mike pushed his burden the final few feet. He left the files momentarily in the hall while he poured himself a stiff brandy. He savoured the sensation as the warm liquid seeped down his throat. While Mike was distracted, the two mites scurried into dark corners where they settled down to wait. Mike's thoughts returned to his diminished Capstan stash and almost on impulse he left the half-full glass of brandy on the bar and went back out into the night.

It was cold out and soon he began to wish he had brought a coat. Shivering slightly, he increased his pace to try and warm up through exercise. He reasoned that it was not worth returning to the flat for a coat when his errand should be completed in a relatively short time. The streets were emptying quickly of the day time citizens and it would not be long before the night time shift was dutifully engaged in their designated tasks. Mike didn't have long before he was the one on the wrong side of curfew. He headed away from his upmarket district and turned down toward the canal. It was there that he would find one of the few remaining homeless and a trade in Capstans. The wind ruffled his hair and blew his fringe into his eyes. Brushing it away he was sure he saw something scurry away from him in the corner of his vision. The rats were coming out even earlier these days. Turning onto the tow path he almost slipped on a patch of damp mud. He saw a fire lighting his way directly ahead and he felt some relief as he approached his usual dealer. The dealer looked as dealers in contraband always looked, aged beyond his years, dishevelled and on the edge. No words were spoken; the exchange ritual had been enacted between this pair on many previous occasions and by many other pairs in an identical fashion for centuries.

Mike handed over a week's supply of food tokens and in return he received three individually wrapped Capstans. Small talk was not on the agenda for either man. Both needed to complete the transaction quickly. Mike to return to the safety of his home and the dealer to find a safe place for the night. With his stash, safely in his pocket Mike turned back the way he had come and, whistling jauntily, he began to make his way home.

The wind blew leaves from the trees overhead and sent them tumbling down the street ahead of him. Few people had been out when Mike had started his errand but now the street was completely empty. Mike did not think he was past curfew, but he was a little disconcerted by the vast emptiness of the night. A rat ran across the street ahead and disappeared into a drain. Mike momentarily wondered how many were down there waiting for their comrade. He was not sure exactly what had changed while he watched the rat disappear but when his attention returned to the street ahead, he felt a subtle difference. The hairs on the back of his neck stood to attention and he shivered slightly as another breath of wind cooled him further. He hesitated when he passed an alley and veered into the road rather than pass directly across a darkened area. Mentally chastising himself for his childishness he slipped back into his building and with a feeling of relief, locked the night out where it belonged. Perhaps next time he thought he should go a little earlier to buy his contraband.

✳✳✳✳

The wolf stepped momentarily from the shadows of the alley Mike had just passed. If he had turned just before entering his building, he would have seen it slink away into the night and realised that sometimes fear had a legitimate basis in ensuring survival. Without Mike knowing, the wolf was creeping ever closer to him and that, no matter how you looked at it, was not good news. For the present time, the wolf was happy to watch but patience would soon run out. Then the wolf would act in accordance with his true nature.

✳✳✳✳

Mike happily mounted the stairs and letting himself back into the flat he retrieved the brandy and slipped onto the balcony to enjoy his guilty pleasures. He was, he decided, addicted to cigarettes and the other pleasures his position could provide. He needed to think carefully before he went too far down a road from which he could not return. He went back inside and contemplated the new files he had taken from the law courts. Perhaps he should turn them all over to Davidson, simply tell him what he had found to date and enjoy the life he already had. Poking the pile with his foot he already knew he would not do that; he was already too far down this new road. Sighing deeply, Mike reached for the top file and renewed his efforts to understand.

Progen had been the first to utilise the cryptid DNA. They had tested it mainly on rats but the very first subject, he now knew courtesy of the subject coding list, had been human. By the time the IGH had abandoned rat trials they already had the results from human and another species trial. They were in a very good position to conclude that combining the cryptid DNA with human subjects would have the maximum profitability because they had tested the process considerably on all available species from the start. Well before Donna Logan had begun to chart the demise of her world.

Mike now wondered if her death had been even more sinister than he had suspected. He wondered if it could have been murder and not suicide after all. Had she stumbled on a secret or a secret experimentation programme that the political powers of the time wanted to remain hidden? It raised the question: did the government of the time have evidence of the great disaster before it happened? Were they allowing the experiments because they knew what was about to happen? Had they suspected that the death of the cryptids would cause the death of so many other species? If they had, could they have prevented any of it? Mike was tired, more so than the strains of the day could account for. The weight of this new knowledge drained his strength even more. He decided to leave the other papers for later and retired to his bed for the night.

Chapter 10

Davidson paced the length of his office. After his visit to Caldwell, he was on edge. He was sure the man knew more than he was letting on and soon Caldwell would try to capitalise on his knowledge. He had hoped that library mites' incident would have scared him off, now however he was beginning to think that more drastic action would be needed. For that he needed the Director's consent and Caldwell had always been one of her favourites. He would have to be careful to convince her that Caldwell was a danger. Exactly how to do that was causing him great anxiety. He also had to inform her about losing the boy, which was also causing him anxiety. If he was not careful in the way that he handled her he may end up re-assigned himself.

Just then the buzzer on his desk sounded. Pressing the button, "Francis, I thought I said I was not to be disturbed."

"Yes sir, but Detective Kapowski is here to see you sir, I thought you would like to know," Francis informed him.

"Thank you, Francis, give me a minute and then send him in," Davidson replied.

"Yes sir," she acknowledged.

Jumping behind his desk and picking up a pile of papers to make it look like he had been extremely busy all morning, Davidson wondered what the detective could possibly want. He did not have to wait long to find out. His office door swung open and in strode Kapowski as if he owned the place. What was even more irritating, completely ignoring Davidson's attempts at manipulation. However, this was Davidson's territory and he did not give ground easily. Glaring at the detective he said, "Take a seat," and gestured toward the smaller chair facing his own over the desk "Close the door as you leave please Francis," he continued in a tone that had chilled many who had been its recipient in the past. Recognising the warning signs, Francis withdrew silently and firmly closed the door behind her. Sitting at her desk she opened the intercom channel on the computer and set it to record. Mr Davidson would make his mind up later if he wanted to keep it or not. Having done that, she busied herself with routine tasks.

Sitting where indicated, Kapowski found it a little difficult to fit his large frame into the small seat. Davidson smiled at his discomfort and fidgeting.

Without ceremony Davidson asked, "What catastrophic event brings you here?"

Wary of his cool tone Kapowski said, "Both a tracker and Sutton have gone missing." Then, becoming aware of the look of incredibility on Davidson's face he added, "I thought it was far enough out of the ordinary for you to want to know right away sir." Kapowski's tone held just enough deference to mollify Davidson slightly and so he replied.

"Possibly, but you could have e-mailed or phoned, why come here?"

"I thought it was important sir," Kapowski reiterated feeling even more uncomfortable.

"It or you?" Davidson asked.

"I apologise sir, I should not have presumed." Kapowski replied in a truculent voice.

Changelings

"No. you shouldn't!" Now Kapowski was in his place he could relent a little. Besides, the detective was so thick he was easy to manipulate and hence once you had seen him squirm for a while there was no fun in prolonging it. A bit like an over enthusiastic pup, he just needed a slap every once in a while, to remind him of his place.

"Ok Kapowski, why don't you fill me in on the details" Davidson asked as he sat back relaxed in his large roomy and comfortably padded swivel chair, which declared his seniority for him.

****

Mike had tossed and turned in bed for some hours before sleep had stopped his thoughts from tumbling, incoherently around in his head. He awoke feeling exhausted and as if he had gone ten rounds in a boxing ring rather than had a restful night's sleep. As a result, he was not in a good mood when he passed the spot where the records of the previous night should have still lain. Instead of the manila files there was a pile of neatly shredded paper which was growing as he watched. He understandably rubbed his eyes in disbelief and then as he moved closer, he swore aloud when he saw the two library mites industriously shredding every file he had recovered. To save even one file he ran to fetch a hammer from the kitchen. Totally unaware of his approach the mites were easily overcome, and Mike had no problem reducing the pair to a small yet satisfying pile of scrap metal. He had however only managed to save a couple of files.

He brought a dustpan and brush and swept the broken mites and shredded files into a neat pile and disposed of them down the waste disposal. Sitting on his settee he decided to familiarise himself with the last two files. The first was concerned with James Westcott, Cerberus' brother. When Cerberus had been changed the boy had been left alone and unable to fend for himself. Rather than be changed too, the boy had elected to become a companion. He was tied to an executive Mike had never heard of, but it would be relatively simple to track him down. Mike was pleased he had, even as a by-product, discovered what Cerberus had demanded of him. He found out what had happened to his brother. The second file was in Mike's opinion much more interesting, it was concerned with the details of the first experiments and the location of the first of the Progen laboratories. It seemed that Progen had originally operated in the Loch Ness area. Mike made a snap decision. He decided to take a trip up there. Having made his decision, he felt the adrenaline flow through his veins; he felt excited. Very few people went on trips anymore.

Firstly, he had to get clearance from IGH. He wanted three days, and that proved relatively easy to obtain. He did not even need to talk to Davidson which was a relief as the man had been acting decidedly peculiar recently. The next problem was transport. He finally decided to take a train to Glasgow and then hire a personal vehicle to take him the rest of the way. He could justify a vacation visit to Glasgow; it was a major tourist attraction as it had been preserved as a giant time capsule, a monument to a decadent past. A visit there would be perfectly normal for a tired executive of his rank. The final piece of the puzzle was Will and Barb, which would take careful handling. He decided to shower and use some of his well-crafted charm.

Over dinner he made sure he paid equal attention to both, complimenting Will on his choice of outfit and Barb on her cooking.

"I am lucky to have you both," he announced, and both smiled then exchanged happy and meaningful looks with one another.

"We are the lucky ones" Will said as he drank from his wine. Barb nodded in agreement.

"I don't want to upset you both" Mike ventured

"Why would you do that?" Barb inquired innocently.

"I was thinking of a few days away" He said bravely.

"Oh, without us?" Will inquired.

"Well, yes, but only because we could not all get the time off together," Mike lied.

"Don't worry," Barb said, "We will be fine."

"I will miss you both, but I feel I need a few days away, not from you, just to relax."

"We understand, don't we Barb?" Will said and Barb nodded her agreement.

"Good," Mike concluded wanting to get the discussion over with. Then, pouring them all more wine, "Why don't you get another bottle?" he asked Will. "Then we can have a romantic evening before I go," he finished.

Will did not need asking twice. He virtually ran into the kitchen and Mike took Barb's hand and led her through to the lounge. It had been easier than Mike had thought it might have been and although he was happy, he was a little miffed at the lack of resistance they had offered to the idea. Still, the logical part of his brain reminded him, they were both relatively new companions to him. He was sure once they grew closer to him they would be more upset at his going away. It was as if Will read his mind as he began to reassure Mike that they would miss him while he was away.

****

At first all Sutton could see was blackness, but as his eyes adjusted, he was able to discern subtle variations. He briefly wondered if he had died, but quickly rejected the notion. Primarily because his body felt as old and stiff as it usually did when he first woke from sleep. Then there was the smell, it was dank and rotten like the stagnant water in a small pool where the fish had died. Gingerly, he stood and tested his ability to balance. He licked his lips and wished he had his usual whisky on hand. He knew though that there was no mileage in wishing for the impossible. He started to move forward carefully. He slid one foot forward across the floor and then slid the other foot across to join it. He experienced feelings of vertigo as he had the sensation of motion while his senses told him no motion had occurred. The landscape remained stubbornly the same. He tried the move again and then again. Each time feeling insecure, as the stage on which he found himself remained unchanged while his mind simultaneously told him he was moving some distance. After a while he became aware of certain dense shadows keeping pace with his progress and this, he found particularly unnerving. He did not know where he was or how he had been brought here, but he knew it was the creatures that now followed him that were the cause. He slowly started to become accustomed to the strange motion and he became aware of a lightning in the density of the blackness surrounding him. His spirits lifted with hope that urged him on. He lifted his right foot to take his first step on this alien terrain and almost stumbled when he misjudged how far he needed to press down in order to reconnect with the floor. Flailing, he tried to steady himself and failed. He fell to the ground with a large thud. He lay where he fell and felt tears of frustration sting his eyes.

"Come on!" he shouted, challenging whoever was watching him to come out and introduce themselves. "Come on you bully!" he shouted again. He may as well not have bothered as his words fell like useless stones to the bottom of the pond. They did not even project very far in this strangely lifeless world. Getting no response, he curled up in the foetal position and rocked back and forth in order to comfort himself and for a time allowed his mind to take a rest. If the boys back at headquarters could see him now, he would be forcibly retired. There really was no fool quite like an old fool; and an old fool was what Sutton knew himself to be.

✶✶✶✶

Mike kissed first Will and then Barb before he entered the first-class compartment of the train. He was as excited as a child and both companions thought he was endearing. The whole experience was new to him and he savoured entering the compartment and sitting in the velour clad seats. He looked out of the tinted window and as the engine began to draw out of the station, raised his hand to wave goodbye to his two companions. He briefly wished he could bring them with him, but only briefly.

He was the only traveller. People seldom had the clearance to travel these days and when they did it was almost never in first class. Mike was one of the elites and pleased to be so. He watched through the window as they passed through the city wall and sped into the less certain countryside beyond. He watched the ploughed fields pass by and was a little shocked at the numbers of changelings toiling for the city dwellers. He had not realised they had created so many creatures to assist in the struggle to survive. As the cultivated fields began to give way to more wild and unkempt greenery, Mike began to drift into a dreamlike state lulled into a sense of security by the repetitive motion and solitude provided by the train.

It could have been anytime later when he was jolted from his reverie. Logically, it had to be about three hours as they were due to pass through Manchester. It had once been a city that could have even exceeded Birmingham, but the famines had hit hard in the north and people had fled fast. The result was a graveyard of huge proportions where those intent on looting and hoarding had flourished. By the time they realised that money and goods no longer had the same currency, they had nowhere to flee. Now Manchester was a huge septic tank, a receiver of the waste of society. A place where all the renegades of the human or changed variety could run and hide. Although the newer batches of changelings had limiters which meant in order to survive, they had to stay in their designated geographic zones. It was a useful introduction that ensured the changelings remained productive and on task the whole of their lives. It meant that the IGH saw the greatest return for the investment that changing them had cost. The changing process was not a cheap one. Only those who managed to run before changing could now hide here. It was a place you passed through, and even then, you did it quickly in daylight.

Mike sat up in his chair, instinctively alert, even though he knew the train had reinforced windows and locked doors. At first all seemed calm, but as he watched, movement could be seen between the buildings. Nothing concrete just flashes from time to time and Mike realised something fast was keeping pace with the train. Mike looked round to see if anyone could confirm his impressions, but he remembered he was the only one in first class and he would have to move to another carriage to find another traveller. He did not want to take his eyes away from the window and so stayed where he was instead. The train approached the old central station and had to slow to pass through. The platform was dilapidated and strewn with rubbish. Apart from the fact that he knew this was a ghost town, it could have been a platform in any functioning city. Then, just as he began to relax and his senses started to come off alert, he caught sight of further motion at the far edge of the platform and suddenly the creature was fully visible. Mike froze, and his jaw dropped open. He had difficulty accepting the vision he could clearly see and as quickly as it had appeared it disappeared. Mike could have sworn it had recognised him, but that of course was impossible, he had never been here before or seen a creature like the one he had just viewed.

✶✶✶✶

Kapowski pulled his coat around him as he left the IGH. The wind had changed, and he felt a little chilled. He did not like the way things were going, and Davidson was a complete idiot only interested in his own skin. Although that was fine in Kapowski's book, it was Davidson's complete cowardice that was unacceptable and made the man a complete plank. That aside, Kapowski wanted to know what had happened to the tracker for his own peace of mind. He wanted to know who had dared interfere with police business. From the same sense of outrage, he also wanted to know what had happened to Sutton, even though he didn't like the old man. How dare anyone interfere with police business synonymous with his business; how dare anyone interfere with him, was really the important question. At least Davidson had seen something had needed to be done.

Kapowski had agreed to set the trackers free again tonight. He liked the trackers, the clean efficiency of the death appealed to him. Nothing of the miscreant was wasted, it was ultra-efficient and completely anonymous. He wondered what Davidson would do if he ever encountered a tracker. The thought made him smile as he walked away.

****

Sutton sat upright and wiped the tears from his eyes. He was a little ashamed of his own weakness but felt somehow refreshed from his outburst. He once again tried to get his bearings and he became aware of the constant motion around him. It was almost as if he was underwater. Then he realised that he was entirely correct. He was immersed, but not in water, he was immersed in shadows. He had fallen into the shadow world and he had no way of knowing how to find his way out, but if he got in, he was sure he would be able to get out again.

As he sat in the moving shadows, he heard of a mournful low sound as if something was calling and calling specifically to him. It was, he realised, a sound he had heard before, but he could not place where. Standing once more, he decided to find whatever it was that was singing, and he headed in the direction the sound seemed to be coming from. The sadness in the call almost started his own tears again and then he realised the darkness was decreasing. He saw the source of the light and the sound not too long after. Moving faster now, he headed toward the light. Suddenly, he came to a painful halt and stretching out his hand he felt what he could only describe as glass, although he knew this was not quite accurate. He was watching the world as if he was looking through the glass of a shop window rather than experiencing it directly.

The scene that unfolded had a dated quality about it, as if it had occurred a long time ago and he was watching on a film that had become aged. The view was of a lake filmed from above and as he watched, the viewpoint zoomed in, bringing the lakeside into focus. He was close enough to see the water gently splashing on the shore and it had a hypnotic effect. The mournful cry from across the lake broke the spell and he raised his eyes to see the creature swimming toward him. He recognised it as the popular conception of the Loch Ness Monster. Intrigued, he continued to watch, and the perspective changed again.

This time, to the opposite shore and what appeared to be a camp. On the van parked next to the tents was a logo which was vaguely familiar and then as the camera or whatever it was zoomed for a close up, he recognised the Progen logo. The view changed once again, this time to the scientists out on the lake. They seemed to be taking samples. Then, the creature surfaced close to the small boat and the scientist became very excited and aiming what looked like a gun, fired directly at the creature. The animal let out a shriek and Sutton realised he had heard the sound before and the blood went cold in his veins. This animal swimming in the lake was the same creature he had tagged as a shadow. Sutton was sorry for harming it in the same way as these others. Looking back at the drama in front of his eyes, he saw the scientists reeling in a cartridge. They had not fired at the creature; they had taken a sample from it.

For the last time, the scene changed, and he watched as the group packed away its camp. The last person to climb aboard the van was a small red headed woman. The only colour on the film was her hair and even before she turned to face the camera, Sutton knew it was the Director. Then the picture faded and instead of credits, the same shape shifting darkness filled his view.

Changelings

✳✳✳✳

Once they pulled out of Manchester, Mike relaxed. He was now able to enjoy the rest of the trip. Between Manchester and Glasgow there was very little discernible life. Plants that relied on wind pollination thrived, but no crops grew. There were not enough farmers and associated changelings to cultivate this far North. Once past the Scottish border, the farmlands began to appear once more. The Scottish population had suffered less than the English, primarily because they had less people to feed when disaster struck and relatively more land. However, they had still suffered extensively, and derelict dwellings were evident all along the rail line. Entering Glasgow was a completely different experience to entering Manchester. Glasgow had been entirely revamped as a huge holiday resort and museum. The wall constructed to define and protect was sheer polished, metallic, solar panelling that both acted as a barrier and a producer of energy. The train glided through the tunnel and came to a stop at the newly created station. Everyone disembarked at the edge of the city, then communal trams took visitors to their destinations. Mike had booked into a mid-range hotel available to his rank and he boarded the appropriate transport. Used to the individual units back home, Mike was unsure as to the expected etiquette of travelling with others. He headed toward an empty seat and found himself next to a stern slim blonde whose breasts stood to attention as if they were afraid to do anything else. When she saw him looking at her, she deepened her scowl and looked disdainfully away. Turning to his right, he saw his other companion was a nervous looking gentleman who giggled slightly at his attention and looked at his feet obviously embarrassed when required to connect with people. Mike decided the safest thing was to look straight ahead and he found himself gazing into deep blue eyes and an amused smile. Behind both was the cheeky countenance of a beautiful brunette. He wondered briefly if his attraction was disloyal to

147

Phoebe or indeed either Will or Barb. He spent the rest of the short trip to the hotel smiling at her like a fool. Fortunately, she did not seem to mind his attentions.

The hotel turned out to be the former Royal Hospital and rooms were all decorated as if they were for individual patients, authentic down to the bedding and hospital corners. The reception staff were dressed as nurses and guests were taken to their rooms by porters with luggage being transported in wheelchairs. At another time, he would have been taken with how quaint it all was, but at this moment all he wanted was to shower and rest.

****

Cerberus was on edge. He had been unable to sleep and kept fidgeting in the nest. Maia had finally sent him out so she could get some sleep herself. Whatever was on the way, Cerberus could feel it was not going to be pleasant. Toward the end of the day a light breeze had stirred, and a faint odour had been blown across the roof tops. It was the odour of death and Cerberus suspected it was coming his way. As the sun descended to hide in the hills, he wondered if they really ought to join it. As his people woke for the night, his apprehension communicated itself to them, and they waited until he realized that they stood behind him. Turning to face them he looked at each one in turn and he remembered his love for them. Then he spoke.

"Something is very wrong," he began, and they all nodded, having felt the strain in the air and aware that speech was not required or even desirable now. "Last night I helped a boy escape the trackers and I think tonight the fee for this act will be due, we may all have to pay." Cerberus continued.

"We will all stand with you," called Theo as others murmured their agreement.

"It might be best if I run for the country," Cerberus offered.

"No, we are all with you," several shouted together.

"What if they send more trackers?" Cerberus asked.

"Then we fight," Theo shouted, "We are sick of being slaves to the day walkers," he continued.

"But the personal risk to you all?" Cerberus tried to remind them, and then the newest and smallest owl changeling stood and shouted, "We are all with you," and they all joined in agreement.

"So be it," Cerberus concluded.

He sent four sets of two fliers out, one each, north, south, east, and west. He instructed them to fly to the city limits and back reporting any movements. Theo, he sent to contact Thanatos. If they were coming for the owls, it was likely they would also try to cleanse the city of him, their main ally. Why they had allowed him to remain in the city so long, Cerberus had never understood. He paced the length of the roof and began to wonder if he was overreacting and then he heard the baying of the tracker hounds and knew the reality he had lived in fear of for so long was about to violently arrive.

The scouting parties returned almost simultaneously and each reported tracker activity, not just one or two but approximately twenty in total. They were beginning the hunt from the city limits and working their way inward. They already knew that what they hunted was inside the city. The tactics Cerberus proposed were simple. The initial force of the trackers came from the hounds. Cerberus instructed his people to hide in the shadows and take the hounds out first, it would be like silencing the sonar of a submarine. Without the guidance of the hounds the trackers would themselves be less effective. Then the second wave was to concentrate on shredding the trackers wings. Without flight, they would be easier targets. It was imperative that they steered clear from the trackers' poisonous fangs.

Changelings

Chapter 11

Mike found the car hire shop without difficulty, but acquiring one was a different matter. If he was on vacation, then why would he want to take a risky and difficult journey outside of the city limits? It had not, in his arrogance, occurred to him that he would be restricted in any way or that anyone would question his motives. It seemed that his plan was going to fail at the first hurdle because he had not fully prepared. Leaving the shop and feeling dejected and foolish, he worried about what his next move should be.

He wandered around the streets for a while and then spotting a coffee shop, he decided to think over lunch. He was tucking into a fresh salmon salad when one of the many excursion sales reps approached him. Mike was going to wave him away when he spotted a picture of the Loch Ness monster. He quickly called the man, or more accurately, the notice board hybrid over to his table. The hybrid slid over in one fluid movement and started its advertising script. Mike listened politely with mounting excitement.

His trip included train travel and a two-night stay at Castle Urquhart. Why he had not thought just to book directly into the castle in the first place he did not know but he was extremely pleased with himself now he knew it was possible. He was excited that he was going to see Loch Ness. It made sense really, since Loch Ness was where it had all begun, and of course they would have a visitor's centre. He had until the following morning to enjoy Glasgow. He wondered where the brunette was and if she wanted an interlude with him. In the mood for a little fun, he went in search of a one-night companion.

Mike found a house of delights. They were all regulated these days so there should be no worries about cleanliness. He walked through the beaded doorway which had been a feature of similar places for hundreds of years and past the guardian on watch. At first glance in the dim light, others may have mistaken the guardian as fully human, but Mike knew better. The large frame and huge paws were borrowed from the black bear that had once roamed the old forests. He could just see its snout in the shadows, and he smiled to himself as he recognised one of his earliest transformations. It had been produced as a body guard and although he was a little surprised to see it on guard in this establishment, he was still pleased to see how well it fitted its function. He'd always had a flare for the codes that moulded the biological clay he used.

Reaching out to stroke the light fur that covered its body, he was surprised at the threatening growl that issued from the changeling's throat and, withdrawing, he continued into the house. He would have to check if it were legal to have something so dangerous and aggressive around normal citizens. He might even insist it was removed legal or not.

Once inside, he sat on a deep red couch and eyed the available companions for the evening. They ranged from dark beauties to young men displaying impressive six packs. While viewing the available merchandise, Mike accepted a drink from a veiled waiter and sipping the pseudo champagne he relaxed into the upholstery. Another customer chose a tall redhead to disappear with into the more intimate rooms. Mike, however, was finding it hard to make a choice and requested they dance for him. It started slow and seductive as they moved in a circle with light silk attire, all colours of the rainbow intertwining. Slowly the circle moved with each of them turning on their own axis of orbit around his sun. Once he was surrounded the circle began to gain speed, gaining momentum much the same as a roundabout. He watched as if from a great distance and realised he had consumed more than simple wine. Rising in slow motion as they spun ever faster around him, he could not maintain the upright position and fell back into the softness of the upholstery. All he could now see was the whirl of mixed colours forming a veil around him and he laughed loudly as he enjoyed the show.

****

Cerberus waited nervously for the converging trackers. At first all appeared calm, but he knew that this was an illusion and that they were on the way. Then, suddenly, the hounds broke free of the buildings surrounding the law courts and as if on cue, the bird people swooped to silence their howls. The hounds were easily dealt with, the battle was swift and violent, steel talons tore throats from the necks that had housed them. The dogs lay dying in the streets with streams of blood flowing toward the sewers. Cerberus felt sorry for them, they had simply been serving their masters and did not deserve such a fate. It was something else he blamed on the IGH and its director. Twitching noses emerged from subterranean haunts, attracted by the smell of death. The rats hesitated, wanting their share of the available flesh but unwilling to risk injury or death of their own. They waited for the hostilities to cease and formed a macabre audience drooling as they anticipated the feast. The beaks of the owl people ripped at the approaching legs of the trackers. As Cerberus watched, he saw Maia tear a hound to pieces and rip its heart from its body mercilessly and he felt pride rise in his chest. He also saw Aries grasped by the ankle and brought down to the street by one of the trackers and before she could struggle free, several others leapt upon her and ripped and devoured her flesh before his eyes. Shuddering he dove from the rooftop to join the fray. Blood flowed in every gutter and the stench of freshly slaughtered meat rose into the night air. Rats began to pull portions of meat into their dark lairs. This kill would feed many of them for days to come. Death had arrived, but it was obvious that the owl people had the advantage. The advantage that was, until the second wave of trackers joined the fray.

They did not enter the fight visibly; suddenly, they were just there and fighting. Their appearance was a complete surprise, a second wave had not been foreseen and cursing his naivety Cerberus called his people to attack from above. They aimed to shred the wings of the trackers so that they had to run along the ground, a way of traversing the world that they were even more ill-suited to than the owls. Their huge talons sparking against the paving stones in protest at this unnatural posture, it made them vulnerable. Theo chased one disabled specimen into a side street expecting to valiantly defeat the creature but instead he came face to face with two others who were not disadvantaged. He fell almost before the shock could register on his face.

Cerberus was aware of the changing tide and he saw several of his key people fall to the trackers' poisoned fangs. Calling to Maia, he signalled a hasty retreat but before he could take flight himself, he became aware of several trackers surrounding him. They began to circle him as if he was the centre of their orbit, each one slowly turning on its own axis with leathery wings stretched like torn grey curtains drawn around the body in a funeral entourage. Slowly they circled and then they began to speed up as if on a hidden roundabout, faster and faster, keeping Cerberus transfixed as if held by invisible wire or mesmerised. He tried to rise, but the dizziness from the increased motion and a small amount of poison still in his system made him fall back onto the hard concrete. Folding in upon himself, he felt his grip on reality receding, and still they turned faster, forming a grey veil around him. He called out in confusion and fear and Maia turned to see his fall.

****

The colours mixed to form a new world for Mike, and he slipped momentarily into unconsciousness. Then the dancers stopped and fell to the floor on their haunches, each in their own place and looking at him as he looked at them, a little bewildered. He realised it was expected to choose at least one. He chose two girls that could have been twins and with one supporting him on each side, they escorted him into the depths of the house.

****

The grey shrouds melted together to form one curtain and Cerberus momentarily lost consciousness. The trackers stopped and fell to the floor on their haunches, each looking directly at him with malevolent eyes as he observed them with bewilderment. They should attack and finish him and yet they held back. He realised something was expected of him, but what that was, he was not sure. Then two came to each side of him and half carrying, half supporting him, they escorted him into the depths of the night. They had, their prize and Maia feared she would not see him again. She set to follow him, but three trackers formed a barrier across the street. Even so she determined to follow until Eos pulling at her wing convinced her of the uselessness of direct attack. Instead, with tears streaming down her face, she flew into the night with the rest of her kind. She flew in retreat to safety and left him to sure death. The tears blinded her sight and she followed Eos through pure instinct.

****

Changelings

The wolf walked through the remnants of battle. Such was his authority that the feeding rats gave way to his passage. Blood stained his paws and he was excited by the sights and smells surrounding him. He watched the owls retreat and thoughtfully licked the flank of a fallen hound before entirely giving in to his carnal nature and falling to feast upon the carrion. Assured that he would not seek satisfaction in their flesh the rats returned to feed around him and for a time the night was filled with the sounds of gnawing and crunching of bones.

****

Mike stirred and felt the silk sheets move below his form. He became aware of the daylight and rose quickly, afraid at first that he had overslept. Checking the time, he relaxed a little and went into the adjoining bathroom to shower and refresh himself. Once finished, he was impressed with the breakfast that greeted him. Toast dripping with butter and eggs fried to perfection, the white solid and the yolks ready to drip a yellow blanket over the toast. His taste buds salivated at the sight. Hot coffee enticed him to his seat and the twins from the night before were ready to serve him. He wondered if he ought to go to Loch Ness the following day, after all it might be considered rude to leave too soon. Perhaps, he thought, he could stop over on his way back. The thought cheered him as he attacked his breakfast with gusto.

****

Cerberus stirred and felt the straps bite into the tender parts of his arms and thighs. They were placed to cause maximum discomfort. He became aware of daylight and tried to rise but fell quickly back onto the table to which he was secured. Dimly, he recognised the lab environment in which he had first awakened as a new changeling. He turned his head slowly so as not to aggravate the headache he could feel, lurking behind his eyelids. He became aware of the two trackers from the night before leering at him as if about to devour him.

Smelling the aroma of freshly brewed coffee, his salivary glands kicked into overtime and he became acutely aware of the hunger and fear playing games with his stomach. However, he also knew that the coffee would not be on offer to him.

Looking at the ceiling and contemplating what this could mean for him and his tribe, he was unceremoniously swung into an upright position and he came face to face with the owner of the coffee.

"Good morning Cerberus," Davidson drawled "Did you have a good night?" he enquired sarcastically and then without waiting for an answer continued, "I think you have been a very naughty boy, haven't you?"

"I don't think so."

"Unfortunately for you" Davidson smirked, "it's my opinion that counts."

Cerberus knew Davidson was very dangerous. He did not expect to get out of this alive and that knowledge gave him a bravery beyond the circumstances. "What is it you want?" he asked.

"Information, what else?" Davidson replied. Cerberus waited, unwilling to play the game and ask what information. Davidson also waited, enjoying the obvious realisation in Cerberus' eyes he was going to die. But Davidson also knew he needed to give him a reason to co-operate.

"I hope you appreciate that we let your little Maia fly away last night?"

Cerberus strained a little against his bonds and Davidson knew he had his full attention. "We could bring her in," he continued. "That is if it were necessary."

Understanding the meaning completely, Cerberus replied, "that won't be necessary, I will co-operate."

"Good," Davidson drawled. "Then we can get rid of the trackers and get down to business. Breakfast?" he enquired, as if they were conducting any normal early morning business meeting.

****

Maia flew high above the battle where Cerberus signalled the retreat. She went swiftly to the park where they had agreed to re-assemble. Worriedly, she searched the sky for her returning people. Hermes landed softly next to her. "I am sorry Maia, but some of the others saw them carrying Cerberus away." Unable to reply, she simply nodded with tears streaming once more down her face. Hermes confirmation of what Maia had seen herself brought the emotion back tenfold and she took a minute to compose herself. Looking at her people she was further shocked to see their condition. It seemed that none had escaped unharmed and blood seeped from a variety of wounds. She knew that they would have to act swiftly. She told Hermes to take the newer changelings who were tied to the city and return to the nests to rest. She prayed that they would be safe. The IGH could not afford to purge all of them. Then, gathering the older ones, she sent them to exile in the streets of Manchester. She did not think the IGH would waste its resources chasing a few renegade changelings so far. She decided to seek out Thanatos whom she had not seen since the start of the battle. Perhaps he would know what could be done, if anything for Cerberus. As the bird people limped away in defeat, the shadows shifted on a mission of their own.

****

Still trapped in the shadow world, Sutton now understood why they had wanted to communicate with him. To inform him that the experiments had started a long time before any species started to die. The IGH had not discovered the miraculous solution to the problem in the carcass of the old world they had already known that shape shifting was a possibility. He suspected that there were more revelations to come. Still, he had plenty of time to contemplate the universe in this darkened reflection of reality. As he mused and felt sorry for himself, the shadow reflection of a woman walked unnoticed to his side. Gently coughing to attract his attention, she held out her hand to him. Almost falling over with shock, after goodness knows how long in silence, the gentle sound appeared as harsh as a gunshot. Sutton reached out to her to steady himself. Although her features were completely indiscernible, he could have sworn she smiled and more than that, he was also sure that this was what was left of Caldwell's companion. He asked her directly but of course she was unable to reply, and she just nodded as an inky black drop fell from her eye and slid down her cheek. Sutton had not known they could cry but then he had never known a woman who was unable to either. He had all kinds of questions running around in his mind and so did not notice that he was following her. The landscape still offered no clue as to motion.

It was not until he saw the growing light once more that he realised he was walking. Glancing at the light, he saw a woodland glade once again at the banks of a great lake. This time as he watched, a man emerged from the moving waters. Water streamed from his hair and gave it the appearance of seaweed. His chest was bare, and Sutton could see that his hair grew in a point down to his navel. Sutton wondered if he would be wearing swimwear and as he continued to rise from the water, he realised the man would not need it, for instead of the legs of a man, there followed the torso of a horse. Sutton felt as if he had stepped directly into Greek mythology as he stared at the Centaur before him and he could not stop himself from expressing his surprise.

"Good lord, what were you produced for?" he asked.

Throwing back his great mane of hair, the Centaur laughed heartily. "Welcome, Detective," it said.

Sutton tried to step forward but was stopped by the invisible barrier. "How come you can talk to me?" he asked, "the last time I could only watch."

"Welcome, detective, to my world."

"Your world and your rules," Sutton hazarded a guess.

"That's right," the creature continued, still clearly amused.

Sutton sat down in his shadow world facing the Centaur. "So, will I be able to get out of here?" he asked.

"Of course, you are only here to talk with me, the shadows are simply the fastest, most secure way to travel," the Centaur continued reasonably.

"Then who are you and why do you want to talk to me?" Sutton asked with a little hysteria evident at the rise in tone of his last word. Recognising the hysteria in himself, he made a conscious effort to remain in control.

"The name is Keanos, but I suspect you want more than my name?"

"Why you were created would be useful" Sutton answered.

Still amused, Keanos continued. "Why I was made I do not know and like you will probably only find out when I meet my maker."

"That's a bit cryptic." Sutton commented.

"Cryptic, that's a good one you see I am what you call a Cryptid," Keanos laughed.

"All changelings can claim that. Who made you, who wrote the codes that changed you?" Sutton pressed.

Sighing deeply as if trying to explain a difficult concept to a particularly unintelligent child, Keanos simply turned and dived back into the water and as he dived, he changed shape to that which was commonly accepted as the Loch Ness monster. While Sutton gaped, he swam up and down a couple of times and then re-emerged as he had been.

"Clear?" he asked. Nodding, Sutton cleared his throat, "We thought you were all dead." He said.

"You were supposed to," Keanos replied. "After your science killed several of us, the rest returned to the shadows to wait for the right time to return. After all, we had hidden from your kind for centuries, a couple of decades posed no problem."

"Then why show me, why am I special?" Sutton asked.

"Actually, sorry if this offends you but you aren't, we want you to help Caldwell expose the truth. We think he may be useful," Keanos informed him.

"Great, I should have known, just the lackey as usual." Sutton sighed.

"No, not just detective, you have a part to play that no one else would be able to play." Keanos was earnestly reassuring Sutton.

"Ok, I'll let Caldwell know what you showed me. Can I come out of the shadows now?" Sutton asked almost plaintively.

"Certainly detective, you only had to ask," Keanos informed him. Still clearly amused and holding his hand out, he gestured to Sutton to take it. Hesitating, Sutton asked "Can she come with me?"

"Unfortunately, she is a shadow of your making not mine. I cannot restore her to your world," Keanos said as he tugged Sutton through the barrier.

✳✳✳✳

Mike was impressed with the castle. They had restored it with obvious empathy and with an eye for luxury. He was going to enjoy his stay. He decided to eat before taking a walk down to the shore. Food did not appear to be an issue in Scotland, and he wondered why more people did not move here. Once outside, he had the strongest sense of déjà vu and supposed it was the Donna Logan tapes that had made a deeper impression than he originally thought. Walking down to the edge of the water, he spied a small row boat and feeling more adventurous than usual, decided to row out onto the loch a short distance. Pulling hard on the oars, he wondered why the boat did not seem to want to go anywhere. Stopping to catch his breath, he realised he was rowing backward into the flat end of the boat rather than the pointed end. Switching sides, he found the boat much easier to handle and began to enjoy the rhythmic motion and gentle lapping of the water on the side of the boat. After a short time, he drew the oars from the loch and sat back to enjoy the calm peacefulness of the area.

As he lay back with his arms behind his head, he noticed a disturbance just below the surface, as if something was rising from a great depth. Leaning over for a better look he saw a myriad of rising bubbles as if heralding the arrival of a noble at court. Instead of a noble however, it was a familiar face that burst through the water's surface to flap around and struggle in a most ungainly fashion. Although he knew it could not be, Mike recognised Sutton the second he broke through the surface. Acting quickly, he held out one of the oars to him and with considerable effort hauled him on board.

Sutton collapsed on the floor of the boat next to Mike and Mike leant back almost wheezing from the effort.

"Either you need to lose some weight, or I need more exercise," he managed.

Nodding and holding his hand up to indicate he needed more time, Sutton stayed where he was while he hung onto the fact that he was still breathing and back in the real world. Finally, he managed, "A little of both, I think," with an edge of his old sarcasm. Now the world was restored, his usual confidence was returning. Heaving himself into a sitting position he asked, "Where the hell is this?"

"Loch Ness," Mike replied simply, "and I take it you came by some unconventional means?"

"You could say that again," Sutton said, "Do you think we could get off the water?" he asked, remembering the Cryptid and the implication that there were in fact a lot of them lurking below the surface. He did not feel entirely safe exposed out on the loch. They could, if they wished, carry him back to the shadows at any time. Besides, he needed dry clothes and food. He realised he was starving and that he had no idea how long he had been in the shadow world. Mike pulled heavily on the oars and Sutton was grateful to feel the motion and see the shore grow visibly closer. He was also grateful that Caldwell did not ask any questions. Sutton needed time to make sense of his experience and time to decide what to tell and what not to tell this man. He also wondered by what coincidence Mike had been just at the right spot to rescue him. Sutton was very suspicious of coincidences and he critically eyed Mike who rowed in silence, lost in his own thoughts

Changelings

Chapter 12

Maia entered the Law Courts and was immediately aware of the chaos around her. The trackers had already been here, and it was also evident that Thanatos was no longer in residence. Wherever he was, she now had to concern herself with her own safety. She would probably need to fly to Manchester and join the others. Entering his quarters, she swiftly looked around for anything that would be useful. Most of his belongings were strewn across the floor having been slung carelessly from drawers and cupboards. He had always been very particular about his surroundings and she was glad he was not here to see his life being treated with such disregard. As she turned to go, she noticed the bedroom door stood slightly ajar and feeling the urge to check, she went in, just to be sure Thanatos was not injured and was not in need of her help she rationalised to herself. She walked over to the bedroom door and peered in. The same destruction greeted her, but no dead body was evident and for that she was grateful. Glancing towards the bed, she saw the corner of a book just visible beneath the disturbed covers. She uncovered it with her foot and, realising it was a diary picked it up. With an urge to preserve something of Thanatos she flew with it out of the city.

*****

Thanatos sat under the Law Courts in the city's sewers. They had always provided safe passage for the less desirable residents and less desirable was what he knew himself to be. He hunched down on his haunches and leaned back onto the sewer wall. He felt the damp travel through his shirt, and he accepted he would smell disgusting for some time to come. He thankfully could no longer smell the aroma down here, he was on sensory overload. The sewers did have one advantage, they were peaceful, the calm before the storm.

He was here to contact the 'mistakes' the IGH tried to hide. Not the unfortunate shadows caught between existences, but the early changelings, none of which had been entirely functioning. They had been thrown into the effluent to die, they were not even worthy of the effort needed to extinguish life entirely. It was time the Director faced the consequences of her actions and Thanatos was determined to help her do just that. They came as they sensed his unspoken call. They were drawn by the unmistakable call from a brother. They came slowly, crawling on deformed limbs with minds twisted and disturbed by the experiences they had suffered. Some shuffled and others scurried but however they came, Thanatos was pleased that they were drawn to him. Reaching his hand out, he stroked the creature nearest to him and it began to purr as he did so. Looking down at it, he was repulsed but continued to stroke it none the less. It appeared even the least attractive creation appreciated tender contact. He called them to use them and, in that way, he knew himself to be no better than the Director.

*****

Cerberus was not proud of his actions. He knew he would have withstood any amount of pain to protect his people but had betrayed them in seconds to protect Maia; and the truth was he had probably not even achieved that goal. Deeply depressed, he leant against the wall and, tilting his head back, stared directly at the ceiling. Wallowing in his own misery, he failed to notice as the sewer cover on the floor of his cell had begun to move. Cerberus tilted his head and watched as the cover scraped across the floor; and in disbelief he saw Thanatos emerge though the opening.

"You really smell!" he commented.

"Is that all the thanks I get for coming to the rescue?" Thanatos asked.

"It's no use," Cerberus lamented, "all is lost."

"Pull yourself together," Thanatos said as he shook Cerberus "It's only lost if you give up."

"What are they?" Cerberus suddenly asked, as he became aware of the things emerging from the sewer behind Thanatos. Some were small, some large but all deformed and reeking of a decade spent living in other people's excrement. Cerberus felt the tears in his eyes, sorry for the lost lives they represented, but even as they started to flow, they froze on his cheeks as something impossibly huge began to emerge. Several tentacles came first, and Thanatos guided one appendage to pull the chain holding Cerberus from the wall. Then the edges of the access hole began to bulge as the creature forced itself from the sewer. The floor cracked and gave way under the immense pressure and then, popping like a cork forced from its bottle, the body emerged, and the room suddenly became claustrophobically small, both from the sheer bulk of the creature and because of the pure stench which accompanied its arrival. Gagging so much, Cerberus began to wretch. This was a depth of decay he had not encountered before, even corpses did not smell this bad. He was suddenly appreciative for the lack of solid food in his gut, then when the desire to throw up had reached its peak, he began to adjust and accommodate the sight and presence of the creature.

"What! Is it?" he enquired again.

"A changeling, like you," Thanatos said in a matter-of-fact tone.

"But the man converted to that must have been huge." Forgetting his misery, Cerberus was awed by the thing in front of him, it resembled a squid albeit one designed to live on land.

"I believe it was in fact several men," Thanatos told him helpfully and as he said it, Cerberus saw several eyes blink across its surface and the urge to throw up returned vigorously.

"Anyway, are you ready to go?" Thanatos asked.

"Where?" Cerberus countered, still mesmerised by the thing in front of him and confused as to what Thanatos was planning.

"Attack," Thanatos replied with evident relish.

They spilled out of the basement cell and immediately confronted a medic. She turned ashen at the sight of the oncoming menagerie and dropping the tray she held, fled screaming down the corridor. Thanatos's army brought terror purely because of the way it looked. The small creature he had been stroking earlier jumped up and down giggling manically and pointing at the fleeing IGH staff.

****

Back in the room at Urquhart Castle, Sutton ordered a stiff brandy and availed himself of Caldwell's shower. He then borrowed some of Caldwell's clothing. Once warm and feeling much more like his usual self, he was ready to face any questions Caldwell might have.

"So far you are doing a good job being patient," he commented.

"I was just, wondering if you ever intended telling me anything?" Mike countered.

Looking for a minute into his glass, Sutton seemed to be considering his options "If I tell you everything, I think you will be able to secure my early retirement," he commented.

"Really?" Mike was intrigued.

"I don't suppose you have a cigarette on you?" Sutton enquired further.

Looking a little panicked, Mike glanced around the room as if suspecting a trap.

"Don't worry," Sutton continued. "If I was going to arrest you over it, I would have done so the first time we met."

"Was it that obvious?" Mike asked.

"Afraid so," Sutton giggled a little. He thought it must be the stress getting to him, but it did break the atmosphere to more relaxed. Mike produced two Capstans. They stepped onto the balcony to smoke.

"My whole holiday supply in one," Mike couldn't resist commenting.

"Much appreciated," Sutton spluttered, trying to get used to the feeling of smoke in his lungs once again. He felt wonderfully light headed. He started to tell Caldwell where he had been.

Later, when they had talked for hours and dusk began to settle, they decided that darkness would be a good time to explore the IGH facility in Fort Augustus at the very foot of the loch. Abandoned now, it was still monitored, and stealth was needed. They decided to take one of the motorised row boats at the castle mooring. This would give them a quiet and efficient way of travelling. Sutton could handle a boat reasonably well but was still nervous after his earlier encounters. He stayed close to the edge of the lock in order to give them an escape on foot if anything came out of the water. He constantly scanned the dark surface and bank as they travelled. Mike knew better than to try to chat to him when he was so focused. They travelled in a charged, rather than comfortable, silence with the noise of the boat masking any other sounds that might have been heard.

When they arrived where they should have moored the boat, they had to go back and forth a couple of times before they identified the overgrown and half rotten jetty. Tying the boat to a reasonably sound piece of timber, Sutton helped Mike onto dry land.

"Careful, it's more overgrown than I thought," Sutton commented.

Mike just grunted. City living had not helped develop a physique that would cope well with this kind of exertion and he was puffing rather hard. Sutton was faring better, his occupation providing him with a greater opportunity to keep fit. After five or ten minutes, they scaled the top of the bank and found what was left of the once main road that connected this place with the rest of the civilized world. An owl hooted, and Mike jumped, holding onto Sutton's arm briefly until he realised what he had done. "I didn't expect anything," he tried to explain.

"Don't worry about it," Sutton said, "Just don't do it when we get back. I don't want anyone thinking we might be an item."

They turned right and went up the main thoroughfare and when the moon came out from behind the clouds, the whole area could be plainly seen. As they crossed over a small bridge they could see where shops had once been. Many windows were now long gone but merchandise was still on the shelves. Walking a little further, they could see old houses, dark and forlorn. It was like walking through a ghost town. It did not take very long to reach the old IGH facility. It had at one time been a hotel.

Walking up the drive, Mike strained to see if he could hear any more sounds but the owl, if that is what it had been, and it seemed now it had obviously moved away from them. He supposed if it lived up here it had to be an early runaway and would not want contact with anyone it met. It would presumably value its solitude and that would suit the two of them as they planned an illegal entry.

They walked up to the main door and were confronted with an electronic lock. Unwilling to announce their presence by keying in a code, Sutton decided on the low-tech option, and swinging the heavy torch smashed the mechanism open and twisted wires together. Miraculously in Mike's opinion, the door swung open. Inside, they expected to find a similar state of decay to that which they had both seen in the law courts, but the place was pristine. Not even dust marred the surfaces. Automatically closing the door behind them, they both began to explore the premises. The entrance hall gave way to a bar and then a dining room and a kitchen before circling back to the main reception area. Further investigation revealed several offices and a surprising amount of functioning technology. Turning on a terminal, Mike could verify that it was a separate system to the IGH mainframe. It was also not encrypted.

Armed with the information from Keanos, they looked for files from before the breakdown. The image on screen solidified into a young and very feminine Director. Both jumped involuntarily backward unsure at first if this meant she could see them. When they were satisfied it was simply a recording and not a connection they cautiously returned to the screen.

"Philomena Green here, reporting for the Progen cryptid search project. Today we encountered the first recorded cryptid. For some months now, we have been recording sonar songs somewhat similar in nature to those produced by the whale. After extensive research, patterns emerged, and we soon became able to reproduce what appears to be a crude form of communication indicating a low level of intelligence. Using that we could call the creature and we were even able to gain a tissue sample. This has now been assigned for evaluation."

Changelings

"I think that is what I saw when I was in the shadow world," Sutton informed Mike.

Nodding Mike clicked on the next journal entry.

> *"Philomena Green here, reporting for the Progen cryptid project. On analysis, the biological sample retrieved has unique qualities, not least the amount of energy it appears to be radiating. This energy appears to be coming from the constant forming and breaking of molecular bonds. Over time it would be consistent with the known theories of physics that the energy within the organism should remain constant. Energy does not appear to be created or used as the animal maintains overall stasis. Only further research will be able to conclude if this constant change will be able to be capitalised on by the company. On a less positive note David Grey, the tech that retrieved the sample, has been placed off active duty after contracting a flu-like virus. The specimen will be handled as a possible biological hazard until more is known. Access will be restricted to research staff only."*

The next entry turned more sinister.

> *"Philomena Green here, reporting for the Progen cryptid project. David Grey's fever has taken a turn for the worst and two technicians who initially handled the cryptid sample in the laboratory have also begun to display flue like symptoms. The sample has been designated as a full bio-hazard and will now be handled under secure conditions only. Access will be restricted to senior research staff only."*

At each short entry, Sutton lost a little more of his colour. Thanatos was, he could only assume, a central rather than a peripheral player as he had originally judged. He began to feel decidedly played himself and he did not like the feeling one bit.

> *"Philomena Green here, reporting for the Progen cryptid project. The two technicians have died, giving us an invaluable opportunity to examine infected biological tissue. Incredible as it sounds it appears the virus has unzipped some of their DNA strands. David Grey remains in a critical condition. Although he was infected first it seems for some reason his body is accepting the changed structures much more readily. Blood samples show disconnected DNA in free flow within his system. If questioned I would have said that this was an impossibility. Clearly, I would have been wrong as it is happening before my eyes."*

Sutton could clearly see the lust for fame reflected in those cool eyes and wondered if it were at that point that the Director had been born. The entries continued.

> *"Philomena Green here, reporting for the Progen cryptid project. David Grey is slowly recovering and has now emerged from a coma, with what appears to be no ill effects from his experience. We are determined to collect more level one samples directly from the animal itself. However, to date, our attempts at attracting it have failed. It appears the animal has learned from the brief initial contact to stay away from us. David Grey remains a viable source of secondary material. Creating other secondary sources may also be a possibility."*

"Cow!" Sutton could not help himself exclaiming.

"You want to work for her," Mike countered. "She has lost some of her softness with age believe me she will do anything to stay in control."

"I believe it," Sutton replied grimly.

"Philomena Green here, reporting for the Progen cryptid project. Initial contact was four months ago with no other attempts proving successful. David Grey has been under constant observation with no ill effects being observed. However, the virus appears to have left a deposit in his blood and analysis is continuing. It may become necessary to analyse all of his vital organs before a full picture can be formulated. Several other possible secondary sources have been identified and a cross selection of individuals will be exposed to the material over a staggered process. If they all enter a coma, we will be able to cease exposure so that too much pressure is not placed on our medical facilities. The smooth running of the company is always foremost in our thoughts. David Grey is to return to normal duties, he will be closely monitored. It has been decided that more drastic methods should be used to gather a level one sample. Any excess will be cryogenically frozen for future study. It has been decided to deliver a high range prolonged burst of sonar directly into the loch. This should confuse the animal and produce a period of unconsciousness. It is hoped that a complete animal will be harvested."

Sutton could think of nothing to say and he and Mike simply exchanged disgusted looks as the entries continued.

"Philomena Green here, reporting for the Progen cryptid project. An unconscious animal has been captured. Its sonar has been disabled, mainly because the constant sound it was producing was unnerving the workforce and disrupting normal working patterns. This animal is genetically different to the one the first sample came from. Given there is more than one, we must now assume there is a colony. Just how such large creatures could have remained hidden is a

mystery. David Grey is displaying worrying behaviour, insisting the creature is crying and needs to be released. Security has been assigned to monitor him closely. He may need to be harvested for future study."

"Philomena Green here, reporting for the Progen cryptid project. David Grey was caught trying to release the cryptid. When arrested, he changed form into what can only be described as a wolf. At the same time, the cryptid changed into a horse. It is clear the two were in secret communication. It can also be concluded that the cryptids have shape changing abilities with which Grey has been infected. He has been removed for study."

"Wow!" Sutton exclaimed "How much of this stuff is there?"

"A lot," Mike said.

"So, the first changeling was an accident, not quite how the IGH would have us remember it."

"Things are rarely what they appear to be," Mike commented

"Yeah, you don't say," Sutton replied sarcastically. "Tell you what Doc, you continue with the technical stuff and I'll finish looking around."

Now a little aggrieved, Mike just grunted and returned to his screen.

Amused, Sutton took his flashlight and started to explore the rest of the building. Why he did not want to turn the main lights on he was not sure, except that advertising his presence did not seem like the best of ideas. You never knew what kind of undesirable was hanging around a place like this. He was also still a little unnerved by his recent trip to the shadow lands and a little guilty he had not yet told Mike about his companion.

****

Changelings

Maia landed in Manchester and a chill that had nothing to do with the wind made her shiver. She needed to find the others and set up some kind of watch. She was not convinced they had seen the last of the trackers. Fortunately, she did not have to look for the others as they had already begun to gather. It was not just her own people either, the variety was incredible. One looked almost identical to Maia and her people, but it was much closer to an original owl and when it looked at her it hooted. Shocked, she realised it had no speech at all. It was obviously an early, less precise conversion and she realised that many of those gathering were also early changelings. Some had uneven limbs while others had visible deformities. Initially she felt revulsion and then guilt at rejecting her own kind made her look again. They were not as bad as she had first thought. They were deformed, but were friendly enough, just curious about the newcomers. Looking up to the sky, she said a silent prayer for Cerberus before she turned her attention to getting to know these new friends. She prayed that God would keep Cerberus safe and bring him back to her. While she was distracted, even more new creatures had joined the throng. These had a very different feel about them. They were not unfortunates, but proud and strong specimens come to take their place at the head of creation rather than at the tail. Maia stared at them with awe, they were truly magnificent.

"Welcome, little lady," said one of them.

"Thank you," Maia whispered, and she looked up into the deep pools of his eyes and felt herself being drawn into the cool depths in which she saw him swimming. She knew it was him in the pool, but he had a different form. Shaking her head as if to clear it from some fog, she whispered once again, "Impossible, completely impossible."

Smiling, Keanos replied, "No, improbable, but not impossible. Come, you need rest." He turned, presuming she would follow, which of course she did. His right to lead was not in question and so she followed him while the rest followed her. Through darkened streets and dusty ruins, they soon came to what looked like the smallest building ever built. Keanos opened the doorway to reveal a stairway which descended beneath the city. Every fibre in her body rebelled at the idea of entombing herself below ground she was a creature of the skies. She wanted to soar to the highest clouds to feel free and dance with her one true love. She wanted to fly once more with Cerberus, to feel the warmth of his body next to hers. For the hope of that outcome, she turned away from her skies and descended into the depths of the city.

****

As much as the city above was dead and decayed, the city below was alive and vibrant. Every corridor had dwellings off to the sides which were occupied by every type of creature imaginable and even more that were unimaginable. Many peered at them as they passed by, with the wide-eyed curiosity off the young. It took some time for the truth to filter into her tired brain. They were not all changelings. Incredibly, they were young, the offspring of the changed and that, she had been told, was impossible.

Finally, they came to a large chamber and in one corner they had built her a nest. Amazed at the thoughtfulness, she sank exhausted into the soft down and swiftly drifted to sleep as her own people took up watch around her. Thankfully, she accepted the respite that was offered, and she drifted into a new world; one where Cerberus was once again by her side stroking her feathered head with the side of his beak, protecting her from any possible harm. In her sleep, she circled her own body with her own great wings and felt comforted by the dream of his proximity. Her dreams took on a life of their own, her belly swelled with life and as it grew so did her desire for the freedom of her kind. She had thought that her own life was all that could be her destiny. Now she knew eternity was in her grasp; the children she had seen in previous dreams could be hers after all. Hope could flourish from the smallest of seeds and hope was in the continuance of their legacy through the combining of their genes in the form of their offspring. which it now seemed was a possibility.

As she slept Phoebe came to watch over her and it was then that she saw the diary. Leaning over she took it gently from Maia's keeping and retreated to a corner to read. It was the diary of a wolf, a wolf both before and after changing. It detailed the life of David Grey a technician in the employ of Progen. He had been on the original Loch Ness project and had helped retrieve the first cryptid specimens. He had taken the job under false pretenses. He had not disclosed his qualifications and preferred to work as an anonymous technician. That way he had access to all areas. It was the science staff they watched with suspicion and not the glorified cleaner. As a result, he had been the first to handle the cryptid tissues. It was relatively easy to take a small sample of his own and because he took the sample before any weights and measures had been taken no-one noticed the discrepancy. He had then been able to analyse the tissue at his leisure.

It was David Grey who had first discovered the changeling properties and it was he who had realised its potential. He devised a vaccine and inoculated himself. He also slipped a dose to two other technicians to cover his actions. As it turned out it was a good job he had. The other two died relatively quickly and he slipped into a coma. They thought all three had become infected by accident and began treating the tissue as a biohazard. If any of them had been truly intelligent he may have been in trouble but none of the so-called brains on the project put the pieces together. Instead they monitored him, it was almost comical really. They nursed him back to health and then they tried to kill him to study the change. Fortunately, he was ahead of them, as usual, and he metamorphosed into his new form.

He found it an exhilarating experience. When he ran through the woods as a wolf, he felt a new power. The world was full of intense sights, sounds and smells. Everything he experienced was intensified and he wondered how men survived with their limited sense of such a wonderful world. He was pleased to be a wolf. Indian legend believed everyone had a spirit animal and that you could become that animal in extreme circumstances. He believed it no coincidence that he had changed into a wolf for he saw his own spirit as that of the lone wolf. He saw himself as a powerful lone maverick unafraid of taking any risk.

Phoebe shivered; this David Grey was a dangerous man, one willing to take any risk just to see what would happen. He had no thought for those who were caught in his designs when they did not wish to be. A maverick who would try anything without considering the consequences could cause a thousand tragedies, one of which may be Phoebe's own.

Chapter 13

Kapowski was overseeing the loading of the trackers himself. They had never been outside of the city before and he did not want anything going wrong. This was his chance to impress the Director and perhaps secure his future. In his opinion, Davidson was finished. All the Director had to do was realise that he would be a much better prospect to help her maintain the status quo. Maintain her stranglehold on everything in the civilised world.

They had blacked out the windows of a whole carriage for the trackers use. They preferred the dark, a preference that probably stemmed from their bat inheritance. Personally, Kapowski found them intriguing, repulsive and attractive all at the same time. Like most people they made his skin crawl, the very darkness of them seemed to slide over you when they were close, and they made everyone who came into contact with them nervous. They activated some primordial instinct that required fight or flight for survival. His biology responded with revulsion at their proximity, but his mind was fascinated by the creatures. He was attracted to the power they had; it was a dark power, but he would take darkness if it meant he could rule. The ability to inspire fear in others was something he wished he possessed.

Kapowski took his seat in the carriage next to the trackers. He would have liked to have been in first class, but the trackers needed watching. The power they had to instill fear in others could be misused and he did not trust others to stop them from breaking away from IGH control. So, he was stuck with second class; at least they had emptied the carriage for their exclusive use. When they stopped in Manchester, only the doors of these last two carriages would be opened, thus protecting the public from possible danger. He sat at a table and took a file from his briefcase. He wanted to at least appear busy and in control; it gave him an air of authority. He concentrated on the file. It described the renegades that were known to have taken up residence in Manchester. It could prove invaluable to know what he may be up against.

****

Sutton's search of the second floor provided no more information than was already in their possession. It was well kept and obviously looked after by someone. It was the someone was looking after it that worried him. Whoever it was could appear at any moment. That particularly worried him. He continued to the third floor and it was here that the hairs on the back of his neck told him something was watching him.

"Keanos?" he whispered, "tell me if it's you."

Silence greeted his request and he wondered if he was wrong, maybe it was not the shadows this time, maybe it was something else.

"Who is it?" he called, with a little more boldness in his voice than he felt. In answer, he heard a slight rustle that confirmed his suspicion. It was indeed the shadows, just not Keanos himself. "Ok, as long as it's you guys," he said into the darkness and continued his reconnoitre. To his own surprise he felt completely at ease with the thought that the shadows were watching. He had come to consider them on his side, friendly as opposed to unfriendly. As he recognised the feeling consciously, he surprised himself. He finished his search of the upper floor and while deciding what to do next he walked over to the window. Looking out, he had a postcard view of the Loch, a peaceful, beautiful scene; it looked calm and tranquil, bathed in calming moonlight, and yet it was at the centre of some of the most monumental events to have shaped history in centuries. He wondered what other secrets lay beneath its smooth surface. As he stood, he felt the shadows gather behind him and wondered what it was they wanted. Returning downstairs, he looked in on Caldwell, he was still engrossed in the computer records.

✱✱✱✱

Maia woke in the new nest and sat bolt upright. She looked above and instead of the expected starlight her eyes fixed on the brown earth that formed the roof of the large chamber. Hermes brought fresh meat over and she ate ravenously, focusing solely on the food. She became aware of being watched and when she looked up saw a small Butterbee looking over the side of the nest. Smiling at it, she wondered if this was the one Cerberus had escorted out of the city. Opening her wing she invited the Butterbee to come and have a cuddle. Smiling, the creature shook its head and flew into the air with a giggle. There were several answering giggles from all around the nest and she became aware of several small beings running away together.

"Forgive them," Keanos said "They are simply curious about you, they mean no harm"

"It's ok, I find them charming," Maia replied with a smile.

"Probably your maternal instinct," Keanos said kindly.

"I didn't think I had one," She admitted.

"All females have one," Keanos commented "How are you holding up?"

183

"Good, I think. What happens next?" She asked.

"We are readying ourselves for attack," Keanos said calmly.

"Why?" Maia asked, and she reminded herself of the child she had been, forever curious about the world around her.

"They are bringing the trackers from Birmingham," Keanos calmly stated.

"Oh," she said deflated. "I am sorry, we should leave now, that way they will leave you all alone."

Keanos stroked the top of her head affectionately as she had often dreamed that Cerberus would if he had the hands to do so. Keanos made melodic calming noises.

"Sh, don't blame yourselves, they would have come eventually, we are a threat to them keeping their power." He told her.

"But if you had more time," she tried.

Shaking his head, he continued, "No, we are ready to face them. Will you stand with us?" he asked her.

"Yes, but do you have news of Cerberus?" she asked, bracing herself for the worst.

"You do not know?" He asked, surprise obvious in his tone.

"No, I was hoping he was still alive even though it is not likely."

"He is in the IGH dungeon. I know you feel he is still alive. You should trust your instincts more; they are good ones." He assured her.

Her heart soared, there was still hope and she would hang on to that hope. Feeling elated she nodded, "We are with you Keanos, you can rely on us."

"Good, I will get one of our owls to show you where to position your people. The trackers will be here within the hour, we believe."

"So soon?" she asked, disappointment evident in her voice.

"Yes, it appears they are anxious to bring things to a close. Let us hope it goes the way we want it and not the way they desire."

Maia hoped so too.

****

Thanatos squeezed into the lift with the composite creature, there was no room left for the others. Cerberus was extremely thankful that he had suggested that he follow with some of the creatures in a minute or two, at least he would not have to get up close and personal to the slime or the stench of the composite creature.

Thanatos thought that it was the best idea as he could act as reinforcement if needed. He intended to confront the Director by himself and backup would give him extra leverage. Cerberus was to wait ten minutes before ascending and joining Thanatos. It felt like he was waiting an eternity. The silence didn't help either. Ever since the tech had dropped its instruments and fled, they had heard no other signs of life and that bothered him. He was also worried about the confined quarters. He was at his best in flight but in these small hallways he was not even able to stretch his wings to their full extent never mind use his talons to their best capabilities. He found himself constantly looking over his shoulder. With all their equipment, the management must know he was free and how he had become so. Looking again over his shoulder, he wondered what they were doing above. Surely, they had some preconceived policy for just such an eventuality. He wondered what Thanatos was walking into.

The lift which held Thanatos sped upwards without interruption. The Director monitored its progress and waited for it to arrive. Davidson nervously paced her office. He would much rather have them dealt with in the depths of the IGH rather than let them become exposed. Once Cerberus was observed entering the second lift, she froze it mid-floor and drew a certain amount of amusement from the ensuing confusion. Satisfied that he would be occupied for some time and pose no threat, she turned from the monitors and straightened her jacket. She wanted to look her best when facing Thanatos.

The lift stopped, and Thanatos stepped out, the huge creature emerged behind him. Looking straight ahead, he saw her through the double doors that allowed entry to her inner sanctum. Smiling broadly, she beckoned him forward and returning the smile, he stepped through the doors and into her world.

"David," she said warmly, "it's been such a long time."

"Phil," he replied equally as syrupy, and he held out his hand to her.

"To what do we owe the pleasure?" she enquired

"I thought it was time we had a chat," he replied.

"I'm always available to old friends," she assured him, placing her fingertips together and sitting back relaxed in her chair. Always poised and in control Thanatos thought and yet there was weakness in her unwillingness to use his new name. She wanted to only address the human part of him. It was evident the wolf made her very nervous and this pleased Thanatos.

"I think things are getting a little out of hand," he continued.

"Really?" she encouraged him innocently and he found himself falling into the trap.

"Yes, I don't know if you know?" he said warming to his theme under her encouragement.

"Know what?" she enquired.

"The shape shifting ability has leached into the general population." He took pleasure in informing her.

"Oh that," she said almost offhandedly. "Davidson is dealing with it I believe."

"That's just the thing," Thanatos continued, "he is not dealing with it very well."

Davidson could contain himself no longer "Hey, I say, you have no right to slander my abilities." Appealing for support, he looked toward the Director herself then immediately fell silent. She had one of her dangerous looks about her. It was as if she was about to explode but you had to know her to recognise the signs. He physically withdrew to the edges of the room and found a very interesting piece of carpet to explore.

"What makes you think that David?" she almost whispered. It was a tone designed to make the hearer strain to hear the words properly and it made Thanatos draw even closer to her.

"My companion for one thing. Did you know that this creature was once Oldfield and Maxwell, amongst others?" he asked her.

"You give me very little credit old man. I know everything that happens on my watch." she told him with emphasis on the word everything.

"Very confident of you, but I wonder?" he mused.

"It is sweet of you dear David to presume my innocence however I think a little naïve." She informed him as she leaned forward.

"You knew about the double conversion?"

She simply raised an eyebrow and nodded.

"Do you also know about the limiters?" he enquired and again she nodded. "and the boy?" another nod told him everything he needed to know.

"Is that all you know?" she asked in return, and from her desk she withdrew what appeared to be a weapon, aimed it at the huge creature and fired. Something whistled past Thanatos's ear and he turned to follow its progress. There was a light thud as it sank into the creature's flesh. The result was as swift as it was savage. The great bulk that had seconds before been living, began to fold in upon itself and as it grew ever smaller there was a hissing decompressing sound that signalled the extinction of life. The escaping gasses stank even more than the creature had in life. Davidson had to throw up in the waste paper bin and the Director produced a handkerchief which she used to shield her nose. Very quickly all that was left was a small piece of matter in the centre of which blinked a single eye.

Shocked, Thanatos watched as she walked over and picked up the remains and handed it straight to Davidson "Dispose of this, and this time do it properly and then get rid of the others in the lift, David and I have some catching up to do." She ushered Davidson from the room, closed and locked the doors behind him. "Wine?" she enquired.

Nodding, Thanatos sat in the chair facing her impressive desk. "Do sit down," she offered sarcastically.

"Was that entirely necessary?" he asked.

"No, but it made my point. Back to my question, is that all you know?"

"I know where the boy is." He told her.

"I also know that," she said mocking him. "Come on, why come here if you did not want to trade for something." She asked.

Thanatos looked toward the locked doors and again she mocked him "I'm afraid your reinforcements are otherwise engaged," she informed him, pointing to the monitor that showed Cerberus trapped in the stalled lift. "Fairly soon now they will meet with a tragic accident."

"But why Phil, it makes no sense for you to condone these actions, the changelings would be more compliant if you were kinder," he told her.

"I haven't condoned the actions, I orchestrated them you fool," she said, her patience running out. "It will be good to tell you everything before you, too, meet with a tragic accident. No one really appreciates the beauty of it all or how much hard work it has taken," she lamented.

"Ok, I'm listening." He wanted to occupy her while he figured out how to turn all of this around for his own advantage.

She began by reminding him of the research station at Loch Ness. If she had not had a lethal weapon in her hand any casual passer-by would have thought them old friends reminiscing about past glory days. Indeed, even in these stressful circumstances he could not stop himself from smiling at the warmth of shared memories and old friendships. The atmosphere changed when she mentioned the first cryptid. He wanted to tell her it was he and not her that had discovered the truth behind the changeling technology, but she wanted to believe it was all her own doing. He had always had a crush on her, her flame red hair and petite frame made him view her as a creature of perfection, an Irish angel and still he could not bring himself to hurt her too deeply. His soul began to cry for his loss. Not the loss of the woman herself as she had never been his, but for the loss of the love he always thought could have been. They should, in his opinion be ruling together. The fact that he was relatively powerless was a result of her very real betrayal. She let him infect himself and had then stolen his ideas and presented them as her own. He had fallen into the same trap that men had fallen into since the beginning of history. If a woman looked beautiful and pure on the outside, then she was beautiful and pure on the inside. He learnt his mistake at this late stage in the play. She was not as he had amused himself thinking she was over the years. He had thought her to be an innocent dupe of Davidson's charms. It was more likely that Davidson was an innocent dupe of her charms as David Grey had been. She was good at what she did. It was suddenly obvious why she surrounded herself with men. Women would have seen through her games much more quickly than any man. The realization of this repulsed him in a way that not even the rotten stench produced by the Oldfield/Maxwell creature could have repulsed him. He pulled visually away from her and into the back of the seat in which he sat.

"Why David, I do believe I may have gone down in your estimations," she commented nonchalantly, while she demonstrated her indifference as to his opinion of her by waving the gun in his general direction. He saw now what a fool he had been. He had thought to free her so that they could rule together as he thought it should have been from the very beginning. She on the other hand was simply laughing at him.

Changelings

Gaining pleasure from the length of time she had been able to play him for a fool.

$$\star\star\star\star$$

The first thing Cerberus did when the lift stopped was panic. Once that was over, he was able to think a little clearer and focused his energy on escaping the metal coffin. It did not take him long to find the roof hatch and climbing through it, he flew up the vertical shaft with ease. He would return to help the others once he found out what was happening. Reaching the top of the shaft, he pried the lift doors open and stepped out into the foyer of the Director's office. He watched as Davidson left carrying something carefully in his right hand and a wastepaper bin in his left. He saw the Director lock the doors of her office and turn to talk to whoever was inside. He presumed it was Thanatos, but the situation did not look good. Opening the window, he stepped out onto a slim ledge, spreading his wings to give him extra balance he made his way along to her office. From this vantage point he could observe what was happening between Thanatos and the Director. He saw the tube in her hand and although he had not seen the weapon before, it was easily identifiable as a weapon. Concerned for the safety of his ally he flew away from the window and then turning, he flew hard in the direction he had come and instead of stopping at the barrier of the window he closed his eyes and, feet held out in front of him, continued at the same speed slamming into the window.

The effect was dramatic, the window shattered inwards with the impact, tiny shards flew in all directions and Thanatos who had seen him coming dived for cover. With his autonomic nervous system response kicking into action and releasing the right amount of adrenalin, he changed into his wolf form. The Director was surprised and tightened her grip on the tube which she carried causing it to fire at the space which seconds before had been occupied by Thanatos. As glass shards shot toward her desk, she was protected from their full impact by the high back of her chair. It was momentary respite as within a fraction of a second, Cerberus slammed into the chair himself forcing it forward into the desk. She hit at waist level and was immediately winded, losing all control the strange tube shot forward across the room. Cerberus was brought to a halt by the chair and the excess energy sent him tumbling head over heels towards the wall. Recovering quickly, mainly because he had initiated the chaos and had not been taken by surprise like the others, he was able to regain his feet in what appeared to be one fluid action. Pounding toward the now open window, he jumped on top of the Director's desk and using it as a launch pad headed toward freedom and the night sky. On the way, he grabbed Thanatos and they made their escape. As he flew, the Director's doors burst open and security started to fire at them, but they were already out of range.

✳✳✳✳

Maia stood atop an unfamiliar building and watched unfamiliar streets, but the action had a very familiar quality about it. She watched as Keanos directed the ground troops and prayed that this battle would have a more favourable outcome than the last one. She was not entirely confident about the outcome though, as she was now fighting with untried allies. They had failed already with great owl warriors. Many of these new allies were small and timid. They hardly inspired confidence.

She had seen the train stop at the station, a monumental event as no trains had stopped here for years. She had then watched as the security force complete with trackers had disembarked and she had felt the chill in her blood as she observed them once again. The trackers were re-entering her world far too soon for her own liking. She found it particularly disquieting when she observed one officer stroke the head of a tracker as if with affection. Who, she wondered could love such a creature? They began to enter Manchester,

191

but it was with considerably less confidence than they had displayed in Birmingham, their home hunting ground. The hounds sniffed in circles around one another, cautiously moving forward as they reconfirmed their ownership of each centimeter of ground. It was painful watching the slow progress, painful to wait while they inched their way toward conflict.

****

Sutton was bored. Caldwell was engrossed in the computer system and watching someone surf was simply not engaging. In addition, the longer they stayed the more edgy he became. He decided to have a look round the kitchen. If this place was occupied, then maybe he could find something interesting to eat. Enthusiastic now he had a focus, he almost skipped to the kitchen and soon he was engrossed in creating a gourmet delight otherwise known as beans on toast. He hadn't known there were any tins of beans left in the world.

Mike was focused on the computer; it confirmed his belief that whatever had happened began here on the shores of Loch Ness. Long before officialdom would have the rest of the population believe. Rubbing his tired eyes, he had the feeling there was still a large piece of the puzzle missing. Rubbing his eyes again, he looked toward the door, wondering where Sutton had gotten to and then he saw her just to the left of his vision. At first, he thought she was a figment of his imagination but finally his conscious mind accepted what his subconscious was screaming at him, Phoebe was here. She was here, and she was a shadow. Tears started to flow down his cheeks and once they began there was no stopping them. He cried for his loss and then he cried for her loss, as he realised, she was not the person he had known.

Chapter 14

Kapowski placed a handkerchief over his nose. The smell of decay was everywhere in this place and the quicker he eradicated these vermin and returned home the better it would be. As far as he was concerned, the changelings were simply dumb creatures created to fulfil certain needs. They were the property of those who had produced them and as such could be disposed of when their usefulness ceased. He was just cleaning up and this particular clean-up was long overdue.

He followed the trackers, grim-faced, into the heart of what had once been a thriving city. Not usually a fanciful man, he imagined the throngs that had once lived here as he walked. The people he imagined were pale representations, dancing in the lost corners of time, echoes from a forgotten source that confused his perceptions. That was why he almost missed the changeling fleeing just ahead of their progress. The hounds however missed nothing, and they began to strain on their leashes. The trackers freed them to pursue their quarry and they shot into the night howling with pleasure as they went. The chase had begun, and the trackers followed with the humans bringing up the rear.

Changelings

The hounds emerged from a side street into Albert Square where Keanos and his people were waiting. Immediately, they stopped both running and howling. Milling around at Keanos' feet, they began to wag their tails and sniff his hooves. One lay down and rolled onto his back, clearly indicating his submission. The pack leader lowered his head and growled to indicate that he was not yet ready to submit to a new authority. Reaching out, Keanos stroked its huge head and it immediately fell silent, recognising its genetic origin, and took its place in line behind the main assault. The ownership of the pack had been established.

One second the hounds were howling and the next, apart from one whimper, the night fell silent. The silence was ominous, mainly because of its suddenness and totality. The trackers and Kapowski's men all stopped and looking around confused, they waited for his direction. Kapowski sensed that if he did not urge them forward soon enough, they would lose their nerve and so he galvanised them back into action ordering man and tracker forward to discover the fate of the hounds. He strategically hung back, no point putting himself in danger if it was not necessary.

The next to emerge into Albert Square were the trackers. They glided swiftly forward, just inches above the debris strewn pathways, ready to enter battle and tear their foe to pieces, slavering at the thought of the pleasure to come. There was not much left of the brains they had once owned but what there was became overloaded very quickly. The scent of the changelings was mixed with hound and that served to arouse their feral instincts; but suddenly dominant, was a third, much older scent. It was the aroma of ancient dominance, a hierarchy that spoke to a primeval order that was not to be overturned on a night such as this. They owed allegiance to the source of their power and this knowledge stopped them dead, just as the hounds had done. Battling their nature to kill and the instinct to submit left them turning confused in circles. Unlike the dogs, they had no genetic history of submission and it soon proved to be an urge that was too distant in the collective memory to be obeyed. One at a time they began to move forward as their nature gained dominance over collective ancestral memories.

Keanos held his people back while the outcome of the trackers battle with their own nature was being resolved. He did not wish any creature destroyed before they had the chance to choose their own destiny. He watched while the trackers chose to die for their human masters, and he felt saddened that they were unable to recognise that they were closer to those on this side of the conflict. Really it was just another wrong that the IGH and its Director needed to account for; the tally was growing.

As the first tracker turned to fight, Keanos ordered his people forward. The changelings did not have to move at all. The cryptids emerged swimming from the shadows in their ancient form but changed into the physical form of the Centaur as they entered this world. They literally galloped from the shadow world into the present realm and as they came, they changed the air around them, throwing the trackers deeper into indecision and confusion. The trackers floundered, and the cryptids galloped by and gathered the trackers up as if they were the catch of the day. One used a net, others used tangle and grappling equipment and still others, their bare hands. Whatever they used, the trackers were subdued swiftly and dragged into the shadows wailing and howling their terror before they could taste a single drop of blood. The venom so deadly to human and changelings alike had no effect on the cryptids and the trackers were gathered as easily as if they were errant children being sent to bed for being naughty.

Maia watched the whole bizarre scene unfold below and although she was ready to join the fight, she could clearly see that her efforts were neither sought nor needed. She particularly watched Keanos and she could have sworn he was enjoying himself. She was fascinated with his physical presence and drawn to his essence that pervaded the world around him as an almost tangible aura. She was a little embarrassed at her fancifulness until she observed that many of her kind had similar feelings. It was clear all the changelings could feel his power and their own connection to his bloodline. His right to lead seemed completely natural and their right to follow, unquestionable.

****

Sutton entered the office, triumphantly bearing his gourmet offering, but when he saw Mike's face, he was a little taken aback.

"What's wrong?" he asked.

Mike pointed at the corner and Sutton said "ah," as he unloaded the contents of his tray onto the desk. "I was waiting for an opportune moment to tell you about that."

"Any time in the last 24 hours would have done," Mike grumbled, "and how did you know?"

"I met her when I was in the shadow lands, come on eat, it tastes great," Sutton replied, as he tucked into his beans with evident relish.

"Is your stomach all you think about?" Mike asked.

"Hm, no, but there is no mileage in fretting about what you can't change, is there?" Sutton asked as he shovelled more beans into his mouth.

"You eating that?" he asked, as he reached for a piece of Mike's toast. Smacking his hand back Mike too began to eat, still aware that Phoebe was watching closely.

When they had finished, she gestured to them to follow her and Sutton rolled his eyes.

"Oh no, back to the shadows I think."

"What?" Mike said a little slow on the uptake.

"She wants us to follow," Sutton offered helpfully. "Come on, let's go girls. The sooner we go, the sooner we get back," and heaving himself from his seat while simultaneously wiping his mouth across his coat sleeve he walked directly into what should have been a wall. Momentarily stunned, Mike was galvanised when Sutton's head re-emerged from the flowery print and said from the centre of a frame of petals, "come on then, I'm not doing this on my own again." Rather disconcerted with the conflicted images of Sutton as both a slob and a flower, Mike followed him to play in the shadows. He was, Mike realised, the closest thing he had to an actual friend.

The transition was strange, a little like being in the back of a car as it sped over the summit of a small hill. There was the same lurch in his stomach and he tripped as if over a threshold. Looking back, he saw the room they had just exited and as he watched, it drew away from him, reducing in size as if it were now a distant memory. He briefly wondered how the owner would feel about cleaning up after their meal and conversely, how they would feel at someone stealing their food. Shrugging, he turned away to embrace a new realm. The change in perception was disorientating and he shook his head to clear it. He took a step forward and stumbled again, not yet used to the lack of visual clues as to his position. Then Phoebe was by his side and supporting him as she had always done. He felt the warmth of her hands around his arm and turning, he took her into his own arms as if she had never been missing in the first place. He wanted to hold onto her if he could and closing his eyes, he leant forward to kiss her, to regain what had been his. As his lips met hers, he could almost believe that there had been no change in her, almost, but not quite. What should have been a passionate embrace turned cold before it had begun and although she responded, the experience still resembled kissing a wet fish. Pulling away, she burst into tears and covered her face with her hands. Mike stood arms empty, unable to offer her any comfort and perhaps cruellest of all, he did not want to re-embrace this sad half reflection of a woman he believed he had loved. In the end, it was Sutton who walked over to her and held her, not as a lover, but more like a father while her tears ended. Mike watched the two of them, partly jealous, partly relieved and when she had finished crying, he was glad her once, deep, blue eyes were now the same grey as the rest of her. He could not see the abandonment she evidently felt, emanating from these new orbs to accuse him of the betrayal. He felt ashamed of himself and for Mike that was altogether a new experience. Sutton took one look at his stricken face and knew words were not necessary. Mike did not need telling that what he had just done was perhaps the cruellest thing he had ever done. Once Phoebe regained her composure, they followed her lead and swam through the shadows in a parody of the breaststroke rather than walked as Sutton had previously done. This was a much easier way to travel, and almost effortless, even it did appear ludicrous.

Every now and then, they passed windows that reflected colour from the real world and Mike wondered how many of these portals between the two existed. They were so clear from this side looking from dark to light, grey to colour, but he wondered how you identified them from the other side. After a while his arms began to ache, and he called for a rest. Phoebe stopped with grace, rolling over from swimming to standing in one beautiful motion. Mike tried to copy the action and instead fell like a stone from the sky. Meeting the floor with far too much force, he cried out as his body and what felt like concrete came into sharp contact. Sutton fared better, half skipping and half running, he slowed his momentum and was able to stop in a more dignified fashion keeping his feet at least. Mike could have sworn Phoebe was laughing at them, but by now he did not care and sitting in an upright position he took the time to regain his lost breath and check his extremities for injury.

* * * *

Maia became aware of a presence above her and, ready to fight a tracker, she launched herself into the air almost turning a complete summersault to bring her face to face with her enemy. Talons outstretched and beak open to inflict the maximum damage, she had to veer away at the last second as she realised it was no enemy that approached. The force with which she was going to attack propelled her forward to contact with a chimney stack instead. The impact with immovable stone winded her and partly demolished the chimney. She fell to the roof top amidst stone and rubble and next to her landed Thanatos, dropped from Cerberus talons.

"As delicate as usual, I see my love," Cerberus teased.

Standing and shaking dust from her plumage, she glared at him and wrapping herself in her wings threw her head toward the sky and turned her back on him. Walking up behind her, Cerberus wrapped his own wings on top of hers and pulled her to him. Whispering into her ear and gently stroking her head had the desired effect and she turned to embrace him as best she could. A little embarrassed at witnessing their intimacy, Thanatos walked to the edge of the roof to amuse himself and lick the wounds where Cerberus' talons had pieced his skin. Maia and Cerberus were oblivious to the immediate events completely wrapped together. They were transported to another world and time where only the two of them existed. They drew strength from the warmth of one another and felt complete, not as two joined together but as two halves of the one being, functioning completely in harmony as they were always meant to be.

$$* * * *$$

Kapowski and his men entered the square just in time to see the trackers hauled away screaming in terror by the Centaurs. Kapowski knew what a Centaur was but had never expected to see one. They were not on the list of creatures that were known to be living here and he made a mental note to himself to find out who was responsible for not informing him of their existence. Whoever it was would find themselves straight down the changing booths. It still had not occurred to him that he may not find his way back to what he considered to be civilisation. Without the trackers, his task was going to be a little more difficult, but still possible, and he gave the order to charge.

He and his men ran forward brandishing their weapons, but the line of changelings remained unmoved. He even thought, he saw one of the Centaurs laugh at him, and enraged, he began to fire to show them who was in charge. The effect was instant, a whip was launched through the space that divided them and entwined around his wrist in a painful grip. He had not expected to be exposed to pain, how dare they attack an officer of the law and he gripped the whip with his free hand and tried to unwind it from his wrist. He felt himself being dragged forward and he looked around to see if help would be possible. Unbelievably, it seemed all his men were engaged in similar struggles and discarded weapons were strewn at his feet, but he was unable to stop and reach for them. The uneven ground resulted in him losing his footing and being pulled along on his back. He bounced painfully over pieces of rubble and would sport several bruises when this was over. He reached his free arm out to try and gain a weapon, but this proved too painful as the limb hit against all manner of immovable objects. He also found he needed to hold the whip with his free hand to prevent his arm being wrenched from its socket by his own weight. He had, for now lost control.

Finally, the pulling stopped and exhausted, he looked up into the face of Keanos. He started to regain his feet but was pushed back down by something behind him. He was then lifted and unceremoniously thrown into what could only be described as a cage. Humiliated, he promised himself they would pay for this insult. They obviously did not know who they were dealing with and he gave the bars a vicious kick to underline his displeasure.

****

Phoebe walked ahead. Leading the way in silence, she did not turn to see if they were following as she wanted only limited contact. Anything more would only serve to reinforce the sadness and remind her of all she had lost, and Sutton saw the occasional inky tear drop as they walked. On occasion, Mike reached his arm forward to touch her shoulder. However, he always stopped himself before physical contact was made. He did not want her as she was and yet he wanted her to want him. Sutton thought Mike was completely selfish and wondered, not for the first time, what he was doing so involved with all of this. Still he trudged behind them, the three of them walking through a land of grey, while each was truly in a world of their own making trapped with past decisions and present consequences. They were together yet, functioning in their own loneliness, separated by unseen chasms they could not cross. Each one was incomplete in a different way. Each one unaware of what they needed to gain happiness, but each one searching none the less.

The intrusion, into these separate yet connected worlds, was subtle when it came. The strains of sound drifted in as if on winds that brought no refreshment. It was Sutton who identified them as sounds. Stopping, he called to the others to do the same and straining, he tried to find the direction they would have to go to find their origin. Impatient at first, Mike thought Sutton had finally lost it but then he too began to hear the echoes. Moving once again toward the sound, they unconsciously picked up the pace. This time it was Sutton who took the lead. Soon they began to hear the song more clearly. It chilled and attracted each of them, to the same degree. They followed more cautiously now, not really wanting to find what was producing it but also unwilling to remain in this dark realm with an unidentified creature that wailed in this fashion. For all they knew it could be behind them stalking instead of them walking into its path.

It was not long before the shadows ahead began to solidify into definite objects and images of the creatures began to crawl into their minds. They recognised them as trackers. Fortunately, Sutton could see the trackers were caged. All they had to do was stay out of their reach and because of the instinctual revulsion they engendered that would not be a problem. As they passed each cage, the trackers contained within began to reach through the bars and Mike had the impression that they were starving, reaching out not for comfort and food but rather with a desire to kill. For all the revulsion he felt, he also felt sorry for them. He identified his own guilt in the production of these creatures, and he cried more out of pity for himself than them.

"Oh, for goodness sake man," Sutton exploded.

"I can't help it if I am sensitive," Mike replied.

"Just save it" Sutton said shaking his head in evident disapproval. Uncharacteristically, Mike stopped himself crying and did as Sutton directed.

They rounded the last cage; the jailers in charge of this dungeon were revealed. Sutton felt relief flood over him. He was surprising himself recently. He much preferred the company of the changelings than those who were supposedly more human. Perhaps he was less human than he had thought or perhaps the changelings were more human than he had been led to believe. Not a view he realised the IGH would want to promote. Thinking like that could lead to the changelings being given citizen rights; a proposition which really was verging on the heretical.

✳✳✳✳

Maia, Cerberus, and Thanatos made their way down to join Keanos and his army in the square. They had won what was perhaps a battle, although it was a very strange one indeed. The hounds had defected almost without hesitation on first contact. The trackers had been dispatched to the shadow lands without much effort at all and the men were all caged almost without casualty on either side. One man lay dead, accidentally shot by his comrades and two others were injured. They would receive treatment soon. Three shadows lay dead already their forms seeping away to merge with the natural shadows for eternity to come; all were victims of the men's weapons. They were always more vulnerable than creatures who were fully on the side of the changeling divide. Other changelings had minor wounds, all victims of the initial confusion rather than direct attack. None were seriously injured. Picking her way forward toward Keanos, Maia could not wait to introduce Cerberus and Thanatos to him. Her heart was soaring to a beat of its own, and she felt for the first time that freedom was within their grasp.

＊＊＊＊

Walking toward the jailers, Sutton, Mike, and Phoebe crossed the threshold to the night of the real world and tripping once more at the boundary, Mike started to curse. Then, as his surroundings crowded into his mind, he decided it was best to keep quiet. They were in the centre of what had all the appearances of a battlefield and, led by Phoebe, they were walking toward the middle of the altercation. Mike momentarily wondered if it were her intention to betray them and this feeling was strengthened when he saw the cages occupied, this time not by trackers, but by the IGH's security force. He caught up with Sutton and tugged the back of his coat to get his attention.

"What," he responded, demonstrating some of the frustration he felt with Mike.

"Do you think this place is entirely safe for us?" he asked.

"Probably not, but what else do you suggest?" Sutton asked him impatiently.

"Going in the opposite direction," Mike offered.

"And you think they would let us?" Sutton asked him gently. The man really was impossibly naive at times, he thought.

Mike looked around unhappily and had to admit Sutton was probably right. They were surrounded by changelings and shadows of all shapes and sizes.

"Oh, and stay away from the cages, if anyone recognises us we may end up in there with them." Sutton suggested.

"Good thinking," Mike replied.

Cerberus was making his way through the debris and seemed to be working his way at such a tangent that their paths would cross. Nudging Sutton once again Mike pointed them out.

"I know," was all Sutton said, for he was focused on the point at which they were both heading. Focused, as it seemed all were focused, on the form of Keanos.

****

The Director paced across her office. The window had been replaced with toughened glass and she gazed across her city. She was waiting for news from Kapowski. She expected him to contact her soon with the details of how he had destroyed the changeling camp and retrieved the boy. She had a special lab prepared for his study. She could not risk the public discovering that a changeling had occurred naturally. It would lead to unrest and that had not happened since the food riots during the early shortages. She could not allow it to happen again. It was this small possibility of unrest that caused her anxiety. She disliked events happening outside of her control.

Kapowski had taken all the trackers with him and only her beautiful banshees remained to protect her. Davidson thought he was next in line but truthfully, she saw him as no more than a lackey, a servant of the lowest order.

The banshees served as her private guard and secret police rolled into one. They were both her protectors and her children. If she loved anything in this world it was them, a reflection of her own ego.

Davidson came snivelling into the office to tell her preparations for the boy were ready. Once in their custody they would hold him in suspended animation. That way they could keep all his organs alive while running a variety of tests. For once she was pleased with Davidson's efforts. As a reward, she decided to let him take her to dinner.

Changelings

＊＊＊＊

The restaurant was crowded but that was of little interest to the Director. It was an honour that she had decided to dine there and so they set a new table as soon as they could. They placed them by the window overlooking the tow path of the canals. The canals were a little-known beauty spot in the very centre of Birmingham. They had always attracted tourists even before society had changed so drastically. The director saw them entirely as her property. She owned everything in her universe. Davidson was annoyingly attentive but tonight she allowed him to bask in her reflected glory. After all, very soon everything would be back in order and so she could afford to be magnanimous.

She ate her soup with an air of distraction as Davidson prattled on about codes. Glancing out of the window she saw a shuffling mound of discarded clothing approach along the tow path. Initially, she could not believe her eyes and she thought incredulously a tramp was walking toward her. She stared intently and then kicking Davidson asked, "What is that thing doing walking on my tow path?"

Not understanding what she was asking Davidson squinted into the night and it was a surprise to him to see the decrepit shape moving ever closer. "Err," was all he could manage. He cursed himself and the tramp. This was his chance to impress. He should have had the police clear the canal before they sat down. Now this degenerate could ruin his plans for gaining her favour.

"Well?" she pushed. "What are you going to do about it?"

"I'll send some men along to get rid of it," he assured her.

But she was in no mood to be patient. Calling an officer over she demanded his weapon and stalking out of the restaurant went to deal with the man or whatever it was herself. For a minute Davidson was overtaken by surprise then

205

"Oh No!" he exclaimed and throwing his napkin on the table jumped up to run after her.

The cool of the night sent a shiver through her body. The flimsy evening gown she wore was no protection against even the slightest breeze. She could not see the tramp to begin with, but then she became aware of him standing directly next to her.

"You're brave," she told him.

"Not really lady," he replied with none of the deference she expected.

"Don't you know who I am?" she asked indignantly.

"I know," he replied with a sneer in his voice. "The fact is, I do not care."

She could not believe her ears., No-one, never mind an outcast, ever talked to her like this. She began to raise the weapon she held but instead of crumbling in fear, he simply laughed at her. Becoming red with anger she aimed in his direction, but he reached out and taking her wrist swung her round and into his arms. He held her tightly from behind and took the gun from her. "Ladies should not play with weapons," he told her as he tossed it into the water. She was now beside herself with anger and she screamed as Davidson came through the restaurant door, "Arrest this fool!"

Davidson looked around for backup but the security detail he had ordered was nowhere to be seen and the Director was almost apoplectic. "Get this stinking idiot off me!" she demanded. The stinking idiot simply laughed. "You will regret this," she informed him. "When they bring you in I will make sure you die very, very slowly and very, very painfully." She promised.

"You need to stop the changeling experiments and stop messing with what you don't understand," he whispered in her ear. Then without warning he was gone.

She was completely shaken. Had things gotten so out of control that she could be molested in such a fashion? Davidson was grovelling, and the action simply sickened her, but for now she needed the familiar around her and so she let him usher her back into the restaurant. Security did an immediate sweep of the area but all they found was a pile of rags next to the canal. They had obviously been worn to hide the scent of the owner. No dog would be able to track him, and all the trackers were in Manchester. She did not want to risk her personal guard. They had to chalk this one up to experience. As they turned away the sergeant could have sworn, he heard the mournful cry of a long extinct creature in a swamp ... but that was impossible.

Changelings

Chapter 15

They were all gathered around the table waiting for Keanos to join them. Kapowski nursed his injured wrist and pride as if they were both in need of sympathy. He would not, allow a changeling to dress his wound and amused himself by thinking of the worst expletives with which to address the Centaur when they talked.

"Is he always like this?" Mike asked. Sutton just nodded wearily and played with the food which had been prepared for them. He was unhappy that Kapowski knew of his involvement at all. He suspected he would pay heavily for this eventually and that made him decidedly gloomy. In contrast, Cerberus and Maia ate with gusto and obvious enjoyment. They were elated to have found one another again. Thanatos, now in his human form, ate delicately with an air of detachment. When Keanos came in, they all paused and allowed him to claim his seat before continuing with their meal. Mike could not help sitting up straighter in his chair. Sitting to attention, he noticed Sutton do the same. Kapowski on the other hand shrank into himself and seemed to become smaller. He even stopped cursing and Sutton was grateful for small mercies.

Keanos directed his initial attention at Kapowski.

"Not hungry Captain?" he enquired.

"I would not eat any muck prepared by your kind," Kapowski spat. "Why don't you just kill me and get it over with?"

"We don't intend killing you Captain," Keanos responded. "On the contrary we were hoping you would take a communication back to the IGH."

"What's in it for me?" Kapowski asked.

"Your freedom," Keanos replied in a very even, almost friendly, tone while holding out a communication cube to Kapowski. "Now would you like us to make your arm more comfortable before you go?" he asked reasonably.

"I'll get it looked at by a real doctor when I get back," Kapowski growled with noticeable lack of grace, while snatching the cube from Keanos with his good arm. "I don't really want your slimy hands all over me," he concluded.

"Whatever you wish Captain," Keanos gestured to two Centaurs and instructed them to take Kapowski back to the train station. "You will be blindfolded; we don't want you to see all our secrets." Much to Sutton's relief, Kapowski was escorted from the great chamber before he could respond further. The tension in the room visibly decreased.

"What next?" Sutton asked in a much more buoyant tone.

"We give him time to return to the IGH and get an answer to my letter." Keanos told him. "We relax while we wait."

"What I don't understand," Thanatos interjected, "is with all your powers and abilities to move where you want, you have not contacted the Director and sorted this before?"

"She is a lady who is well protected," Keanos replied.

"But what does that mean?" Thanatos pushed.

"Doctor," Keanos said sharply "You were there at the start, you know what she can do," he continued. "She is the only one who has managed to kill one of our kin and when she did, she nearly wiped us all out. If she knows that the cryptids are still alive there is no telling what she will decide to do next. We feel distance is best kept between us." He concluded.

"Hang on," Mike interrupted. "Are you saying she deliberately caused the death of the cryptids?" Sutton, Thanatos and Keanos all sighed together.

"Come on Caldwell, keep up," Sutton instructed "The rest of us are way past that one. The only question left is what else she did and what will she do from now on to keep her power?"

"What do you suspect?" Mike asked.

It was Thanatos that replied. "We suspect she engineered the eradication of all the species that died."

"That's impossible," Mike stated, but as he said it, he knew he did not believe it. The species that had left the earth were central in ensuring food supplies and the survival of humanity itself, but they were not directly connected. He knew there was no real reason as to why those particular species had been affected. If the reason was not obvious then it had to be hidden. It could be that the cryptids went first because they provided the biological material to make mass changelings possible; then the sequence was entirely logical. Logical, that is, if the crisis were manufactured and you were going to save the world and become extremely powerful in the process.

"How long did you change before the cryptids died on mass?" Mike asked Thanatos.

"About five years," he replied, and Mike suddenly felt sick. He had known the experiments had all been the wrong way around, but he still had difficulty believing the whole thing was deliberate. Hell, if it was, the Director was worse than Hitler; at least he had only killed millions. If they were right, she had orchestrated the death of billions. Even worse, he and others like him had been her accomplices. For the second time in his life he felt a deep shame as he realised, he owned at least a part of the guilt that was the Director's. He had never questioned what they were doing or the cost to people and their loved ones. It was only when he had lost something he had thought of as his that he had started to look at the way things truly were, and he realised even that had been selfish. Rather than retreat into self-pity as the old Mike would have done, he decided to try and do better and help these people with no reward for himself. Yes, he would do this unselfishly, and perhaps redeem himself in the process.

Mike directed his next comment directly to Keanos "Won't she know when Kapowski talks about Centaurs, that the cryptids are alive?"

"Yes, but we need to take the risk if we are to negotiate," Keanos stated. "The boy proves that she is not in as much control as she thinks. Things are developing on their own. She may now be scared enough to want our help."

"Forget negotiation," Mike said, "It's time we fought back. She needs to pay for her actions." His anger was directed at her, but Mike knew it was also a result of his own complicity. He needed to make amends. He looked to Keanos for approval and he was not disappointed as several voices asked in unison, "How?"

"I need a microscope and some samples to start with, how about the old university?" Mike stated emphatically.

"It is still intact," Keanos informed him "What do you intend?"

"To fight back, perhaps produce a way of reversing the changes or perhaps blocking her ability to change anyone else." Mike said as he jumped up from the table getting ready to put his plan into immediate action.

When the others left the main hall, Sutton stayed where he was. He was a little suspicious that Caldwell had suddenly become a revolutionary. A few days ago, he was a self-obsessed dandy and he did not think people changed that quickly. He was sure Mike was in it to maximise his own fortunes. Then he relented a little, perhaps he was being a little harsh, but he had found caution had served him well in the past. He was also unsure if this was the right side to be on. Kapowski would assume he had defected but that was not a reason to stay on this side. He had been a company man for a long time and old habits were difficult to break. Sighing heavily, he rose from the table and decided to take a walk to clear his thinking.

He walked the hallways that made up most of this facility and marvelled at the variety of creatures that lived in the tunnels. Mostly he was taken with the children, second generation changelings who should not have been possible and he wondered what humans would look like in the future. The thought made him shudder and he realised he was a xenophobe, having a strong dislike for those with different genetic material to himself, but he also realised how close they really were to one another. He saw mothers nursing infants, children playing together and young people walking hand in hand as they discovered who was important to them. He thought about the obvious love Cerberus and Maia had for one another and the selfishness with which Caldwell had treated Phoebe. Eventually, he made his choice and having made it he would be loyal to the end.

✴✴✴✴

Mike walked through the streets of the abandoned city of Manchester. Brief stretches were strewn with debris, a result of the initial panic and looting. Mostly, however, the impression was one of surprising order. The highest degree of disorganisation could be seen around the major commercial outlets. These had been ransacked by those looking for wealth. The things they had taken were later discarded as the people of the time had realised that the boundaries had moved. Money, jewels and designer goods no longer had currency. Bread, rice and potatoes were what people valued most and so there was no point expending energy carrying what had once been lucrative luxuries.

The overriding impression was one of orderliness. Most shops still advertised their goods in window displays designed to attract the shoppers. A gentleman's outfitters drew Mike's attention and he walked over to have a closer look. Two mannequins stood in the window facing each other as if in conversation, each wore a suit and carried a sign advertising twenty pounds off in the sale. He knew that pounds were the currency they used to use but he wondered what a sale was. He would have to ask Sutton later. He thought that he must be old enough to remember those kinds of things. Pushing the door, he was not surprised to find that it was locked, but he was not ready to give in just yet and putting some weight behind his efforts, he found it relatively easy to force the door. Stepping inside, he began to look around. Outside, the others were becoming restless and he was aware that they wanted to move on. He made his way to the back of the shop where the changing rooms were hidden from view with heavy curtains. As he drew one back, a thick cloud of dust made him cough. He was about to search further when Thanatos came to the door.

"Come on, you can explore as much as you want when we have settled things with the Director but right now, we don't have time."

Mike nodded, disappointed. He recognised they should move on, but as he turned away, he had the feeling he had missed something and that feeling remained with him for the rest of the journey through the city. In the darkest corner of the shop a pair of eyes blinked and then disappeared into the shadows.

They arrived at the University and they stopped to marvel a second at its majesty. Even now silent and empty, it cut an impressive figure in the landscape. Mounting the stairs, they entered the main lobby. Cerberus and Maia positioned themselves on either side of the doorway to guard against any intrusion even though none was expected. Truthfully, they were much more comfortable outside than in. They looked from a distance like two sentry gargoyles. Mike and Thanatos looked for a campus map and it was not long before they found one.

"What do you think will be the best faculty to head for?" Thanatos asked.

"Medical science should have everything we need," Mike said and then, "look, it's in the building over there." Leaving quickly, they re-emerged into the sun and once again set out together to find the right place.

This time they all entered. Even though Cerberus and Maia were more comfortable outside. It was felt, particularly by Mike, that they should all stay together. It did not take long for them to find the labs. Switching on the lights, they were surprised that the electricity still worked. A quick recon yielded all the equipment they needed. Test tubes and analysing machines were all easily available. Computers booted quickly as if they were happy to be in use again. Once set up, Mike began drawing blood from everyone assembled. He then gathered a blood collection kit together. Someone would have to go back and get samples from the boy and from some of the second-generation changelings too. Maia and Cerberus were happy to take on this task but were unable to draw samples themselves. Thanatos wanted to stay with Mike and begin the analysis of the first samples but eventually gave in as he was the only one with the expertise to draw the samples. They set off immediately, as even going as fast as possible, they would be pushing it to return by nightfall.

Mike began busying himself with the initial analysis and tried to forget his disquiet at being left completely alone. Perception seeped into his consciousness slowly, one minute he was happily busying himself with his samples and the next he was continually looking at the door.

"Expecting company?" a voice asked.

"Where are you?" Mike demanded.

"Right here," the owner of the voice said, as they stepped out of the shadows. Mike knew immediately he was in trouble.

"I didn't know trackers could speak," he said outwardly, keeping his cool.

"They can't," whatever stood in front of him informed Mike smoothly. It was obvious that this was no tracker, the wings were lighter, and it had more discernibly human features.

"Then what, are you?" Mike asked, coming straight to the point.

"Unique," the creature informed him and then it continued. "Like the situation we find ourselves in."

"What's that meant to mean?" Mike asked.

"Well, here you are valiantly trying to find out how the changeling ability has leached into the general population, so you can heroically rescue what is left of the human race, obviously with no thought as to how you can benefit," it purred.

"Something like that," Mike said cautiously, "and what are you here for?"

"Oh, I'm here to stop you." It informed him.

"Why?" He asked.

"It is a little complicated, but as you noticed I am not entirely human, and I really don't want the rest to be saved as you're planning." While it was talking, it walked forward and took a test tube from Mike with one hand and stroked his cheek with the other. Mike realised it was female and as she breathed on his neck, he understood that a strange one-sided attraction may be happening.

He wanted to scream and run away. He wondered if her kind had been around when peasants had reported seeing demons. She fitted all Mike's impressions of demons that was certain.

"What have you got against humanity?" Mike asked, as he stepped backwards retreating from her.

"I was beautiful, before I went through the process," she partly explained as she advanced further and reaching forward, she drew him to her. Kissing him, he nearly gagged, and she laughed, "but as you see the process has adversely affected my attractiveness rating."

Still coughing, Mike asked "so it's personal?"

"Oh no, I was sent to kill you," she informed him, as she reached for him once again, this time running a talon down his cheek and licking the blood as it appeared. Ending up at his ear, she blew gently into his lobe as if they were engaged in foreplay. "It's almost as good as sex," she added as she thumped him in the stomach.

"Fear tastes so good and it's exciting too."

Then, as he fell to the floor, she sat on top of him. He frantically tried to think how to get out of the situation when a large flask shattered against the back of her head. Screeching her fury, she leapt from on top of him and as she moved, he saw Phoebe behind her. Taking the opportunity offered, he rolled away and searched for a weapon but all he could find was a chair. Turning back to face her he was just in time to see her literally rip Phoebe to pieces. He hit her hard on the back with the chair and although it collapsed into pieces the blow seemed to have no effect on her.

When she had finished with Phoebe she turned once more to him and this time it was very evident that she meant to complete her mission as soon as she could. Working his way around the benches, he tried to keep something very solid between her and himself. His latent cowardice and natural self-preservation impulses proving very useful. She had other ideas and she leapt on top of the work bench. As she did, he rolled underneath to the other side and armed himself with one leg of the shattered chair. Then, taking the situation in hand, he attacked her and by the expression on her face she had not expected bravery from him. Using the leg, not as a club but as a stake, he launched himself into the air pushing forward with all his weight. Miraculously, the wood breached her flesh and he heard the cracking of her ribs as it pressed deep within to pierce her heart. Blood spurted from the wound in rhythm with the slowing heartbeat. He was showered with the warm red liquid. Her weight fell heavily against him and once again he heard the cracking of bone but this time it was his own arm rather than further damage to her. With the last of her strength, she tried to bite his throat, but he managed to hold her at bay with his remaining good arm and the intense desire to live. As the life left her eyes, he had the strangest feeling of recognition. It was as if he had known her, but that was impossible, he had never seen such a creature before. He pushed her from him and crawled over to the form that had been Phoebe. As he cradled her in his arms, he was glad that she was aware of his touch before she slipped away for good. "Don't die," he whispered. "Please don't die." He could have sworn he saw her smile before he felt the last breath of life leave her body. He clung to her, unwilling to let her go.

Unsure how long he sat cradling her in his arms the sun had started to sink below the horizon when the door opened to admit the others.

"Had a party?" Thanatos joked but his tone changed when he tripped up over the cadaver of the creature Mike had been fighting. Bending to look closely, he could not help exclaiming, "Oh lord, it's a Banshee".

"A what?" Sutton exclaimed, and then he saw Mike. They all galvanised into action. Thanatos and Sutton persuaded Mike to leave Phoebe and took him into the next room where they began to clean up. Finding some old sheets, they wrapped both Phoebe and the Banshee in them and carried them down the hall.

"What's a Banshee?" Sutton asked.

"It was an Irish spirit that heralded death, but now it's a variation of the tracker."

"A deliberate variation?"

"No. Usually when transformed, trackers lose their ability for independent cognition. The Banshee retains all cognitive ability. A fluke I think." Thanatos replied. So much had changed it was no longer entirely clear as to what was, and was not, by design.

"Poor thing," Sutton commented.

"Hmm, she will have known what she once was. Not a happy existence," Thanatos agreed, "But she did have a choice. She chose to bring death to those her controller wanted killed."

"Perhaps she thought she had to," Sutton said wanting to believe the best of all creation. He really was a romantic at heart and had harboured a vain hope Mike and Phoebe would be reconciled after all. Now it would never be. Then they both lapsed into silence.

The physical strain of moving two bodies and then cleaning up was proving to be a considerable drain on their energy. When they finished, they sat down with Mike. Sutton found drinks in the supplies they had brought, and Thanatos encouraged Mike to talk.

The Banshee had been sent to escort Mike to the afterlife. Although Sutton still thought the man was an empty-headed coward most of the time, he was glad Caldwell was still with them. The self-absorbed megalomaniac was growing on him. Patting Mike on the shoulder, to demonstrate his growing affection, he went to make sure the perimeter was secure. Even though he was unable to help with the technical stuff, he was very capable of ensuring Mike and Thanatos remained safe while they searched for the changeling mechanism.

Keanos was unable to settle. He was worried that the Director would simply attack in retaliation and he was not sure as to the allegiances of any of the outsiders. Caldwell and Sutton were men and as such their chemistry was beyond his knowledge. He was unable to read or influence their reactions in the way that he could know any changeling. They would decide their own fate and he spent little time worrying about their actions. No, it was Thanatos that most worried him. He should be easily influenced by Keanos. After all, he was perhaps the most directly related changeling of all and yet Keanos found him almost impossible to read and definitely impossible to influence. The fact that he was also there at the beginning added to Keanos' disquiet. He thought the wolf man had deeper connections to the Director than he did to his own kind.

These worries combined to make sleep an elusive state. Wakefulness was all he could look forward to that night.

He prowled the hallways of his own sanctuary and fretted about the fate of his people; not just the other cryptids but also the changelings. These new creations were like lost cousins and he felt as responsible for them as he did his own kin. As he prowled, he came across the human hybrid child and his now inseparable Butterbee companion. They looked sweet and vulnerable, entwined together in their unconscious travels. The boy twitched and moaned as if his dreams were unpleasant and the Butterbee twitched as if in echo of the boy. Keanos watched them for some time and he knew he needed to protect them. Making his decision, he started to rouse his people, they had very little time. Kapowski had not seen any of the children and so the Director would also be unaware of their existence. Keanos was determined to keep it that way. He was arranging for them to be removed, to Loch Ness. Hidden away, so if the worst happened and the Director won, the species would still live on.

Kneeling beside the pair, he reached out and stroked both of their foreheads. Gently bringing them to consciousness, he placed them both on his back for a last ride around the compound before sending them with the others. Both boys laughed and urged him to go faster as he almost flew through the hallways, his hooves sounding out a rhythm as he galloped, announcing their approach to all who may be in their way. Finally, he headed back to the main hall and the boys recognising the fun was over, slid, one after the other from his back. Then, hugging each in turn, he watched as they entered the shadows. Both boys waved as they disappeared into the darkness and Keanos felt sadness in his spirit at the loss of the children even for what he hoped would only be a short time. Then setting his heart to a new hardness, he began to plan the next move in their campaign with his generals.

Chapter 16

Kapowski was pleased to be back in civilization. His first stop was at IGH health centre to get his wrist set and then after freshening up, he headed over to report to the Director.

It wasn't until he was outside her office that he started to become nervous. She was not well known for her tolerance and he had just lost a whole station of officers. It was with trepidation that he entered and stood in front of her desk waiting for attention. She looked at him over her glasses a couple of times and he felt he should start to talk, when she turned back to the file she was reading. He knew it was a control technique designed to put him at a disadvantage but knowing what it was did not make it any easier to handle. Davidson stood by her side and frequently gave him what were supposed to be meaningful looks. It was just that Kapowski did not know what the meaning was meant to be and when she finally put the file down, he visibly jumped at the sound of her voice.

"Why not take a seat," she said, as if it had been his decision to stand all this time. Folding his arms, Davidson stood to one side behind her as if he was needed to witness what was about to occur. Kapowski suddenly felt his mouth go dry and he had difficulty replying in a way that did not betray his nervousness. He needn't have worried because it was evident that his disquiet pleased her.

"Thank you, ma'am," was all he could manage as he pulled a chair up to her desk. He could have managed better without the look of pure contempt on Davidson's face. Holding her hand out, the Director indicated she wanted the communication cube he was holding, and he handed it to her. Placing it in the computer, they all watched as a mini hologram of Keanos came to life.

"Greetings from the cryptid nation," the hologram began. Then, as they all watched, it continued. "As I am sure you are now aware from your emissary, not all cryptids were annihilated under the first wave of attack you orchestrated some years ago. Suffice it to say that we were temporarily driven to a secret location to regroup. We now believe that hiding is no longer the optimal solution and wish to negotiate our return, unmolested, to our previous haunts. In return, we will find it unnecessary to encroach on your territory. We await your response."

"What do you think Kapowski?" she asked almost innocently, but he knew it was a loaded question. How he answered her now could seriously affect his future.

"He isn't to be trusted," was the answer he decided to go with.

"No?" she continued with her innocent tone.

"No ma'am, he effectively turned the hounds to his own side and dispatched the trackers in minutes. The battle was over before we entered the square." His report was succinct and to the point. The longer he talked the more comfortable he became and the deeper Davidson's scowl. Kapowski took that as a good sign as Davidson had never liked him. If this wasn't what Davidson wanted to hear, then perhaps it was going his way after all.

"It wasn't your fault then?" she asked.

"No ma'am, there was nothing we could have done." He told her.

"What would you recommend we do next?" she asked.

"I think we should hit them hard ma'am." He replied without hesitation.

"Hit them with twice or three times the force?" she enquired.

Nodding now and feeling excited that she was not blaming him, he became a little over enthusiastic "Yes, yes," he agreed.

"Why would you want us to send virtually all our security forces. If what you say is true then they could end up the same way as your men, could they not?" There was warning in her lowered tone if Kapowski had been smart enough to hear it and Davidson was visibly wincing as the sergeant walked straight into the pit.

"With more officers I am sure we could win" he reassured her.

"Really, and when you say we, do you mean you and your new friends, Captain?"

Genuinely puzzled, Kapowski enquired, "New friends ma'am? I don't have any new friends."

"You expect me to believe that this creature, Keanos did not know you were coming? He was not forewarned. He was obviously waiting for you; wouldn't you say so Davidson?" Davidson simply nodded his agreement knowing from experience that his opinion was not really being sought just his affirmation of her view.

"I'm sure he wasn't. I mean how could he have been?" Kapowski asked unsure once more as to where he stood.

"I am glad you asked," she said, opening the file in front of her, "I have a citizen's report stating you were consorting with a strange shadow, you disrupted their barbeque to do it." Kapowski just looked at her with no comprehension or understanding on his face and this served to infuriate her. She exploded,

"Either you are acting, or you are very thick and frankly Kapowski, whichever way is the truth you are useless to me. Davidson lock him up somewhere while I think what to do with him." She ordered.

Nodding, Davidson moved forward and called security. Kapowski was dragged out backwards protesting his loyalty. Leaning back in her chair the Director announced, "I need chocolate." Davidson jumped to fulfil that desire as he did to fulfil all her wants. There was nothing he would not do for her and she was aware of his loyalty.

****

Will hummed as he dusted the apartment, he wanted it to look nice for Mike's return. When the buzzer sounded, he wondered if Barb had forgotten her key again; that girl was seriously dizzy. He opened the door to two uniformed officers.

"Hi boys," he greeted them but neither even raised a smile. Thinking a sense of humour was not too much to ask for he continued, "What can I do for you two handsome specimens?"

"William Dryer?" the one nearest him asked. Will replied, "Friends usually call me Will, but I guess you can call me William."

Looking up as if he was trying to keep calm, the officer continued, "You are under arrest, you do not have to say anything but what you say or do not say will be used in evidence against you at your trial."

"But I haven't done anything," Will wailed unable to believe it was anything other than an elaborate joke. It was probably the office staff having fun at his expense, any moment these two would to start to strip and Coleen would be heard giggling from the hall.

"Not our problem," the second officer informed him and then a little more conspiratorial, "We could let you have a phone call." The first officer nodded his agreement. "I knew you were gentlemen," Will enthused.

"Yeah, the first one agreed, we let you have a little consideration if you show us some."

"That's right," the second one agreed, "a little consideration," and he winked at Will.

Will had never been slow at catching on. "The world turns on consideration," he almost purred, and batting his eyes at both, he suggested, "Why don't you both wait in there, just while I slip on something more comfortable." They could not contain their excitement as they almost fell over one another to get to the bedroom. Fun with a companion was a rare occurrence for those at their rank. Will took his chance and, leaving the apartment, he dead locked the mechanism as he went. It would take them hours to break out and he did not think they would be in a hurry to report he had given them the slip. He could probably count on a couple of clear hours before a general alert went out. The first thing he needed to do was contact Barb, hopefully they had not picked her up yet.

****

Barb was in Mike's office when Will called. He quickly told her about the arrest. She was more than a little sceptical.

"Are you sure it wasn't to do with a past indiscretion Will?" she asked.

"Come on Barb, what do you think I am?" he asked innocently.

"Frankly, loose most of the time and impetuous," she informed   him.
"Barb! You wound me," he exclaimed and then continued "Listen, girlfriend, I would seriously get out of there if I were you." But she did not reply, and he began to get worried about her when he heard her say,

"Mr Davidson, you made me jump, I was just cleaning Mr Caldwell's office."

"Really," he said acidly and who were you on the phone to?"

225

"Just my brother sir," she lied "I know I shouldn't during office hours, but he gets lonely, I am sorry sir." She told him as she looked downward with a contrite expression.

"Don't worry, Barbara," he assured her almost kindly, "I want you to come with me."

"Can I ask why sir?"

"The Director wants a word," was the last thing Will heard as someone broke the connection.

Scared, Will, began to run from the apartment. He was not as empty headed as people thought. For the most part, it was a convenient act. When others thought you were a fool they did not think you could cause them harm. Will had survived many an awkward situation with the ruse, he also had a plan to leave that he'd devised some time ago. When you lived in an uncertain world where anyone can disappear at any time it was wise to have a plan you could follow in an emergency. He knew exactly where to run and how to do it undetected.

****

Barb wiped the palms of her hands down her thighs and then crossed her arms in front of her stomach. She could feel the butterflies inside and they were making her feel sick and light headed. She was not worried that she was nervous, anyone with any sense felt nervous when facing a meeting with the Director. She shuffled her feet and wondered what was taking so long, but then, she supposed, she was very low down on the Director's list of importance. When the double doors finally opened, she was relieved to have the anxiety of waiting removed and she entered the office eagerly. She walked straight up to the desk, sat down, before being asked and let out a sigh. Despite herself, Philomena was taken with Barb's naivety and she smiled an almost genuine smile. Seeing the Director smile at her made Barb feel much better and she smiled in return and felt the butterflies fly from her abdomen.

"Hello Barbara," and while speaking she walked around the desk and shook Barb's hand. Then, rather than returning to her seat, Philomena perched on the desk and faced Barb. "I thought it was time we became better acquainted, after all you are one of my best crypto-biologists significant other."

"Thank you," Barb virtually simpered.

Patting Barb's arm, Philomena continued, "Tell me how you made Mike notice you?" she asked. Barb went through all her little tactics. She even confided that she thought he liked her better than Will. She finished by saying, "I think he felt obliged to take someone of the same sex, you know in the name of fairness."

Philomena nodded in sympathy "Where is Mike now?" she asked innocently.

"Some relaxation trip," Barb told her.

"Would you like to join him?" the director asked.

"Oh, yes please," Barb replied, jumping up and down in her seat.

"Good, I would like you to go with Davidson and get a couple of inoculations before we send you up there," she said as she lifted Barb's elbow and steered her toward Davidson and the door.

"Injections?" Barb said, a little of her nervousness returning.

"Nothing to worry about dear," Philomena replied. "You never know what's hanging around outside the city. It's just a precaution, of course, if you want to risk catching something?" she left the decision to Barb but there was really only one option and Barb did not disappoint. Cute but entirely thick, the Director decided.

"No, no I don't want to catch anything," Barb said as she was literally handed over to Davidson. Now with him in control of her elbow, she was guided out of the door. They continued to the lifts and then all the way down to the lowest level. Down here Barb's butterflies returned, and it felt like they had brought reinforcements with them. She pulled back as if wishing to return to a safer floor, but it was evident that Davidson was in control and he propelled her forward. When she heard the lift doors close behind her, she jumped and looked nervously at Davidson. She realised there was no comfort to be had from him and all he was interested in was pushing her into the lab at the end of the corridor.

She was literally placed into a chair in the centre of the room. A technician fastened straps around her arms and legs to hold her in place. Then, both the technician and Davidson left her alone as Phoebe had been left in this place before her.

After a while she started to call out, "Hello, can anyone hear me? Hello." Finally, a voice from the darkness replied, "For goodness sake can you just be quiet?"

"Who's that?" Barb demanded.

"We're not at a tea party where polite introductions are the order of the day you know," the voice replied with obvious irritation.

Getting angry, Barb retorted, "Well forgive me. I only wanted to know what was happening."

"You may be happier not knowing," the voice informed her.

"I think it always helps to know," Barb finished as a technician re-entered the room.

"It's nice to see you are both getting along" she commented.

"Yeh, sure," Kapowski replied. "Loosen the belts and I will introduce myself properly."

"Just ignore him," Barb said, "I think someone got out on the wrong side of the bed this morning. He is Mr Grumpy." she told the technician in an almost conspiratorial fashion.

Kapowski groaned "Look woman, we are not on holiday here, we are about to be changed."

"Don't be silly," Barb retorted, "we are only getting jabs, so we don't get anything nasty when we travel."

Kapowski gave up, she would find out soon enough. He watched as the tech drew fluid into a syringe. Interestingly, it looked completely innocent, and yet he knew it would lead to him becoming something completely different. He prayed that he would keep his mind intact as he found the thought of becoming a tracker driven only by instinct very repulsive. Becoming one would be simply vile. The tech approached Kapowski first and he closed his eyes while tensing his muscles. He was unable to stop himself peeking as the needle slid into his arm and then he held his breath as the tech pushed the plunger and the clear innocent looking liquid entered his veins. He believed he could feel the progress of the fluid through his veins and he began to sweat. His pulse rate increased, his heart beat faster and his breathing became fast and shallow. From experience, he expected the changes to start within the hour and he leaned back in the chair. Sweat dripped down his face as he waited for it to start. He vowed he would get his own back for this betrayal.

In contrast, Barb expected an inoculation and being a little on the squeamish side, looked toward the corner of the room and hummed lightly as the tech slid the needle into her arm. She was unaware of it being over and had to wait to be told that it was. Relieved, she leaned back in the chair and somehow drifted into sleep. Kapowski even heard her snore lightly and wondered who she was and why they were being processed together.

Davidson slipped into the room silently and approached Kapowski from behind gaining pleasure from his vulnerable state.

"Comfortable detective?" he whispered. Kapowski jumped and asked,

"Where did you come from you backstabbing mongrel?"

"Now Captain, sour grapes do not suit you, you are usually a man of such dignity."

"Cut the rubbish, we both know you're a snake. What are you changing me into?" Kapowski demanded.

"Nothing, we aren't actually changing the two of you," Davidson informed him.

"I'm not as dumb as the woman behind me. I know you have given us something other than vaccinations".

"Do you know the story of Troy?" Davidson asked.

"What's history got to do with this?" Kapowski asked genuinely confused.

"Let's just say Captain that the cryptid camp is our Troy and you are our horse"

Becoming noticeably paler, Kapowski replied, "Cut out the theatrics and just tell me what you've done?"

"You ruin my fun, you know that Captain? You are taking this so seriously, but I suppose you are not as relaxed as I."

"For God's sake Davidson, what have you done to me?" Kapowski shouted.

Barb jerked awake and gave them both a disgusted look. "What's wrong?"

"Nothing to worry about Barbara" Davidson reassured her in a patronising tone. He unfastened her restraints. "Why don't you go with the tech Barbara and finish your rest?" Barb went out without any complaint at all.

"Back to you Captain," Davidson said brightly, obviously enjoying the cat and mouse game he was playing. Kapowski just glared at him. "Really, you aren't any fun. We have given you a virus detective, something to take to the cryptids."

Kapowski cleared his throat and spat on the floor. "What makes you think I will play your game?" he asked, with obvious contempt in his voice.

"Well, I can cure you, if you get back in time that is."

"Traitor!" was all Kapowski could manage.

"Absolutely," Davidson laughed as he started to leave, and then to the tech, "release him when he calms down." With that he left.

****

The lab appeared small when filled with the bulk of Keanos and his discomfort at being in such close quarters was tangible. It was the first time Mike had seen him not entirely comfortable. He had with him a sealed jar and he held this out to Mike.

"Treat it with respect," he instructed. "It is all that is left of my kinsman, the first to fall to the virus." Taking it gently, Mike simply nodded clearly communicating his understanding. As he turned, Keanos placed a hand on his shoulder and said, "I am sorry for your loss."

Still not trusting himself to speak, Mike set the jar on a bench and began to lose himself in his work. He felt her passing much more keenly than he would have thought. Phoebe had saved him, and he would be grateful to her for a very long time. The equipment was antiquated, and everything took twice as long as it should, but he could still see progress as he worked. The virus was basically a derivative of Actinomycosis. It had been genetically manipulated to attack the cryptids only and it had been enhanced to produce a strain that resulted in extreme abscesses forming. The bacteria had the unique property that it could move from one layer of tissue to another, regardless of the site of the infection. The result was the organism developed abscesses both internally and externally over most available sites. The bacteria literally turned the infected into one huge walking sore. The infected creatures died quickly. It was merciful they did.

Mike was glad he had treated the tissue as a biohazard. Although the bacteria were developed to attack cryptids, he knew from experience that once released, such genetically manipulated diseases could mutate of their own accord. If this one attacked human DNA it could result in a plague as devastating as the Black Death had been in the Middle Ages. It bothered him that the boy they had come across was a naturally occurring changeling. More specifically it bothered him that if the boy became infected then it could feasibly cross the species barrier in one leap. He needed to know if the bacteria would now attack the cryptid DNA in the changelings. If it did then cross infection of human DNA was a real possibility. If the changeling ability had leached into the eco system, then so could the bacteria and they could have a serious problem. That had not been a factor when the bacteria had originally been released as changelings had not yet existed, but now it was possible the human population could be wiped out. Whoever created it had been very short sighted. On the bright side, these bacteria could unite both sides when they started dying in their thousands.

Mike first introduced the bacteria to Keanos' blood and watched as his natural antibodies easily fought the infection as he had been previously exposed. He then introduced it to a sample of Thanatos's blood, and this was quickly overcome with the bacteria multiplying and overwhelming any natural defences. It appeared that the bacteria would attack any organism that had a percentage of cryptid DNA. Just out of curiosity he decided to see what would happen if he introduced the bacteria to his own blood. The bacteria seemed to have no effect and he was confident that it attacked cryptid genetic material only, whether that constituted whole or part of the genetic material in question. He really wanted to try the bacteria on the boy's blood but without more data dare not. He did not want to risk creating the very virus he was afraid may develop unaided. It was best if he waited until they could set up a functioning isolation lab. It would minimise the risk of releasing something nasty of his own creation. He now needed to concentrate on developing a vaccine to protect the changelings. That however was not going to happen while he was so tired. Gathering all the petri dishes, he placed them in the fridge and went to lie down for the night.

****

Will waded through the sewers. He kept his eyes fixed ahead as he did not want to become too well acquainted with the debris that shared the water with him. Getting up close and personal with excrement was not what he had in mind when he moved in with Mike. It had been fun for the short time they had together, but he hadn't really wanted it to last much longer. Pulling a face, he moved sideways to let a particularly large object float by. It was better to avoid contact with some things. After a while, he saw daylight ahead. It was the exit he had always known was there. As he approached the end of the pipe, he withdrew a screwdriver from his pocket. He would need it to detach the wire mesh that stopped any creature without a permit entering the city. Once on the outside, he reattached the mesh. He did not want anyone finding the misplaced cover and following him to where he went next.

The sewer flowed into a small stream which made its way to a river. Will followed it to the river entrance and then wadded upstream until he felt it was safe to scale the banks and walk on dry land. On his way up the bank he caught his hand awkwardly between a rock and a tree stump. Shaking his right hand, he sucked his second finger and pulled the remains of the nail from it. He was not pleased; it would take a while to re-grow and that may prove to be a nuisance. This whole day was proving to be difficult but, unfocusing on his own problems, he was very worried about Barb. He did not trust Davidson one bit and the fact that he had picked Barb up worried him deeply. Trudging through the undergrowth, he alternated between worrying about Barb and worrying even more about Mike. By the time he reached his intended destination he was exhausted, and the day was almost over. There was still a while to go but the abandoned petrol station was where he had chosen to hide his motorbike and with this, he could reach the farmhouse without too much exertion.

It had been his grandparent's house. When things had first started to decline, they had refused to retreat to the city and when the wall had gone up around Birmingham they had stubbornly remained in their farmhouse. Will had discovered the farmhouse much later, after his grandparents and mother had all died. His mother had inherited his grandparents' stubbornness and had retained a key to the property. For many years, she had sneaked out of the city to keep the place in order. When she died, she had left him a map of the place and the key. He had immediately seen its value as a place to run to if trouble ever found him. Now was a good time to disappear for a while. It had always been a little remote and as such had its own independent generator. His grandfather had, at one time, been worried about a nuclear war and he had stockpiled enough canned food to feed a small army for about fifty years. The stockpile had never been discovered as it had been legitimately purchased years before any shortages. Those trying to stockpile after shortages had become a problem and were usually executed without trial. His grandfather had technically committed no crime and with the remoteness of the farmhouse there were no neighbours to complain either. It really was the perfect spot.

When he first arrived, despite his tiredness he made sure he put the bike in the barn well away from any prying eyes. You never knew these days if any wandering changeling would try to trade knowledge of this place with the IGH. Having secured the bike, he let himself in the house and headed straight up to the main bedroom. He needed a shower. He particularly hated the stench of the sewer and wanted to rid himself of it as quickly as possible. Refreshed, he wrapped himself in a dressing gown and busied himself in preparing a light meal. He felt perfectly relaxed and at home here and thought he would not be too upset if he never returned to Birmingham.

✳✳✳✳

Confident in her plan to rid herself of the opposition, Philomena poured herself a red wine. It was a luxury she allowed herself on rare occasions but tonight she felt justified. The continued stability of established order needed celebration. Once the changelings were back in their place, she would have a tracker assigned to the vagrant that had annoyed her earlier. She would she thought have him brought back to headquarters, she would enjoy watching him squirm as she allowed her banshees to play with him. The only slight sadness was the lack of a companion with which to celebrate. She knew she could have called Davidson at any time but although he was useful, she detested the man. He had even been slimy as a child which was saying something. No, she had hoped that something would have developed between herself and Caldwell. He was a lot younger than she, but she prided herself on making the best of what nature had given her. The odd tuck and lift had assisted.

What really attracted her was Mike's mind. He was the best code writer they had. He had an ability which verged on the artistic. Every change he made had been successful. That was why she had assigned Phoebe to keep an eye on him. Although she liked him, she trusted no-one, particularly no one that might have the ability to outsmart her. She had removed Phoebe because she was becoming too attached and Philomena could not allow that. It was a shame that Caldwell felt it necessary to leave the protection of the IGH in search of something as ludicrous as love. Drinking deeply, she mourned the loss of what could have been with him, still there was time for him to return home. She would not make it too easy though, he would have to grovel before she forgave him. Calling for Davidson, she ordered a single night companion, a young man to amuse herself with.

Davidson complied as usual. He would do what she asked, but he did not understand why she did not see his love for her. He would give almost anything to feel her lips touch his own and her breath caress his neck. He wanted to run his hands over her firm body. For a woman her age, she had kept her body firm and always made the best of her features. His heart ached to hold her close and breathe in the essence of her beautiful, powerful, dark and twisted soul.

Changelings

Chapter 17

Kapowski glared at his escort as they all sat on board another specially commissioned train to Manchester. Barbara was across the table and prattled on about Caldwell. She still had no idea what they had done to her. He almost felt that she deserved to die if she were indeed that stupid. Kapowski wanted to tell her and ruin their plans, but he wanted to have a good chance of escape when he made his move and having her upset may slow him down. He decided it was best to say nothing for now. Davidson had made it clear that if he did anything to jeopardise the success of the mission then the cure would become lost to him but Kapowski was positive the man would go back on this promise no matter the outcome of his and Barb's mission. He was left, for the moment, with simply glaring at the world to make his displeasure known.

****

Mike sat looking at the cultures from the night before. All of them had grown bacteria, including the one that contained his blood. What concerned him was it looked like anyone could contract the bacteria and although there was less of his blood for the bacteria to grow on, it was still present. A second possibility crept around the edges of his mind. He could somehow have a small amount of cryptid DNA in his bloodstream and the image of the Banshee bleeding above him as he fought remained stubbornly in his conscious mind. He could not recall if any had entered his mouth. For all he knew he could experience a change like that experienced by David Grey. He drew more of his own blood for further analysis.

****

Will sat having breakfast and looking at his mobile. He had the overwhelming urge to phone Barb but knew if he did, they would be able to pinpoint his position. His conscience would not let him just forget her, and he finally decided to take a trip on the bike and phone her from a safe distance. He decided that the deserted Manchester would provide reasonable cover and although it would take a few hours to get there, it would probably be worth the trip. Carrying petrol to barn, going sooner rather than later seemed best. The quicker he set off the quicker he could make a safe return. He had made a trip to Manchester before, just from pure curiosity and found it to be an eerie place of ghosts. He followed the same old map he had used on that previous occasion. He did not, however, travel at full speed. The old road systems had not been repaired for a long time and most had serious deterioration that could throw him if he hit a bad spot at too high a speed. In days gone by, it would have been a pleasant day trip but now it was a fraught ride.

This far North the country was virtually deserted. Remaining populations had concentrated in southern areas but Birmingham and not London had become the new capital. London experienced high casualty levels during the food riots that proved almost impossible to clear. In the end, it had deteriorated into a giant graveyard which unlike other deserted cities made it almost impossible to reclaim. Once everything became more fully decomposed reclamation would be relatively simple. It was a matter of waiting. For Will it meant that he travelled in solitude and virtual silence. Much of the land further south was farmed by the changelings but the North had reverted to wild land or as wild as England ever became. Will did not pay much attention to the passing landscape, too engaged in his own concerns. Surviving in the modern world took most of his energy and appreciating the beauty of the great outdoors was not on his agenda. Had he done so, he might have noted the butterfly skipping along the hedgerow. An impossible creature that was supposedly extinct.

****

Davidson sat at his desk. He loved working in the early morning before any other employees entered the IGH headquarters. This morning he wanted to recall the information snake from Caldwell's office. It cost a lot to run such sophisticated surveillance equipment and since it looked like Caldwell would not be returning, it made economic sense to recall and repurpose the hardware. He did not want office staff becoming aware that one of the senior staff had been under surveillance. It would make them unnecessarily nervous and that would be counterproductive. They would most likely underperform if they felt insecure. It was in the best interests of the IGH to promote someone into Caldwell's position quickly. The office staff would gossip but continuity would be secure. Davidson intended spending this time going through the possible candidates and selecting one by the time the usual office staff started work. He could have the office door plaque changed in minutes and he intended to do so. He also intended to start a rumour that Caldwell had deliberately high jacked other biologist's codes so that all his changelings were viable. He was going to make it look like Caldwell was a cheat. When Davidson had finished, records showed Caldwell was personally responsible for hundreds of botched changes and guilty of passing these off as others work while recording their successes as his own. It didn't matter what the reality was, just what the record showed. He had also selected his candidate for Caldwell's replacement. It was a young woman by the name of Fay Miller. She was tall slim and blonde, he was sure the Director would approve her appointment. The young woman had looks and brains, a winning combination by anyone's standard. One phone call and the office sign was changed.

****

The train arrived at Manchester and Kapowski and Barbara were escorted to Albert Square. It seemed to be the most logical choice to meet the cryptids. The sergeant in charge was nervous and kept turning to check his perimeter. Kapowski was amused by their behaviour and drew some sadistic pleasure at watching their discomfort. He was already identifying himself as separate to the officers and he supposed, closer to the outlaws which in this case were the changelings. He was a pragmatist and decided to take the initiative as soon as the opportunity presented itself. It did not take long. The sergeant's attention was taken by activity down one of the many side streets. Ordering a guard to watch Kapowski and Barbara, he took the main defence down the street to investigate. Taking a rock in his hand, Kapowski rendered the first guard unconscious without difficulty but the second guard had his weapon focused on Kapowski before he could be tackled in a similar fashion.

"You don't want to shoot me," Kapowski told him.

"Why not?" the officer asked.

"For one thing, I will regain my seniority soon and then I could commission your change." Kapowski informed him.

"Not likely and not if you're dead," the officer replied. Nodding his agreement, Kapowski continued, "Then there's the disease they have infected us with, you wouldn't want to get that," he added nonchalantly.

"Disease?" Barb shouted, fear evident in her voice. Kapowski hoped she would remain quiet and not mess this up, but as it turned out she proved to be a useful distraction. The guard's attention was momentarily drawn to her sudden outburst giving Kapowski the chance to dive at the officer. He forced the rifle upward and by sheer weight, pushed the man onto his back. Then, taking the rifle, he reversed the muzzle and shot. Barb simply stood with her mouth open.

"Come on!" Kapowski ordered, pulling her along behind him.

"But," was all she managed. Kapowski replied, "look, just accept for now we are in the same boat and they are not your friends," then seeing the uncertain look still on her face changed tack and simply ordered her, "Shut up and run, I'll explain properly later." Looking around, Barb could not see a better option. When the sergeant returned, he would be very unhappy to find his men dead, so she started to totter after Kapowski. As soon as they were out of sight, Kapowski took her shoes and broke off the heels. Barb was unhappy as they had cost her, well Mike really, almost a month's wages but she did have to admit she could run faster. Kapowski took as many turns as he could, just to throw off pursuit.

Returning to the square, the sergeant examined his men with his boot, vigorously pushing each in turn. He was sure they were both dead and satisfied he called a return to the train. The dead men's families would receive extra benefits for a month to compensate their loss, but risk was a part of being an officer. Kapowski could have just knocked them out. No one could have foreseen that he would find it necessary to kill them to escape. It was partly the officer's own fault. They did not have to resist too strenuously but then, perhaps it was more realistic that they had. The main thing was that the mission had been accomplished. Escort the prisoner to the square and afford an opportunity to escape. The cryptids would soon take two refugees into their fold and then the bacteria infection would do the rest. Satisfied the mission was a success and had been relatively straightforward the sergeant decided to reward his men with a bottle or two of whisky and perhaps a companion for the night for himself. Walking back, he began to whistle.

****

Kapowski was aware that they were not being followed and he slowed the pace, so Barb found it easier to keep up. He thought it was because they were afraid of venturing too far into this wasteland, but he soon rejected the idea. He was talking about hardened IGH men. He had to accept that they did not want to follow but even that was incomplete logic. He had to admit that they had no orders to follow, which in turn meant they had accomplished their mission. Kapowski could kick himself. They had delivered him and Barb to where they wanted them, fugitives to be accepted into the fugitive group. He had just followed the script the Director had wanted him to and escaped. He cursed his own stupidity. They would be accepted because of Barb's connection to Mike and it was evident the Director had never intended either of them to return and that realisation made Kapowski determined to return and deliver a nasty package back to her and her infernal IGH. After a while Kapowski broke the silence and shared with Barb what he knew and his thoughts on the subject. She began to cry.

"Am I going to lose my looks?" she asked.

"How should I know," Kapowski said, exasperated that she was still so focused on herself and how she looked.

"Don't shout at me like that," she continued, "they are all I have to get by with."

Oh lord! He never thought he would be comforting a woman like this, but he put his arm around her and made shushing noises to offer his support. He hoped she never told anyone he had a soft side. "Look," he said, "you have me and whatever happens. I'll look after you." Drying her tears, she nodded gratefully, and he continued to look for a place for them to stay the night. He realised he really did want to look after her and briefly wondered if it was the virus affecting his brain.

✳✳✳✳

Will entered the outskirts of Manchester around noon. He wanted to make it to the centre to provide maximum camouflage. Parking his bike outside a movie theatre he decided to make the call from inside. That was his first mistake. Entering through the broken glass doors he removed his helmet, his second mistake. As he unzipped his jacket to retrieve his mobile, he was hit swiftly from behind.

He was not out for long and rubbing the back of his head he sat up in what appeared to be a nest. Looking at him curiously was an owl man or in this case, more accurately, a woman. He tried smiling at her but that had no effect at all, so then he said, "Hi!" which made her hop backwards and gave him a view of the rest of the place he was in. Thankfully, he appeared to be in a tunnel. He thought 'thankfully' because he could have been on the top of anything in a nest and he was very scared of heights. He was, as he had already noticed, being watched by an owl. He used the edge of the nest to steady himself as he started to climb out. This did get a reaction and she made it obvious that he was to remain inside the nest. Sitting back down, he was relieved to be provided with a drink and then, with nothing else to do, he closely examined every inch of his temporary abode. It, not being very big, did not take long, but the exercise did provide him with a book to read and pass the time. Leaning against the side for comfort he began to read what looked like a diary. All the time Maia watched him closely. She did not trust the humans at all and for a deserted city there was a lot of human traffic passing through. Looking over the top of the book to check if she had become tired, Will was greeted with her brown eyes fixed upon him. He tried his most engaging boyish smile that disarmed any woman he had ever come into contact with. She simply tilted her head sideways. This he decided could take a while and he settled in for a long reading stint.

Will perused the book. It was a story about some guy called David Grey; he was a wolf changeling who could transform whenever he wished. Will became bored very quickly and the story did not even seem possible. He had never been into science fiction or fantasy. He preferred a good romance. Tossing the book over his shoulder made the owl woman come dashing forward.

"Careful," she told him.

"Oh, now you speak," Will retorted a little peeved.

"It's my friend's diary," she told him in explanation.

"Huh," Will snorted looking down his nose at her and flipping his head in a disbelieving fashion, "pull the other one it's got bells on," he told her.

"What other one?" she asked completely puzzled.

"Have you never heard the saying?" he retorted. "Other leg silly."

Maia peered over the nest, "but neither have bells," she told him still with a puzzled tone to her voice.

"It's not a literal comment," he tried to explain. He had not realised that owls were devoid of a sense of humour. Still the incident had broken the ice and Will felt like he could ask her some questions. He decided to introduce himself, "I'm Will, by the way."

Maia hesitated, she had been asked to watch him … not chat, but he seemed to be quite nice for a human and she thought exchanging pleasantries would be fine. "Maia," she returned.

"Nice to meet you," Will tried.

"You too," she replied.

Now for a difficult one Will thought, "Do you know who hit me?"

Looking a little sheepish, she answered, "It was one of the younger changelings and I think they mistook you for a lone security officer."

It was Will's turn to look puzzled, "but I look nothing like them."

"No, you don't, but what were you doing wandering around an abandoned city?" Maia asked.

"It's a long story hon," Will began. "I was trying to phone my companion; I think she was arrested. Our boss, Mike, has been out of town,"

"Mike who?" Maia asked, it all seemed a little bit of a coincidence.

"Mike Caldwell," Will replied. Maia was stunned and almost fell from the edge of the nest.

****

Kapowski found a hotel where they could sleep for the night. He simply leaned behind the reception desk and took a handful of first floor room keys. For some reason, he felt safer just off ground level; you never knew what kinds of creatures prowled at night especially in a place like this. Any number of early changelings could have been abandoned around here.

The first room they entered had two skeletons in the bed. The second room had a strange smell the instant they opened the door and for that reason they did not even open the next two rooms. They settled on Room 5.

Apart from a little dust, the room was very comfortable and for the first time Barb questioned the society she took for granted. She wondered why everyone was crammed into Birmingham and why they did not start to reclaim some of the other cities now the population was on the increase and food supplies more reliable. Kapowski told her it was about control, but she found it difficult to accept that the Director would make so many lives miserable just to control them.

In a way Kapowski envied her simplicity, while at the same time finding it very naive and very attractive. He wanted to protect her, and at the same time was wondering if she was doing something to him on purpose to make him feel that way. Later they sat together in bed, Kapowski was sure they were being watched but he was unable, to make out by whom or indeed how. He wanted to call out, 'take to me to your leader', but it sounded so lame he was embarrassed. In the end, he told Barb of his feelings. She just told him it was overtiredness and to go to sleep. He dreamt of revenge and a land where he was the king and most bizarrely, Barb was his queen.

They woke early to the sun's rays streaming through the window and to what Barb initially thought was a rat watching them. She was about to scream when she noticed this rat had a cute bushy tail instead of the usual skin creeping rope. Then as the sunlight hit its coat she also realised it had red fur. "How Cute," she exclaimed. Barb was growing on Kapowski and he found her cute. He watched her walk over to the window to get a closer look at the creature and Kapowski followed her with his eyes. It was then that Kapowski saw the shadow of Cerberus pass over the window. He pulled her back into the room.

"Why did you do that?" she asked, "I thought we wanted to see them."

"Not yet," he said. "We need to talk to them at a distance to explain about the infection." Kapowski told her.

"Oh," she said. "I'd almost forgotten."

They dressed quickly and headed down toward the lobby. Stepping outside they were greeted by Keanos. Barb, who had not seen anything like him before, automatically drew closer to Kapowski. He took hold of her hand in a gesture of reassurance.

"What message do you bring?" he asked without ceremony.

Kapowski backed away from him and Keanos started forward. Gesturing wildly Kapowski cried, "Stop!" Keanos stopped, not because he obeyed men but because of the obvious distress in Kapowski's tone.

"We bring death," Kapowski shouted, somewhat overdramatically. "They have made us carriers of a disease aimed at killing all the changelings"

"I know the one," Keanos replied and he ordered all changelings to return to the tunnels. "You can let my people near you," he informed them. "We are immune."

"I think they may have changed it since last time," Kapowski said "Best keep your distance to be safe."

"In that case I will take you to Caldwell and his lab, he is considering the problem for us." With that, Keanos came forward and knelt so that they could climb on his back. Barb now calmer since it was obvious, he meant them no harm commented, "it's nice to meet a gentleman, even out here."

Kapowski asked Kenos, "Is it wise putting yourself at risk through direct contact with us?"

Smiling, Keanos replied, "No-one is indispensable. How do you suggest I ask one of my men to risk themselves if I am not willing to do so?"

"You could order them." Kapowski said. Throwing his head back, Keanos laughed. "It is clear you lack understanding of the terms integrity and leadership. Perhaps if you are with us long enough you will learn what true leadership is." With that, he galloped through the streets towards the University. Barb held tightly to Kapowski's waist and wondered how he was managing to hold on.

* * * *

Maia decided to take Will to Mike's lab. The strange human claimed to know him, and she wanted to find out how well before deciding whether to trust him or not. She however did not offer the human a lift instead she provided him with an escort, a slightly updated model of the guardian which worked on the door at the house of delights. Will eyed him sceptically and leaning over to Maia asked in a conspiratorial tone, "He isn't going to eat me, is he?"

Maia found this most amusing and it took her several seconds to regain her composure. "I think he will be more afraid of you than you of him," she told Will.

"Honey I think you are very wrong on that score," He did obediently follow them to the surface. "Hon, why don't I ride my bike? It will be a lot quicker and a lot less effort than walking." Will asked Maia.

Mai was tempted to say no, she could not guarantee that he would follow her once mobile, but she had to admit that the idea made sense. When he saw her hesitation Will added, "I promise to follow you and bear boy can hop on the back."

Maia gave in and Will's bike was brought to him. He checked the brake and fuel lines carefully. He wanted to make sure the changelings had not damaged anything when they had moved it. Satisfied he mounted and waited for the bear to sit behind him. The bear was very slow and unsure. Its amused Will that such a powerful looking creature could be so unsure and hesitant. He would have thought its nature would be to be much more assertive. He enjoyed the feel of all those muscles wrapped around him and in other circumstances it could have been very pleasant indeed.

They had travelled in convoy across half of the city when Will noticed movement. For a supposedly abandoned place it was incredibly alive. Alive with a variety of creatures he had not known were possible. He saw the same red rat with a bushy tail that Barb had thought cute only an hour ago. If he hadn't known better, he would have sworn it was a red squirrel that he had seen illustrated in books. Then it ran in front of him and in his eagerness to avoid it he skidded across the street and unseated both the bear and himself. Maia seeing the accident flew back to find out what had happened.

****

Cerberus had taken an early morning flight around the city to relieve his boredom. Sentry duty while Thanatos and Caldwell pottered with test tubes and potions which was proving very boring. He longed to take the fight to the doors of the IGH and do battle properly. He was a man of action not thought, but Keanos was behind what Mike was doing. It had not been long since he had landed when he saw the unmistakable form of the cryptid gallop into view. His sight was much keener than a human and he could see two figures on the cryptids back. He did not quite know how he knew but he had the distinct feeling it was Keanos and so he flew to meet them. Keanos, however, ordered him back with uncharacteristic harshness and sent him to fetch Caldwell. Grumbling he clumped around inside to do as he was told.

****

Mike installed them both in isolation. Kapowski and Barb could be together since they were the carriers and Keanos he housed alone. Barb refused to talk to Mike at all, blaming him for her present predicament. Kapowski was in no mood to persuade her otherwise as he had started to fall in love with her and he was also more than a little mistrustful of the cryptid's motives. Not too long ago they had been on opposite sides and now they were unlikely allies.

At first Mike felt pangs of jealousy at the obvious connection between Barb and Kapowski but he quickly admitted to himself that it was not because he loved or even particularly liked Barb anymore. It really was because she belonged to him and he recognised that this was a flaw of his, and he did not want to repeat the same mistake he had made in relation to Phoebe. He was determined to be a better person and in some small way honour her sacrifice.

Sutton kept walking past the isolation rooms and glaring at Kapowski. He did not think the man was on anyone's side but his own. He was also convinced he would hurt the people that Sutton had come to think of as friends, and he was not going to fall for his play acting and let that happen without opposition.

On one of Sutton's passes he was putting on a particularly good display of displeasure when from behind him a new voice exclaimed,

"Barb, honey, what a relief to see you." The person tried to elbow his way past Sutton. Sutton grabbed him and pushed him back, "They're infected you fool, you can't go in." He told Will.

"OK Mr Grumpy, no need to lose your shirt," Will said and then said to Barb. "Is he right hon? Have they given you something nasty?" Barb took one look and burst into tears. Kapowski pulled her into his arms and patted her back until she could bring herself to stop crying and join in the general discussion again. Kapowski was genuinely worried about her. If things were not resolved soon, he did not think she would hold up psychologically. While Kapowski comforted Barb it fell to Mike to bring Will up to speed. Sutton joined Cerberus to scowl some more at the world and they had a companionable five minutes complaining session about all the others. It was not productive, but it made the two of them feel better and by the end they were appreciably happier. Mike was impressed with how self-sufficient Will had proven to be and even Sutton gave him some grudging respect. He walked over and punched his shoulder.

Will held the spot and rubbing it said, "Thanks, I think."

Mike told Will, "I think it means he likes you."

"Yeah, made it at last," Will replied sarcastically, but secretly he was pleased.

Mike and Thanatos were concerned the infection could be airborne and as such it may already be infecting the changelings. Keanos did not agree; if it was airborne then it would have been in the atmosphere and infecting them ever since the first cryptids died. Although Mike liked his optimism, he did not share it. If Mike was going to solve the puzzle in time, he needed better equipment and the only place to get it was from the IGH. Someone needed to go and steal what they needed. It was not without risk and Mike was determined that he personally would take the risk. He had the biggest amends to make.

Keanos agreed to let one cryptid accompany them and guide them through the shadow lands. It was the quickest and safest way to travel. It was also their best chance of gaining entry to Birmingham undetected. Thanatos had also volunteered to take the risk because he knew the equipment they needed. He could collect this while Mike downloaded research files that would be useful. Sutton would come to provide protection. It was decided Will would remain in Manchester to look after the infected.

Chapter 18

Viewed from the shadows, the IGH looked menacing, and Mike wondered how much of that perception was due to his own changed viewpoint. In the not too distant past, he had seen it as his home and experienced pride at working within its walls. Life had strange ways of happening. There was no direct access from the shadow lands to the interior of the IGH and so the group had to exit in a nearby alley. They waited until most employees had left the building for the night and then Mike proposed they should try simply walking in using his access codes. It was Sutton that suggested they use his.

"You have access to the IGH?" Mike asked, shocked.

"The police have authority over everyone," Sutton informed him. "They don't use it often. Most just do what the Director says these days, but it wasn't always like that."

"Not over the Director?" Mike said.

"Technically, even over her." Sutton told him. Mike thought he'd heard it all, but the surprises just kept on coming. He wondered if the revelations would ever stop.

"What do you mean technically?" Mike asked.

"Well we have top level clearance over all files, we are just never expected to use it." Mike's brain was working overtime. "Then with your access we can get everything we need?"

"Yes, but it would probably be safer if we went to police headquarters and downloaded it from there. If we do here inside IGH, it may raise red flags in the IGH itself." Sutton told him.

"Then that's where we will go, are you ok getting the equipment?" Mike asked Thanatos.

"More than," he replied.

"Settled then," Mike said. "We meet back here in two hours, everyone agreed?" They all nodded. "If you don't have everything we need by then, just leave it. We need to get back." Again, they all agreed then went their separate ways.

****

Thanatos and the cryptid escort entered the IGH through the sewers, along the same path Thanatos had used to rescue Cerberus. Anyone else would have protected this route, but the IGH was so arrogant they did not expect it to be used again. They had not even repaired the place where the Oldfield/Maxwell creature had entered. As a result, accessing the lower labs was almost child's play and they were very quickly able to source biohazard suits and the other essential supplies they had come for. Once back at the alleyway, Thanatos sent the cryptid ahead with the supplies while he waited for the others.

****

Mike and Sutton made their way to headquarters and walked inside as if nothing was amiss. Mac looked up from the desk and nodding in Sutton's direction, returned to reading his paper without comment. Sutton walked straight over to his terminal and began accessing and copying all top level IGH files. He confided to Mike that he thought it was better to transfer as much as possible before they were spotted, and someone questioned what they were doing rather than waste time searching for only relevant information. He started several computers in the room and started each one downloading material.

****

Alone at his desk in the IGH, Davidson noticed the sudden increase in computer activity. It took only seconds to realise someone was copying IGH files. Davidson did not immediately think to see where the access was taking place. After all, as far as he knew any opposition was in the wilderness with their new cryptid friends. He set about cancelling Caldwell's security clearance just in case they had any way of accessing files from a remote location. As with all bureaucracies this required the completion of several forms. Davidson was a little angry with himself for not doing this sooner. Finally, Caldwell was removed from the system and designated as non-functioning personnel. Davidson returned to monitoring downloads expecting that it had now ceased. He was disappointed as it was evident that files were still being copied and not just Caldwell's files. Kicking his chair, he cursed and began to trace the location of the download activity. To his surprise it registered as Police Headquarters. He had not expected that result and wondered who over there would have the audacity to check up on the IGH and its activities. It was time, he felt, to show the Director exactly what he was made of. Taking control of this situation, he decided, would make her notice him at last.

****

Having completed downloading all the information, Sutton and Caldwell began readying to leave. As they were packing information cubes into their backpacks Mac came in the office. He was a little hesitant in his manner.

"Sutton?" he ventured. "None of my business I know but you might be as well taking the rear exit."

"Thanks Mac," Sutton said, patting his arm. Mac turned to take his position back at his desk with a tear at the corner of his eye. Sutton did not need to see the tear to know Mac was a loyal friend. It was not something men of their age were comfortable with expressing although they both thought highly of one another.

"This way," Sutton instructed Mike, leading him to the rear of the office building.

As Sutton and Mike left by the back-entrance Davidson came in the front.

"Rather late for a citizen," Mac commented.

"I am not an ordinary citizen," Davidson barked as he pressed his palm against the identification screen. Mac knew who he was but as the name and position were emblazoned across his screen he said, "I beg your pardon sir, I did not recognise you at this late hour. How can I help?" in the most courteous tone he could manage.

Somewhat mollified, Davidson said, "Who is in the building tonight?"

"Just the usual staff sir," Mac replied, unhelpfully

"Exactly who is that?" Davidson insisted coldly.

"I am afraid sir; I cannot give you that information without further clearance. Please take a seat and I will get someone who can help." Mac informed him.

"I... Do... Not... Take... Seats!" Davidson almost spat at him.

"I am sorry sir, but I am not cleared to deal with your enquiry," Mac insisted.

"Just let us in to search then," Davidson replied.

"I am sorry sir, but I am not cleared to make that decision." Mac continued.

"Then let me make it for you," Davidson said losing all patience and levelling a pistol at Mac's forehead. He was not prepared for what happened next. A siren began to wail, red lights flashed and small insect like robots resembling the library mites pounced on Davidson and his men. They scurried up their legs and needles were expertly inserted into thighs. Davidson and his men danced around trying to dislodge them but quickly began to lose consciousness as the sedatives took effect. The robots then carried them to the cells below police headquarters.

Anti-terrorist legislation dictated that anyone threatening a police officer with a weapon received a mandatory life sentence. Since it was no longer cost effective to feed any prisoners, that sentence had been commuted to humane euthanasia as changing such hardened criminals was too risky. The basic personality could remain intact through the process and a suicidal or homicidal tracker or owl was not something anyone was in a hurry to produce. A trial was not even necessary, and sentence could be complete before law abiding citizens rose for the day's work. Mac shook his head. The younger generation really ought to be more careful. They should familiarise themselves with all aspects of the law. No one was above the law and once you broke the law you had to accept the consequences. He didn't think even the Director would be able to get him out of this one. He might even be euthanised before she knew anything about it. The process was fully automated. Mac began to hum as he organised his papers. It served the sanctimonious prat right and it had given his faith in justice a much-needed boost.

****

Unhindered, Mike and Sutton ran through the dark streets. Mike looked up at the hundreds of flats and wondered what the occupants were doing and thinking right now. Just a short time ago he had been one of them and now he was a fugitive and the adrenaline he felt in his bloodstream made him feel alive. All the walking and fresh air he had been getting was already having an effect and he loved the feel of real, unfiltered air in his lungs. The air conditioning, he had previously breathed without thought was a poor reflection of what was available in the great outdoors. He had rarely ventured out before, never mind enjoyed running outside. Now the great outdoors was his home. He also liked the concept of adventure and right now he felt exhilarated as he was in the middle of the biggest adventure of his life. He was on the edge of achieving his goal and saving the lives of perhaps hundreds of cryptids, changelings and even humans. Even better than saving the anonymous he was having the adventure with friends. Not companions he had purchased but people who enjoyed being in his company and would even protect him if necessary. He could have gone his whole life in the company of strangers, and he was grateful he had discovered what a true friend was. Turning the last corner, his happiness was short-lived as standing at the entrance to the shadow world, was Thanatos with pistol raised at both of them. Sutton and Mike came to a sudden halt.

"I have been waiting for you," Thanatos informed them.

"What are you doing man?" Sutton asked, drawing Thanatos's and the guns focus onto himself. Realising his intention Mike asked, "I thought you were one of us?"

"One at a time gentleman," Thanatos told them. "I am not one of you nor am I with the Director." He told them congenially.

"Then what?" asked Sutton, frantically looking around to see if there was anything, he could use to get them out of this.

"I am, gentleman and always have been, looking out for number one. Why do you think she allowed me to live at the law courts all these years? It was because I could ruin her, and she knows it, she is both afraid and intrigued by me." Thanatos told them with pride.

"But you could stop this, be a saviour to your people." Sutton said.

"They, are not my people!" Thanatos shouted, "They are worms and I am a king, I don't want their thanks, I want real power."

"So why stop us?" Mike asked.

"I can't let you find a cure Caldwell. I must find it and I must be the one who controls who gets it. Besides they will all focus on hating the Director when they find out how she murdered you two." Thanatos concluded.

"You are just as bad as she is." Mike exclaimed.

"No. Technically she is as bad as me. You see it was all my idea, which she stole, but don't worry I have plans for her too. When I've finished, she will be begging me for help" Thanatos was obviously pleased with his plan.

"I wouldn't count on it," Mike informed him.

"Who is going to stop me?" Thanatos asked.

Mike nodded. "Behind you," he said

"I am not stupid enough to fall for that one," Thanatos informed him as Cerberus swooped out of the shadows and catching him by the shoulders, shook him with the intention of making him drop the weapon. Thanatos, however, kept hold of the laser and fired wildly as he spun. Sutton fell to his knees struck by a stray beam. Mike fell beside him but had no time to feel for a pulse as Thanatos continued to fire. Then, Thanatos momentarily regained control and fired upward, carving a deep arc into Cerberus' wing. A screech that chilled the soul of anyone who heard it, escaped Cerberus' throat and he dropped Thanatos to the ground. To save himself from injury, Thanatos let the laser fall to the ground and changed to his wolf form. Mike tried to reach the laser, but Thanatos landed, snarling between Mike and the weapon. The wolf leapt, and Mike held his broken arm in front of him allowing Thanatos to bite the pot that protected his flesh. The sharp teeth ripped at the protective jacket and eventually sank into the tender flesh, re-breaking the bone. Mike remembered thinking it was much worse than the library mite's bite. With his free hand, he tried hammering on Thanatos's head, but this did not have the desired effect. In fact, it had very little effect at all and Thanatos spun him around and threw him into the wall of the building. Winded, Mike crawled forward once again heading for the laser, but the wolf jumped on his back and began to bite the back of his neck. Blood poured from the wound and stained the floor of the alley. Just days ago, the old Mike would have given in by now welcoming the oblivion of unconsciousness and as a result lost his life. This new Mike had responsibilities to his friends. With a last rush of adrenaline, he pushed forward and reached his goal as his fingers closed around the laser. Slumping forward, he was unable to turn himself over to fire at Thanatos. Instead, he fired over his own shoulder and hoped the shot counted before he lost consciousness completely.

He could not have been out long because when he came to he had to struggle from under the dead weight that was now Thanatos. Heaving his body upright, he swayed and realised he had lost and was still losing a lot of blood. Cerberus had landed nearby and was in the process of retrieving the backpack full of information cubes. Cerberus' movements were hampered because he was also losing blood from the large gash in his wing. He came along side Mike and supporting each other they limped back into the shadow lands. Of Sutton, there was no sign.

$$****$$

Simon had been scavenging near to the alley and seeing Mike and Sutton run into the dead end he had crept closer to discover what was happening. He saw Thanatos raise the gun and watched as Sutton fell. Once the laser fell to the floor he crept along the edge of the alley to Sutton's prone form. He looked old and broken. Simon pulled him by the leg out of the alley. He did not want to leave him alone, as any one of the scavengers in the streets at such an hour would find him a delicious snack. He could not see his friend end his days in that manner and so he phoned police headquarters. It was Mac that answered and for the first time in his long career he left the station unattended and drove across the city to help. Together the two new allies, united in their efforts to save an old friend and in so doing forged new bonds.

****

Sutton awoke in his own bed and at first it seemed completely the wrong place to be. There was a bandage around his shoulder where he had been hit and in his one dilapidated chair sat Mac.

"Awake at last old timer?" he said.

"I am not an old timer," Sutton protested.

Laughing, Mac walked over to the bed and sat on the edge. "Seriously I am glad you didn't die" and then, before it could get any more sentimental, he went on to tell Sutton how Simon had come to the rescue. "I think you hit an ambush, you let your guard down old man. Anyway, old Simon picked you up and called me in to help. We brought you home and patched you up a little."

"What about the others?" Sutton rasped.

"OK I think, only one body, a wolf was found, along with a lot of blood. You were not even mentioned on the morning news. As far as everyone at the office knows you have just been on annual leave. Seems Kapowski has fallen from favour and no-one else is interested in the night shift guy." Mac finished.

Sutton pointed to the bottle of whiskey on the sideboard. Mac swivelled, grabbed it and obligingly handed it over. Sutton took a swig and chortled. He had come out of the whole thing without any long-term damage to his reputation. It was good to have friends. He would have laughed for a while longer if it had not hurt so much.

Mac stood to leave and as he put his coat on, he smiled and said, "Your due back on night shift in two days."

"Thanks Mac," Sutton said as the door closed behind his friend.

Changelings

****

Mike and Cerberus fell out of the shadows in a sorry state. Cerberus fell straight into the outstretched wing of Maia and recognising the worry she must have suffered he finally realised he had all he needed in her love. He dropped Mike and collapsed in front of her before he could articulate his thoughts.

Cerberus woke in his nest, the soft down cushioning his injured wing. He sat up stiffly and was immediately tended to by Maia. He opened his beak to speak but no words would come. Making soothing noises as she stroked his head, she helped him take a much-needed drink. Leaning back onto her comforting form he allowed her to care for him. Without her he was nothing.

****

Mike woke to find himself in bed. His neck was stiff and painful. He was unable to turn it at all and had to turn his whole body to look around him. Will was on hand to look after him and administer pain killers. He had only been unconscious for a few hours. He and Cerberus had arrived back so beaten up that all the cryptids and changelings were unnerved. Rumours were circulating that the Director had let them return as a warning, communicating that she was still clearly in charge and her authority was unchallengeable. They were all unsettled and with Keanos out of action they lacked direct leadership.

Once Mike was clearly in recovery, Will took one of the bear changelings to the city to check out the situation there. He changed his hair colour and borrowed a pair of glasses. It was the best he could do as a disguise. He was not sure what his status was or if they were still looking for him. He had to take every precaution he could. Once inside the city limits, he decided to go to Mike's flat first.

Changelings

✷✷✷✷

Walking up the steps was a surreal experience, not long ago he had belonged here but now it was as if he were a stranger. He tried his pass key on the lock with no success. Then he simply rang the bell. He had to admit the blond-haired person who answered the door was very fine and very at home in her new apartment. Making his apologies for disturbing her Will beat a hasty retreat. It was clear Mike was not going to be able to return to the city any time soon. Next stop was Sutton's place.

Stepping into the small flat Will wrinkled his nose. "Honey, you need help," He informed Sutton.

"I do fine," Sutton growled.

"If poor, dirty and stinking is fine then I agree with your hon," Will told him. Sutton growled some more but did not protest when Will made him go back to bed. Will then began to clean the flat, something that had not happened for a long time. The bear did all the heavy work, carrying years of junk down to the bins below. Will then took the bear on a scavenger hunt to the edge of the city. Using security card to gain access he borrowed the station's van. They then went through abandoned buildings retrieving everything Sutton lacked. Comfortable chairs, extra beds, and a dining table. Once the beds were in the spare room Will and the bear could catch some much-needed sleep. The next morning Will made Sutton breakfast in bed and then continued his efforts in his reformation of the old detective. He left the bear on guard with the strict instructions that Sutton was not to drink; and then Will went to participate in his favourite activity, shopping. He returned to the flat to find a very disgruntled but sober Sutton. Will didn't mind though and ordered Sutton to take a shower before he could eat. Satisfied with his efforts Will went back to report on Sutton's wellbeing.

✷✷✷✷

263

"Hey lover," Will called.

"In here," Mike replied, and Will walked in the room just in time to see Mike giving Barb her last injection.

"Will. Look," she said holding out her arm, "I'm no longer infectious."

"Wonderful Hon," Will replied patting her rear and then he teased, "a little bird tells me you're sweet on someone new." Giggling she nodded. "I don't think I've been in love before," she confided.

"That's brilliant Hon, when do you and Mike get married?" Will teased.

"Oh, it's not," Barb said, and then stopped. "It's not that I don't like you Mike," she continued, flustered.

Mike, Will and Kapowski all laughed. Kapowski took her hand and said, "Don't worry Barb, they are just teasing," and he led her from the room.

"Those two seem happy together," Will commented.

Nodding, Mike said, "Maybe I should be worried losing both my companions."

"What makes you think you have lost us both?" Will asked.

"Haven't I?" Mike countered.

"You know you don't really want a companion anymore," Will commented.

"No, that's true," Mike conceded. "But your newly revealed depths are intriguing."

"That's definitely me, Tall, dark, handsome and intriguing." Will said.

"True, but I'll kind of miss the old Will," Mike confessed.

"Oh, you don't get rid of me that easily lover, I'm going to be the messenger between the cryptids and Sutton. I'll be around for a long time; besides, you need someone to keep an eye on you too lover," Will finished with a flick of his head and a wink.

Recognising in himself the desire to hang onto Will, not from genuine affection but because Will was his, Mike made the conscious decision to let him go. "Come here," Mike said as he gave Will one final hug, indicating that he was truly willing to lose him. "I look forward to seeing you soon," he said and with a tear in his eye he turned to finish giving Keanos his last injection. He was, if he was not careful, in real danger of becoming a sentimental old fool.

****

Sutton entered the station and nodded in Mac's general direction. Mac nodded back; the graveyard shift had begun. Sutton eyed his in tray, it was evident that it had not been touched since he was last on duty. Picking up the top file he read the complaint that a small owl was making too much noise when hunting and it was keeping a family awake at night. He decided to go and investigate this complaint first.

Stepping into the cool night air he pulled his coat more closely around him. His shoulder still ached but his step was light. This was his territory and it was definitely more pleasant knowing Kapowski was not going to be around to ruin his night. He made his way through the familiar empty streets and enjoyed the sound of his echoing footsteps.

He saw Simon searching in a bin across in the alley and waving he started to walk towards him. Simon waved back and then returned his attention to his excavations. Sutton had intended thanking him for his help the other night, but it was obvious that Simon was not in the mood for prolonged human contact. Sutton was aware of his quirks and instead just whispered, "Thank you," as he passed by. He maintained his pace and did not look back, he had said all that was needed and did not need to upset this old friend. Simon nodded several times and then happily changed form and padded away, the lone wolf in full control of his city once more. The wolf that no-one suspected existed. Sutton was also happy, happy that everything was in its rightful place. He continued his patrol, in full control of his city once more.

****

Changelings

Mike was pleased with his efforts against the virus. He had managed to gain access to the sixth amino acid, the IGH had it the whole time. He had been able to produce an anti-virus without too much difficulty and both Barb and Kapowski were as cured as they could be.

Although both now carried anti bodies that may prove useful in the future, neither was in danger of dying. Neither would ever be able to return to the city either, as the Director would have them sent for changing as soon as their presence was detected. They were now part of the changeling community.

Mike wanted to start working on retaliation against the Director and her people but Keanos refused to allow it. He said that the Director's time was limited. Mike was a little unsure what he meant by this as his people had an average lifespan lasting over a century. He was prepared to concede that Keanos perhaps knew more than Mike did. Instead Mike turned his talents to discovering a genetic block, a way of preventing future changelings. In the meantime, Sutton and Will were well placed to keep an eye on the Director and her activities.

* * * *

Philomena stroked the head of her favourite banshee. She was curled at Philomena's feet and her head was laid in her lap. The one she had sent to dispatch Caldwell had not returned and that left her only two. She would have to consider making one or two more.

She wondered what Caldwell would say if he knew her two banshees were his mother and sister. She also wondered if they would kill him if she ordered them to. She had no desire to test their loyalty to her to that extreme, far better to create a couple more who she could rely on to remove Caldwell if it became necessary. She continued to stroke its head as she created the codes that would give her its sister.

Caldwell really did come from a very special genetic line. It was only a small percentage of genetic material that could be transformed into the likes of the banshee. Perhaps if she could trap Caldwell, she would transform him into something new and interesting. She wondered how pleased he would be to be reunited with his family at last.

Opening the file in front of her she began the very necessary process of replacing Davidson. Exactly why he had committed a terrorist act had not been made clear. The man had obviously lost his mind towards the end, especially allowing the homeless to trespass on her territory. His replacement would have to be much more efficient she decided.

✱✱✱✱

Maia was staying very close to Cerberus. She was determined that he would be with her for a long time to come, and after recent events he was not complaining. They all needed to recoup their energy and he was enjoying his sabbatical. He did think Mike could do with a companion. The guy was working far too hard to be entirely healthy. Cerberus had always thought Mike was a little too intense, and although he was a much-improved individual he was still a workaholic.

Mike thought they were all a little too lax and unfocused. They should push home the advantage they had achieved before the Director had time to create a larger army to send against them. Keanos was dangerously unconcerned. Mike was adamant that they would have to fight again, and he for one was determined to be prepared. He had the definite feeling that this was just the calm before the storm and the major war was still to be fought.

✱✱✱ THE END ✱✱✱